CAR

JOHN

"Very few detective stori... ...Carr's always do."

—Agatha Christie

"One of the three or four best detective writers since Poe."
—Edmund Crispin

"You'll never know which one [is the murderer] nor how the trick was worked until old H.M. tells all about it—unless, of course, you happen to be as good a detective as he is. In any case, it's a grand story."

—Kay Irvin
The New York Times Book Review
October 13, 1940

"Customarily excellent Dickson example of turning the incredible into cold fact...tops its class as baffler."

—*Saturday Review of Literature*

"Grade A puzzlement."

—Will Cuppy
Books

JOHN DICKSON CARR
Available in Library of Crime Classics® editions.

Douglas G. Greene, series consultant

CARTER DICKSON

NINE -- AND DEATH MAKES TEN

INTERNATIONAL POLYGONICS, LTD.
New York

NINE—AND DEATH MAKES TEN

©Copyright 1940 by William Morrow and Company, Inc. Copyright renewed 1968 by John Dickson Carr. Reprinted with permission of the author's estate. Cover: Copyright© 1987 by International Polygonics, Ltd.

Library of Congress Card Catalog No. 87-82442
ISBN 0-930330-69-2

Printed and manufactured in the United States of America by Guinn Printing, New York.
First IPL printing October 1987.
10 9 8 7 6 5 4 3 2 1

This story is dedicated, as it should be, to fellow passengers aboard M.V. Georgic, in memory of a crossing we made from New York to "a British port" during the early days of the war.

The crossing took place under much the same blackout and life-jacket conditions as are described here. But there all resemblance to reality ceases. The date was September, 1939; not January, 1940. The ship was not carrying munitions. There were no such regrettable goings-on as occur in these pages. No character in the story—whether passenger, officer, or member of the crew—bears the remotest relation to any living person. In short, everything except the atmosphere is a complete piece of fantasy from beginning to end.

C. D.

London, N.W.3,
May, 1940.

1

Painted battleship-gray, the liner lay by the pier at the foot of West Twentieth Street. She was the twenty-seven-thousand-ton M.V. *Edwardic,* of the White Planet Line; and she was to sail that afternoon for "a British port."

Along the New York skyline, buildings glistened as cold as the frozen runner of a skate. Though it was only one o'clock in the afternoon, a few lights twinkled in their windows. The water of the harbor looked choppy and greasy—and as though it would freeze you in a few seconds if you fell in. Nor was the wind, sweeping through that naked customs-shed, much better.

The *Edwardic* was a stocky-looking liner, squat and broad-beamed despite her length. Her sides curved out like the arc of a bow. From the customs-shed she seemed blank and blind, drained of life, except for the thin brown haze which hovered over her one squat funnel. It was the exhaust of her oil-burning engines, and it was instantly blown wide by that bitter wind. Gray decks, gray masts, gray ventilators, even gray port-holes: blacked-out and screwed down against light.

The dock police shivered beside dirty water. You were not allowed to smoke anywhere on the dock, even in the big dank waiting-room. Though the *Edwardic* had been loaded long ago, the number of guards made it difficult to take a step anywhere without being challenged. Echoes struck back and rumbled along the roof of the shed. A hoarse voice, talking through a loud-speaker, caused a stir among the few dispirited people in the waiting-room. They trailed out, stamping their feet and blowing on their fingers, while a tug hooted from the harbor, and its noise was carried up in hollow vibrations among the girders.

No visitors were allowed aboard. For the *Edwardic,* nominally a passenger ship, was carrying munitions to "a British port." Her cargo consisted of half a million pounds' worth of

7

high explosive, with four Lockheed bombers on the top deck. She carried nine passengers.

*   *   *   *   *

To one man, standing in the fore part of A Deck with his arms folded on the rail, it came as an intense relief when the *Edwardic* at last moved out.

He could not imagine why he should be in such a fever to get started. There was no reason for it. He was leaving America for a doubtful job and a doubtful future in his own country. Being partly lame, he would not even be in the army. For the next eight days (or nine or ten or eleven, according to the January weather and the directions of the Admiralty) he would be living inside a floating powder-magazine. One well-placed torpedo would blow the whole mass to pieces, together with every living organism inside.

Yet nothing relieved his nerves more than when the *Edwardic* began to glide backwards in a slow, wide curve, and he saw the white-streaked water widen between ship and dock.

He hunched himself down into his overcoat, leaning the full weight of his body on the rail. He was a dark-haired, rather grim-looking young man in his early thirties, compact, pleasant-faced, but with nothing greatly to distinguish him except a slight limp which he tried to conceal by using a cane. He wore a thick fuzzy overcoat and heavy cap. His name was Max Matthews; once upon a time he had been a newspaperman, and a good one. Also, they said he was a fool for traveling in this ship—there were so many Italian or American liners, which might take a long time in getting you back to England by the Southern European route, but at least were perfectly safe.

At the moment he was excited—more excited than he ever remembered having been in his life.

Thank God, he thought, we're off at last!

The wind across the harbor struck him full in the face, closing his eyes and chilling him all over. He steadied himself. The *Edwardic,* butted and nuzzled by screaming tugs, rolled a little as she swung. But she had taken on that smooth gliding motion, animated by the throb of her engines, which emphasized the space of water widening between them and the dock.

They were moving out into the dark, into a great loneliness ahead. The ship's whistle called against it, against a sky that seemed even emptier away from land, and the tug whistles mournfully replied.

"Cold," observed a voice not far from him.

Max peered round.

Standing by the rail not far away, looking down over the forward hatches and the forecastle which on ordinary voyages housed third-class passengers, was a tall man in a light overcoat. His head was bent forward; and the brim of his soft hat was blown flat over his eyes.

"Cold," he said in a non-committal voice.

Both of them recognized the conversational etiquette of the sea. This was a tentative opening. If Max merely answered, "Yes, isn't it?" and glanced away again, it was a sign that he wasn't in the mood for conversation. But if he said, "Yes, isn't it?" and added some new remark of his own, it was a sign that talk had been joined.

He had thought that he was far from being in the mood for conversation. To his own surprise, he suddenly found that he wanted to talk.

"Yes, isn't it? I expect we shall get it colder yet, though, before we're through."

"Or hotter than we want it," agreed the stranger, genially but cryptically. He dug his hand into the pocket of his overcoat. "Cigarette?"

"Thanks."

This was the final sign that conversation had been joined. The wind whistled at them, even in the lee side under the partial shelter of a companionway; after several polite efforts to hold a match for each other, they concluded by lighting their own.

The stranger, seen in the spurt of the match-flame, was a tall, heavy man with an easy-smiling mouth showing strong white teeth. His age might have been sixty, and the edges of the hair under his hat were clear white; but his mannerisms were much younger, almost bouncing. His shoulders were slightly stooped, and he gestured broadly. But he had a strong, tight-looking face, with a pair of sharp brown eyes which shone like those of a young man. They gave him most of his animation. What puzzled Max was that he looked and talked and dressed like an American. Yet American passports for traveling, Max had been given to understand, were

9

very difficult to get in these days; and, most of all, Americans were absolutely forbidden to travel in the ships of belligerent nations.

"This is something, all right," he continued, shaking out the already spent match. "Only nine of us, they tell me."

"Passengers?"

"Yes, nobody in tourist or third-class. Just the nine of us in first, including two women."

Max was startled. "Two women?"

"That's right," said the stranger, fixing his eyes on Max as though his word had been doubted. "No place for 'em, is it? Hell! But there you are." He spread out his hands. "The captain says—"

"Have you seen the captain?"

"Oh, casually. Just casually," answered the stranger, in some haste. "Had a talk with him this morning. Why? Do you know him?"

"As a matter of fact," said Max hesitantly, "he's my brother. If you've seen him, it's more than I have. I don't imagine we'll see much of him this trip."

"Your brother, eh? Is that so? I suppose that's why you're traveling in this tub?"

"One of the reasons."

"My name is Lathrop," said the stranger, suddenly thrusting out a big hand. "John Lathrop."

"Mine is Matthews," said Max, shaking the hand.

Max had a feeling that the acquaintance was progressing too rapidly, but there was at once a cordiality and courtesy about Lathrop which he liked. Both of them blinked, the fire flying from cigarettes, as the wind swung again.

The *Edwardic* was now forging ahead down the harbor. Her propellors churned with a deeper vibration which shook upwards through the decks. Towards their left, a nondescript huddle of roofs slid past and presently melted into the skyline of lower Manhattan. It loomed white and powerful against a sky grown so dark that the watchers could barely see, except when a gleam of light struck through the clouds; then even those towers grew dwarfish against an immensity of water.

"I was just thinking," Lathrop began abruptly.

"Yes?"

"Well, all nine of us rolling around in this big tub. Sort of

—peas in a hogshead. They must be pretty determined people, most of 'em."

"How so?"

Lathrop leaned against the forward rail, dropping his cigarette, and interlaced his fingers. The wind tore at their eyes and faces, filling the eyes with water. "They must have pretty strong reasons, all of 'em, for wanting to get to England in a hurry nowadays. Or as much of a hurry as you can make it nowadays. Look at the safe sea-routes. But if you've got to go clear down to Genoa or Lisbon, and then come back overland, that takes time. If they're risking this box of dynamite rather than do it, they've got good reason to. What I mean is: there must be some very interesting people aboard."

"I suppose so."

Lathrop opened one eye at him. "Meaning you don't give a hoot?"

"No; not that, exactly. But I've been eleven months in hospital with this." Max touched his bad leg with his cane. "All I want now is sea air and an uncrowded ship."

"Sorry," said Lathrop in a sharp voice, and with immense dignity. "Didn't mean to butt in."

"No, no. You don't understand. A good trip, with good food and good wine—but, by all the gods, not a 'gay' one. Not a social one. And I have an idea that this run is going to be anything but that."

Lathrop threw back his head and laughed.

"You're right there," he agreed, soberly reflecting. "So that's the reason why you're traveling?"

"If you could call it a reason."

"And look," pursued Lathrop, eyeing him shrewdly, "I'm not trying to pump you. No smoke-screen intended. As for me, my story's simpler and yet maybe queerer. I'm after a murderer."

There was a silence.

A hoarse blast of the liner's whistle beat out against immensity. Even here in the harbor, the water was uncertain and choppy. Looking at the cigarette in his hand, it suddenly occurred to Max Matthews that he was smoking on a munitions-ship; he wondered whether smoking were permitted on deck. He dropped the cigarette and ground it out with care.

"Time's getting on," he said. "Better get down and unpack. There's some sort of paper we're supposed to fill out for the purser—"

11

"You think I'm taking you for a ride?" inquired Lathrop. "About the murderer?"

"Aren't you?"

"Nope. Not a bit of it." First Lathrop's shrewd brown eye twinkled, giving animation to his face; then he grew confidential. "Tell you about it later. Where are you sitting in the dining-room?"

"My brother's table, I imagine. Why not join us?"

"Captain's table? Glad to! Right, then: I'll see you later . . . Oo-er!"

This last was added under his breath, and mostly to himself, as Max turned away. And Max saw the reason for it.

Coming towards them along A Deck, across a scrubbed expanse of boards between the dark-gray bulkheads on one side and the line of lifeboats on the other, strode a nearly middle-aged woman in a sable coat.

Her eyes were half closed against the breeze, and her step was firm. Her very light yellow hair, of which there appeared to be a good deal, was bound round her head with a colored scarf whose ends streamed out. The face was full and faintly brown, shiny under the eyes as though it had been vaselined there; the eyes (what could be seen of them) blue; the mouth full-lipped. Though undoubtedly in her early forties, you did not notice this except at close range. Under her open sable coat she wore a silk blouse, caught at the breast with a diamond clasp, and a dark skirt. The wind, blowing full against her, showed that she was wearing no brassière; that she had full, rounded thighs and admirable legs set off by very high-heeled shoes.

All three—Max, Lathrop, and the woman—were elaborately unconscious of each other's presence. At least, the woman was unconscious of them. She swept past, her eyes still half closed, and a snake-skin handbag pressed under one arm.

Lathrop glanced after her, furtively. Max went below.

He was annoyed with himself because the woman's image went with him. A man fully restored to health after eleven months—eleven intolerable months—of the monastic life of a hospital, is susceptible and uncritical. The woman's attractiveness was instantaneous. Max felt it. Yet there was something vaguely unpleasant about her face: something like a small, mean wrinkle past the mouth.

Max dragged open one of the doors on A Deck, hopped

12

inside with difficulty, and let it slam after him in the draft. It closed with a booming noise against the quiet of the ship. Inside, the passages were stuffy and rubbery-smelling: dead still except for the faint creaking of the bulkheads.

That uneasy creaking followed him. He steadied himself down a flight of stairs, which rose and swayed under him with the *Edwardic's* motion. Downstairs, on B Deck, it was still more stuffy. All bedroom portholes—such were the orders— must be kept closed and screwed-down at all times. Even upstairs in the public rooms, and in the daytime, a porthole might be opened only at the strict discretion of a steward.

Max had never felt so much the sensation of being alone.

His cabin, a spacious one with a private bathroom, was on the starboard side of B Deck. He went down a narrow passage; turned into a very short passage, a sort of alcove, branching off it; and opened the door at the left.

All lights were turned on, shining against white-painted walls. An electric fan whirred in his cabin, partly dissolving the stuffiness. His trunk stood beside one of the white-counterpaned berths: it was a double cabin, though he shared it with nobody. There were a couple of wicker chairs, and a pleasant green carpet on the floor. The tooth-glass vibrated in its rack over the wash-basin; in the bathroom, whose door was open and hooked back, a water-tap gurgled with a kind of snort; and over everything the electric fan, moving from side to side on its revolving neck, swept his face with a cool breeze.

All very peaceful. But—

There was one discreet tap at the door.

"Ah, sir," said the steward, putting a grave face round the edge of the door. "Got everything you want?"

"Yes, thanks."

"I brought your trunk in."

"So I see."

"One other thing, sir. When you hear the next gong—it'll be in a few minutes now—all passengers are to assemble upstairs in the lounge."

"What for?"

"Instructions. Please bring your life-jacket with you. Do you know how to manage your life-jacket?"

"Yes."

"Sure, sir?" persisted the steward, insinuating himself

13

smilingly but gingerly into the cabin. He kept the smile steadily in place like a plaster.

There were two life-jackets on top of the wardrobe, whose mirror reflected the steward's smile. Max reached up and pulled down one of them. It consisted of two large oblong blocks of cork sewed up in canvas, with canvas shoulder-straps and canvas strips for the neck. You thrust your head through these latter strips, so that there was a cork block on each side of your neck; then you put your arms through the shoulder-straps, and tightened the whole harness by tying the canvas strings behind like the tails of an apron. Max put on the jacket.

"That's right, sir," applauded the steward. "And *if* you'd fill out that form, sir"—he nodded towards the berth, where a long pink sheet of paper lay beside the passenger-list—"and take it to the purser's office, with your passport, as soon as you can?"

"All right."

Max did not notice the other's departure. Feeling like Goliath in his harness, he was looking down at the gaudily colored booklet which constituted the passenger-list.

He could not shake himself rid of that image: the (nearly middle-aged) blonde, her eyes half closed and the wind blowing against her body, going past with her head in the air. Hang it all, he was free! He would *not* be bothered with people! He wanted only to doze and lounge. He wanted only solitude; and had got to such a morbid state that he was even willing to travel over a cargo of explosives in order to get it.

All the same, he wondered what her name was. He opened the passenger-list, whose space devoted to names was pitifully thin. It said:

Archer, Dr. Reginald.
Benoit, Capt. Pierre.
Chatford, Miss Valerie.
Hooper, Mr. George, A.
Kenworthy, the Hon. Jerome.
Lathrop, Mr. J. E.
Matthews, Mr. Max.
Zia Bey, Mrs. Estelle.

Hold on! That was only eight names, and Lathrop had said there were nine passengers. Probably Lathrop's error.

But it was the last name on the list which caught Max's attention. If ever a name suited the woman he had seen, it was "Mrs. Estelle Zia Bey."

"That's it, for a fiver," he said aloud, to the buzzing electric fan. And then, in a kind of exasperation: "What is she, Turkish or something? She's English if I ever saw it."

His voice came back at him in that enclosed space. Under his feet the deck of the *Edwardic* began to rise slowly, but with inflexible and treacherous vastness. It rose, hung, and then tilted sideways to a sharp creak of the bulkheads; so that he had to seize the side of the berth to keep himself from falling. The movement stirred in his stomach as well.

Then Max Matthews knew the reason for the excitement which had possessed him ever since the ship sailed. It was caused by nervousness—pure nervousness.

He unfastened his life-jacket, took it off, and hung it over his arm. He could now hear, beginning far away and pulsing nearer through the ship, the shivering note of a gong beaten louder and louder until it banged away past his door.

"All passengers are to assemble in the lounge." Max drew a deep breath. He took off his overcoat, which was now uncomfortably hot. He picked up the life-jacket again. Opening the door to the little alcove-passage, hooking it back against the wall so as to get more air, he stepped out into that tiny space; and this time he met the woman face to face.

Her cabin must be directly opposite his across the alcove. He could have reached out and touched the white-painted door, numbered B-37, which faced him. She was just turning into the alcove, walking rapidly, with the light behind her; and they bumped smack into each other.

"I beg your pardon," said Max.

"Not at all," said the woman, after a slight pause. "My fault, I'm sure."

Her voice was lofty, with a cigarette-hoarseness. While he stood by to let her pass, she groped for and found the knob, and opened the door. The lights were burning in her cabin. It was a cabin similar to his own except for the wallpaper, and had a private bathroom as well. It was already littered untidily with the contents of two big trunks bearing the white initials E.Z.B.

This much he noticed before she turned round, in the act of shutting the door, and glanced at him over her shoulder. The thick snakeskin handbag was still pressed tightly under one arm. Again he became aware of the small, petulant wrinkle by the drooping under-lip. But he was not interested in that.

For she looked him straight in the eyes before the door closed.

2

Max, a bit perturbed, climbed the main staircase to the lounge on A Deck.

He has since admitted that if he had paid more attention to his fellow-passengers during the first twenty-four hours out, if he had studied more than the one or two he did study, much blood and brutality might have been avoided. But that is the whole point. You never do notice much of your fellow-passengers at the outset. You are tired, or depressed, or wrapped up in your own concerns. You see people only as blank faces with whom it is later difficult to associate the personalities you come to know. Even after several days it is sometimes difficult to sort them out. Of course, the *Edwardic* was so thinly populated that the passengers might have been ghosts wandering about in an over-decorated haunted house, and observation should have been easy. The answer lies in a cargo of high explosives, which is apt to distract the best detective instincts from watching the behavior of a murderer.

For the third officer made it clear that this voyage was to be no picnic, when he assembled them in the lounge.

The lounge was a huge salon, with lines of mahogany pillars supporting a mosaic roof of colored glass, with green-covered tables and deep brocaded chairs round a dance-floor now veiled by carpet. Its lights were dim and spectrally glassy. Indeed, those assembled had the air of people waiting to hear a ghost story. But the third officer, who reminded Max of Sir Malcolm Campbell, spoke with brisk confidence.

"Now, ladies and gentlemen," he said, perching himself on the edge of a table piled with square cardboard boxes, "we none of us like to take all these precautions, or worry you with them. But needs must when the devil drives." He uttered this *bon mot* with a sinister roll and thrill. "First of all,

I should like you to come up here and be fitted with gas-masks. Steward!"

(Gas-masks? Why gas-masks at sea? That was the question in everybody's mind. But no one spoke.)

"If you don't need 'em here," said the third officer dryly, "you will have to have them when you land in England. So you'll have to get them from us. Write your name and cabin-number plainly on the box. Now, if you please."

Obediently they trooped up. Stewards fitted on the masks, which gave an ugly and pig-snouted expression to people peering at each other in the dim light. If the mask fitted well, breathing in it produced a long and impolite noise like a raspberry, which rolled and bubbled round your ears whenever you expelled air.

Miss Chatfield and Mr. Kenworthy, it then developed, had failed to appear. A steward reported they were seasick. The third officer was a little annoyed at this news, but finally decided to see them in their cabins later on.

"Tomorrow," he went on, "you will be given detailed instructions. There will be a boat-drill at eleven o'clock. When you hear the alarm-bell ring, go down to the dining-room—*the dining-room*, on C Deck—and await orders. Bring your life-jackets, your gas-masks, and a blanket. Remember, if we are ever attacked, by sea or air, you are to go to the *dining-room*. That's all, for the moment." He smiled. "Don't worry about it; let us do the worrying."

And they trailed out.

There had been no comments, no jokes, no laughter. But the *Edwardic* was already pitching and rolling into heavy weather, and blank faces indicated unquiet stomachs. In fact, only four passengers came in to dinner on the first night—and no officers except the purser.

In the dining-room, which was full of mirrors and red lacquer, a funereal hush lay over half an acre of empty white tables. You could hear crockery rattle as far as the kitchen. The stewards were, if anything, more subdued than the passengers. At the captain's table, which was round and seated six persons, were Max, the affable Mr. Lathrop, and a short fat middle-aged man who introduced himself as Mr. George A. Hooper, of Bristol. Some distance away from them alone at a table for two, sat a wiry dark-complexioned man in the khaki uniform, with gold-and-red shoulder-straps, of a captain of French Tirailleurs. Max supposed that this

17

must be the Capt. Pierre Benoit of the passenger-list. His face was completely without expression, and he never raised his eyes from his plate.

Mysterious draughts swept the dining-room. To the accompaniment of a boiling hiss outside the portholes, the whole saloon suddenly rose up slowly like a balloon, and then dropped like an express lift. Crockery chattered and ran together in the center of the table.

"Crab cocktail," said the doughty Lathrop, consulting his menu. "Grilled sole with Hollandaise sauce, steak and French fried potatoes—h'm—after that, we'll see."

"Steak and chips for me," said Mr. George A. Hooper, in the homely and comforting accents of the West Country. He added: "Gawd lummy Charley! Look at the Queen o' Sheba!"

This marked the entrance of Estelle Zia Bey.

She had committed the blunder of dressing for dinner on the first night out. But no doubt she had done it deliberately. Mr. Hooper's whisper had been one of awe.

Mrs. Zia Bey (confound that name, thought Max) wore an evening-gown of silver spangles, cut so low in front as to make the modest Mr. Hooper mutter under his breath. It reflected back the innumerable mosaic mirrors in the dining-saloon. It showed off her superb shoulders, of the same soft golden-brown color as her face. No wrinkles were visible now. She swung a black handbag from a wrist-strap. The ship rolled sharply as she came into the room, and a less steady-pinned woman would have gone skidding and scuttling into a pillar, clutching without dignity at her skirts.

But she only laughed at the steward who hurried to assist her. She pushed him with some jocoseness in the chest, lifted her long skirts, and sat down alone at a table for two. They heard her voice rise, rather harshly, as she ordered dinner.

The three men instantly went into a guilty and whispering huddle.

"That ought to be stopped, that ought," muttered Mr. Hooper, looking at his plate. "Reckon it's a scandal."

"Oh, I don't know," said Lathrop, with a massive and tolerant gesture. His brown eye, the eye of a young man, twinkled paternally. "She's a fine-looking woman, I'd say. Name is Mrs. Zia Bey. She's divorced, or getting divorced. She's American by birth, but her first husband was English.

Her second husband (the fellow she's getting divorced from) is in the Turkish Embassy at London."

(Lathrop, Max was shortly to learn, had more talent for picking up gossip than a whole parcel of women at a village sewing-circle.)

"You talked to her?" asked Max.

"Oh, casually. Just casually. I think she wanted me to stand her a drink; but I wasn't having any."

(The devil she did, thought Max.)

Lathrop chuckled. "There's one of 'em aboard every ship," he confided. "Sometimes they mean business, and sometimes they don't. Mostly they don't. But she does, if you ask me. No, sir: I'm not having any. I don't think Mrs. L. would like it."

Max ate his dinner in silence. Again he told himself, with angry insistence and some jealousy, that he was *not* going to get tangled up with the infernal woman. He would not strike up an acquaintance with her. He would not invite her to have a drink.

Yet he knew that the thing was fated, and that he could not help it. A sort of unpleasant prevision told him that. The worst of it was that he didn't even like the look of her. But, when a person grows rather sick of life, he says to himself, 'Why not?' he says—

A blue-uniformed steward crossed the salon, threading gingerly among the rattling tables.

"Mr. Matthews, sir?"

"Yes?"

"The captain's compliments, sir, and could you have coffee with him in his room after dinner?"

Max could, and was glad of an excuse to go. On his way out he had to pass Mrs. Zia Bey's table. He could have avoided it by taking a longer circuit round, but he thought that this might look conspicuous; and an acute pang of self-consciousness shot through him. As he passed her table, she lifted her head and looked him full in the eyes. Her mouth, which was painted dark red and looked as soft as pulp, wore a faintly mocking expression; as though she were about to smile.

That was all. He limped past.

The steward took him up in the lift to A Deck, and then outside. To avoid any chink of light being seen, such outer doors as could be used were constructed on the plan of water-tight compartments. You opened one blacked-out door,

19

and walked into a kind of vestibule. Then, after closing it, you opened a second blacked-out door, and emerged into whistling darkness.

"Look out, sir!" cried the steward.

Max had never imagined such darkness even in his dreams. The wet deck soared up under him, tilting high. The ferrule of his cane slipped on a wet iron plate, and he nearly fell at full length.

He could hear the wind scream, under a vast flapping and thrumming, behind canvas sheets which they had tied up like screens along the open deck. Even so, it wormed through and lifted his hair. It was literally true to say that you could not see your hand before your face. He lifted one hand and wriggled the fingers: nothing. Not a gleam, not a star: nothing but a blackness which howled you down, deafened you, and stung your lips with spray.

The steward, shouting something in his ear, was guiding him towards a companionway which led up to the boat-deck. At least, he knew it was a companionway when he barked his shins against it. They groped their way among the huge swathed shapes of the bombing-planes up on the boat-deck, and presently emerged, half-blinded, into the dazzle of the captain's room.

"Look here," said his brother, after surveying him in silence for some moments, "what the devil do you mean by taking this ship?"

Commander Francis Matthews had changed little during the two or three years since Max had seen him last. He was forty-five; his face was something less than the color of raw beef; his bearing was quiet (except in family matters), and his manners good (with the same reservation). He sat, stocky and foursquare, in a swivel-chair beside a polished desk. His "room"—not cabin—might have been the study in a suburban villa. Two frosty blue eyes, the lids pinched and wrinkled as though with astigmatism, never wavered from his brother's face.

Then Commander Matthews put his fists on his hips. The four gold stripes on his sleeves lent him a powerful impressiveness.

"Don't you know it's not safe?" he demanded. "Sit down."

Max laughed at him; and the other, after a slight pause, grinned back.

"You're traveling by this ship," Max pointed out.

"That's different. It's my job," said the captain, becoming powerfully stern again.

There was another silence.

"Er—what's been happening to you?" asked Commander Matthews, fidgeting a little. "I hear you cracked up. Sorry I couldn't get in to see you. This bloody war . . ."

"I know."

"Well?" said his brother fiercely. "What happened?"

"I was covering a fire. The photographer and I were up on a scaffolding. It collapsed. We went down in the middle of the blaze. I didn't get burnt; they pulled me out in time; but it got my side and leg, and if I hadn't had the best doctor in the world I'd have been permanently paralyzed. Tom Miller was killed."

There was another pause. Commander Matthews drew a deep inhalation through his nose.

"H'm. Break your nerve?"

"No. At least, I don't think so."

"How are you feeling now?"

"Fed up."

The other nodded. "Why're you going back to England?"

"You don't keep jobs on a New York paper after eleven months in the sick-bay. The paper was damned decent about it, though: paid every penny of the expenses.—This war's going to spread, Frank. I think I can pick up something in London."

"H'm. Money?"

"That's all right, thanks."

"I said: *money?*" snarled Commander Matthews.

"And I tell you it's all right, thanks. I don't need anything."

His brother seemed a little nonplussed. They had skated rapidly over this personal conversation, as they always did, while Commander Matthews creaked back and forth in his swivel-chair. Once a huge lurch of the ship brought Max's heart up in his throat, turning him slightly dizzy. It set the captain's chair sliding, and almost upset the coffee-service on the railed center table. The captain sprang up. He seemed relieved to have his attention diverted.

"Coffee?"

"Thanks."

"Brandy?"

"Thanks. Frank, what's on your mind? What's worrying you?"

Commander Matthews turned away, but not before Max had seen the blood come into his face and into the blue veins of his forehead. He poured the coffee. He opened a wall-cabinet, taking out a bottle and two fat-bowled glasses. After glancing once at the speaking-tube which communicated with the bridge, he poured out two weak brandies.

"I suppose you don't know," he went on, with his eye on the bottle, "that we found two time-bombs planted in the hold just before we sailed."

Again there was a silence.

"Mind! I'll have your hide if you mention that to anybody! But it's a fact. They were set to explode about six hours out of New York. If Cruikshank hadn't found 'em, we'd all be playing harps this minute."

He set down the bottle with a thump.

"But precautions—" Max began.

"Precautions!" said the captain. "You saw that mob of special constables at the dock. We've taken every human precaution that can be taken. Since then we've gone over every inch of this ship with a microscope: no bombs, no stowaways, nothing. And don't worry about it," he added lightly. "We'll get through all right."

"I hope so."

"But it's a responsibility, you know. There's no denying it's a responsibility."

"To say the least."

"Yes. Well. Look here." The captain hesitated, frowning. "Since you are aboard, I'd take it as a favor if you'd—keep your eyes open. You know? I'm sure of my crew, every man-jack of 'em. But I'm not so sure of my passengers."

Max sat up.

"Here, I say! You don't mean somebody might plant a bomb and then stick with the ship?"

"Frankly," said Commander Matthews, with an air of handsome concession, "I don't know *what* the blighters mightn't do if they saw a chance to wreck a cargo like this." Again he put his fists on his hips. He was smiling: but it was his "official" smile, marble-toothed and fishy and unconvincing. He added:

"I can't tell you anything, Max. I'm under Admiralty orders. So mum's the word. But here I am with nine passengers—"

"Eight."

"Eight," the other corrected himself hastily. "Eight, I meant to say." His eyes grew sharp. "Met any of the passengers, by the way?"

"Only a few. There's a big fellow called Lathrop, with a primitive sense of humor. He keeps on making some joke about being after a murderer, and acting very mysterious about it."

"Joke?" said the captain. "It's no joke. True as gospel."

Again Max sat up.

"Do you mean that?"

"I don't say things I don't mean," snapped Commander Matthews, the blood in his forehead-veins again. "Ever heard of a man named Carlo Fenelli? The what-d'ye-call-it—you know—racketeer? He's in jug in England, and wanted for about six murders in the States. They want him back in a hurry, and they're extraditing him. But (it seems) this chap Fenelli is so canny that he ought to have his behind kicked. If they try to take him out of England by way of France or Italy, Fenelli's smart lawyers will serve more papers on 'em and hold 'em up till Doomsday with more red tape. Lathrop is somebody connected with the New York police. He offered to go straight over, and bring Fenelli straight back in an English ship. At least, that's Lathrop's story. He seems all right."

Commander Matthews drank brandy at a gulp. Picking up a passenger-list, he flicked it open. His reddish forefinger moved down and stopped at the name *Kenworthy, The Hon. Jerome.*

"H'mf. Yes. And I know this one, right enough."

"Who?"

"Young Kenworthy. Son of Lord Somebody-or-Other. He's traveled with me before. Too much money. Always seasick the first half of the trip, and drunk the second. He's all right. But the others—"

Max was growing even more puzzled.

"There's a West Country business-man named Hooper," he replied, "and a French army officer. Then there's a Dr. Archer, and this chap Kenworthy, and a Miss Valerie Chatford: whom I haven't seen, any of them. Finally, there's—"

"Mrs. Zia Bey?" asked the captain, raising his eyebrows.

"Yes. You don't think she's a sinister element, do you?"

"She's a . . ." began Commander Matthews; and checked himself. He hunched up his shoulders. "No, I don't know her. But I know all about her." He eyed Max narrowly. "Take my tip, my lad. You keep away from her. She's got queer tastes."

"Meaning what?"

"Meaning just that."

"It sounds interesting."

"Does it, by God!" said the other, picking up his cap, and putting it on with a slash. The gold leaves on its peak gave him a heavy, competent, still more official look. "You wouldn't think so, if you knew her. Now drink up; and off you go. I've got work to do. Just keep your eyes skinned. If you see any sort of unusual thing, *any* sort (I can't tell you any more than that), you come to me in a hurry. Got it?"

Five minutes later, unsteady on his feet and whipped with wind, Max was back inside on A Deck.

The *Edwardic* moved more evenly, so that the pound of the engines could be felt as a steady throb. It intensified the cathedral hush. Max wandered into the gray-and-mahogany lounge, with its lines of pillars and its roof of mosaic glass. Not a soul was in it.

He sat down in a chair, and got up again. Beside the grand piano there was a full trap-drummer's outfit for dancing. Removing the dust-cover, he struck an experimental whack on the cymbals; it banged out with such loudness that he hastily replaced the cover. He was in a fever of restlessness, and would not admit that this was due to nerves. His nerves, he told himself, were as strong as they had been before the scaffolding collapsed under him in the Chemical Works fire.

Tom Miller's neck was broken in that fall.

From the lounge, Max wandered into the Long Gallery that opened out of it. The Long Gallery was all deep carpets, deep plush chairs, book-cases, and small bronze figures holding lights. There was nobody here either.

So he went on to the smoking-room, which opened out of the Long Gallery. The smoking-room was deserted too—except for Estelle Zia Bey.

Of all the public rooms of the *Edwardic*, this smoking-room had the most hushed atmosphere. Its lamps, each in a frosted-glass chrysalis, were deliberately dim. Its design was dark red. The lamps winked on red leather chairs with chromium fittings; on small tables with green felt tops and polished ashtrays; on a red rubbery floor; on a red brick fire-place which had over it a loud-ticking clock, and under it a big black porcelain cat on a red cushion—always a source of fascination or æsthetic agony for the drunks.

In a far corner, by doors leading to the deck aft, was a small bar. The white-coated barman stood asleep behind it. Mrs. Zia Bey sat on a stool in front of it, sucking a gin-fizz through a straw.

He saw her face reflected in the mirror as he approached. She looked half-asleep herself, her shoulders bent forward and covered by a sable coat.

"Hello," said Max.

"Hello," answered Mrs. Zia Bey. She continued to suck at the straw. Her eyes, pale blue under shiny upper lids, opened a little. After a pause she reached out and patted the stool beside her.

"Sit down."

He sat down.

3

That was the first night out, Friday, January nineteenth. And Max slept badly.

Despite bitter weather outside, the airless cabin was too warm and induced headache. The electric fan whirred spitefully through the dark hours. It became mixed up with a long, hissing rise and recoil of waters; the gentle pitching motion soothed Max, but his dreams were unpleasant. Towards morning—or so it seemed—he was roused by a heavy trampling and bustling somewhere. He knew what it was. It was the life-boats being swung out on their davits, where they would remain, ready to be lowered at a moment's notice, for the rest of the voyage. Then he dozed. He did not wake until the shattering clamor of an alarm-bell, ringing steadily, tore sleep from his brain.

"Boat-drill, sir," said the voice of the steward at his bedside. "You'd best *hurry*. It's eleven o'clock."

Without bothering to shave, Max sloshed water on his face and threw on some clothes. He caught up life-jacket, gas-mask, and a blanket, and hurried down to the dining-room while the bell still pealed like a fire-alarm.

Where last night there had been gloom among the passengers, today there was exuberant gaiety. Mr. John Lathrop called jokes across to Mr. George A. Hooper, whose features Max still could not remember. Captain Benoit was there, conscientiously wearing his gas-mask, with his red-and-gold-topped cap over it, and looking like nothing on earth. Estelle Zia Bey appeared, smiling knowingly at Max. This morning they were joined by a new passenger, whom the third officer addressed as "Doctor": a portly, urbane gentleman, with flat fair hair brushed neatly round his head.

"Ladies and gentlemen!" bawled the third officer. The ringing of the alarm-bell stopped abruptly, so that his voice had some power.

"As I told you yesterday," he went on hurriedly, "if we should be attacked by sea or air you will hear that bell, and you will come down here immediately. One moment. This does not necessarily mean that we shall abandon ship and take to the boats."

("Ho!" observed Mr. Hooper, with some scepticism.)

"It is merely a measure of precaution. If it does happen, however, you will follow me up and out on deck . . . so. Come along, please."

They trooped after him, upstairs and out into the air. It was a heavy leaden-and-silver morning, over a choppy sea running with white-caps, and a dead-cold wind. When they emerged on A Deck, where the life-boats were uncovered and swung out ready, Max saw something which struck him sober: it made him ashamed of their fat-witted gaiety.

In two long straight lines, unmoving, erect, and each in his place, the whole of the *Edwardic's* crew stood at attention. The blue coats of the lounge and deck stewards in one block; the white jackets of the cabin and mess stewards; the caps of the stewardesses; clerks, pantrymen, cooks, laundrymen, every person down to the page-boys with scrubbed faces and shining buttons, and the A.B.'s, trimmers, and greasers waiting beyond. Each person wore his life-jacket. Each person kept eyes front. They would stand thus, even though a sinking deck tilted them into icy water, until the last passenger had got away in the boats.

It was the passengers themselves who presented difficulties.

"You now see—stop!" said the harassed third officer, peering round him and counting. "Miss Valerie Chatford!" he called clearly. "Mr. Jerome Kenworthy!"

There was no reply.

The third officer made a trumpet of his hands. "Miss Valerie Chatford! Mr. Jerome Kenworthy! If you please!"

A steward, who had been detailed off to attend him, leaned close and spoke in an undertone.

"I don't care if they are seasick!" said the third officer. "They've got to be here. Rout 'em out, will you? This may be a matter of life or death. They must know where to *go* . . . Great Scott, now the Frenchman's gone!"

"Well, you said 'go,' " Lathrop pointed out, not unreasonably. "Captain Benoit only speaks about six words of English. I know, because I've had a talk with him. He's from Provence. He's trying to read *Gone with the Wind,* with the aid of a French-English dictionary. And it seems he can't even get to first base. He—"

"Quiet, please!"

"Now, now, my son!" said Mr. George A. Hooper, soothingly.

"I am sorry, ladies and gentlemen, but I must ask you to remain here a few minutes more. There is one further instruction. From this time on, we must ask you to carry your life-jackets with you wherever you go."

"Wearing them?" called Mrs. Zia Bey, rather horrified.

"No, not wearing them. Just carry them over your arms. But don't put them down anywhere."

"Oh! Gas-masks too?"

"No, not gas-masks."

"Blankets?"

"No, not blankets."

"Are we going to be convoyed?"

"I have no instructions about that, madam. Perhaps, on second thoughts, it would be better if you all went below after all. I can manage the rest of it."

So, for the moment, Max saw neither Miss Chatford nor the (alleged) roistering Mr. Kenworthy. But he was not thinking about them. He was thinking about Estelle Zia Bey.

What he could not decide was whether she attracted him very much, or repelled him intensely. Some mannerisms said one thing; some said the other. She had a peculiar loud rasping laugh, throwing her head back and opening her mouth wide, which would have grated on anybody's nerves.

27

She consumed gin-fizzes at the rate of one every fifteen minutes, and never turned a hair: except that her fine English slipped away and her intimate conversation became as coarse as a fishwife's. But she had fine "talking" eyes, and a figure which so exuded sex-appeal that the closer you approached her the more it turned your head.

Their conversation in the bar the night before had been a kind of skirmish, an affair of outposts, in which each gauged the other's strength by maneuvering. He saw it in her fierce, snappish eyes. Each remained undecided. Each said, in effect, "I can't make up my mind about you." They parted on almost a note of hostility.

But that was last night: the gloomy first night at sea. In the morning, at boat-drill, she smiled at him so knowingly that it was like a blanket of intimacy drawn round them. She had thought better of that hostility—as he had.

The whole ship, in fact, seemed to be waking up. When Max invited the lady to the bar for a cocktail before lunch, they found Lathrop already there. He was planted before the brick fireplace, his feet apart. With him was the portly, fair-haired man—evidently Dr. Reginald Archer—whom Lathrop had instantly buttonholed. Lathrop beckoned them over, and insisted on ordering Martinis for everybody.

"What we need," he declared, "is more boat-drills. Yes, indeed. That one was a beauty. Did they finally hoist the two contemptibles out of bed, I wonder?"

"I believe they did," smiled Dr. Archer. "In fact, I remained behind to see. Your good health."

Dr. Archer was very much the man of the world. On his face was always an indulgent expression, a half-smile, as of one at peace with life. He never spoke until everyone else had spoken; and then with an air of delivering judgment. He was perhaps older than he looked. They were sitting round the red leather sofa before the fireplace: with lamps burning behind their heads, for few portholes were opened even in the public rooms. As Dr. Archer sat back comfortably, with his neatly plastered hair and his faint double-chin, the yellow light showed innumerable tiny lines round his eyes.

"I hope," he continued, holding up the cocktail, "that this will settle me. I had rather a bad night."

"Seasick?" inquired Lathrop sympathetically.

Dr. Archer smiled. His eyes were looking a trifle sunken

28

and yellowish as well, but this may have been the effect of the lamplight.

"Partly," he said.

"Partly?"

Dr. Archer smiled again.

"Yes. I should rather like to know who is practising knife-throwing in the passages at two o'clock in the morning."

Like a polished raconteur, he expected a sensation; and he got one.

"Knife-throwing?" Lathrop almost shouted, so that the bar-steward dropped and broke a glass he was cleaning.

"I believe so."

"But what happened?"

"It was something of an adventure," said the doctor. His eternally good-humored face, however, belied seriousness.

"Well? Go on! What was it?"

Dr. Archer tantalized them still more before he continued.

"It happened, as I say, about two o'clock in the morning. I was lying in my berth in my cabin. Queasy, ladies and gentlemen, very queasy. The ship was pitching a good deal, and creaking like a wicker rocking-chair. Aside from that, it was almost unpleasantly quiet."

"Yes?"

"Oh, by the way! I ought to explain that there's nobody anywhere near me. My cabin is on C Deck, amidships. Outside it runs a narrow branch-passage, twelve or fourteen feet long, ending in a blank wall with a porthole." He illustrated with a gesture of his well-manicured hands. "Across the passage there's an empty cabin.

"Well, the first thing I heard was a kind of thump. *Thump!* Like that. As though something solid had struck wood. Next I heard footsteps pass my door, go to the end of the passage, and turn round and come back again. They were little, light, soft footsteps, as of a person walking on tiptoe. After a few seconds there was another *thump*. Down came the little soft footsteps again, turned, and went back. *Thump* again. Do you know"—Dr. Archer put his head on one side, and laughed in apology—"I got the wind up? Fact. I did.

"I rang the bell for the steward, but there wasn't any reply. So I got up, feeling horribly ill and giddy, and stumbled over to the door. There were two more thumps while I felt round and failed to find the door. What I didn't like was the

29

stealth of those noises and footsteps in the middle of the night: it was as though the steps were coming for me.

"Then—whisk!

"I got the door open, and something dodged away. That's the only way I can express it. But I was not well, and my eyesight may have been bad. In any case, the little passage was empty.

"There was a light burning in the main passage, however, and shining into the smaller one. Somebody had been using this small passage as a kind of shooting-gallery. Somebody had been throwing a rather heavy knife at a piece of paper pinned up on the end wall under the porthole. On the piece of paper, by the way, was a crudely drawn image of a human face. The knife had hit the face every time, usually through the eyes or through the neck. That's why I say I spent rather a bad night."

He paused.

Taking up his cocktail glass, he drained it and set the glass down. On his face as he told the story was a twinkling expression which said, "I may be joking, you know; but after all I may not." Then he dusted the knees of his trousers.

"Ah, well. Have a Martini with me? No? Sure? Then I must go and brush up for lunch."

Lathrop said with hollow incredulity:

"Is that straight?"

"Perfectly straight, old boy. If you don't believe me, go down and have a look at the knife-dents in the wall."

"Did you see the knife?"

"No. Ah, no. That was taken away."

"I don't believe it! Sorry; no offense, you understand, but I don't believe it, and that's flat!"

Dr. Archer shrugged his shoulders and smiled. He got to his feet, pulling down his waistcoat and adjusting the fit of his faultless coat. Evidently this was the first time anyone had tried out any stories (true or otherwise) on Lathrop; and he, who usually told the stories himself, did not like it. In turn he adopted a smiling and sceptical expression, shaking his head reprovingly, but Max knew he was impressed.

"Maybe the ship's haunted," suggested Max. "You know: like the Upper Berth."

"Maybe it is," agreed Lathrop, and chuckled. "Maybe that Frenchman is a ghost. You never see him except at meal-times. Or maybe poor old Hooper is a ghost. Did I tell you about Hooper?" demanded Lathrop, laying hold of the conversational reins again, and yanking the team back where he wanted it. "He manufactures rubber stamps. His son is—"

"Excuse me," interrupted Max. "But, Doctor, didn't you report this affair?"

"Report it? To whom?"

Max didn't know. He could hardly say, "to the captain," since the whole thing might be a practical joke. Or, as seemed more probable, it might be an invention of Dr. Reginald Archer's. Something told Max that Dr. Archer was addicted to that wide-eyed and donnish form of humor in which you tell wild lies with a straight face, solely because you imagine somebody has tried to pull your leg first. Dr. Archer, who had been talking for some time to Lathrop, probably imagined that Lathrop did nothing but reel off one whopper after another.

Unfortunately, that was the impression Lathrop conveyed.

"But what about the paper?" asked Max. "That is, the paper this face was drawn on? Did you keep that?"

"The steward has it, or did have it," answered Dr. Archer equably. "It was fastened to the wall with a safety-pin. You could ask him, I'm telling the truth, you know. Word of honor, I am."

"By George, I believe you are!" said Lathrop suddenly.

"And in that case," said Max, "we ought to put all the clues before our criminological expert."

Dr. Archer raised his almost invisible blond eyebrows. "Our criminological expert?"

"Mr. Lathrop. After all, he represents the New York police department. He's crossing the ocean to bring back Carlo Fenelli."

Second sensation.

"That's not quite accurate," observed Lathrop, without batting an eyelid. "I suppose your brother told you?"

"Yes."

"His facts were a little rocky," said Lathrop in the same drawling tone. "It's true I'm going after Carlo Fenelli. But I'm not connected with the police department in the way you mean. I'm an Assistant District Attorney. My job is to see that Carlo doesn't get away with another of his celebrated legal Houdini tricks. Great lad, Carlo."

"That's Carlo Fenelli, the racketeer?" inquired Dr. Archer.

"Yes." Lathrop made a gesture which brushed this aside as of small interest. He seemed excited about something else.

Teetering before the fireplace, his hands behind his back and his forehead pitted with wrinkles of concentration, he allowed an urchin's grin to flicker across his face.

"You see—about that knife-throwing business," he went on. "Now, I'm a lawyer; not a detective. Thanks for the flattery, though. And, as a matter of fact, the study of fingerprints was once a great hobby of mine. But there's one thing that might be very interesting about the doctor's story. Somebody was throwing knives at a face drawn on a piece of paper. All right! The question is, was there anything personal in it? Was it a drawing of any face in particular? Could you recognize it?"

Dr. Archer snapped his fingers.

"Ah! Stupid of me," he said, as though some trifle had escaped his memory. "I should have mentioned that. No, the drawing was not recognizable as anyone in particular. Just a crude sketch. But one thing, if this is of any value to you, was definitely indicated."

"What was that?"

"It was a woman's face," said Dr. Archer.

4

"Maxie," said Mrs. Zia Bey.

"Yes?"

"Max-ie!"

"Yes?"

"I'm awfully thirsty. Aren't you going to get me another drink?"

"Look here, Estelle. I'm perfectly willing to get you all the brandy aboard this ship. But, you're tight as an owl already. Can you hold any more?"

"Maxie, don't be nasty."

"Oh, all right. Steward!"

Things were going wrong again.

At nine o'clock that night, the *Edwardic*, butting a head-wind some six hundred miles off Ambrose Light, was running into really heavy weather. So was Max Matthews.

In the spacious Long Gallery, where the chairs were too

thick to slide easily, Max sat back in one and braced himself. Mrs. Zia Bey knelt on the seat of another, pouting. He had come up here just after dinner, to drink his coffee in peace and comfort. His bad leg had begun to ache with the sleety change in the weather, nor did his insides feel too comfortable under a combination of pitch-and-roll. Estelle Zia Bey joined him half an hour later. As soon as he saw her enter from the other end of the Long Gallery—skittering on the heaving carpet, holding wide the flounced skirt of her white silk evening-gown—he knew what was wrong. Estelle waved a bulging white handbag at him.

She told him about it, volubly. Lathrop and George A. Hooper, it appeared, had been in a skittish mood at dinner. When they passed her table on the way out, they had sat down and invited her to drink. Hooper, she said, had "made a pass" at her. Max considered this very improbable; but in the inflamed state of her imagination she was apt to say anything. She told the story with a combination of immense dignity, crowing laughter, and arch coquettishness.

He kept her quiet with one hand, and beckoned to a steward with the other.

"Steward! Two brandies."

"Double brandies, Maxie."

"Double brandies. For God's sake, sit down in that chair! Don't kneel in it: sit down."

"What's the matter, Maxie? Don't you like your little Estelle?"

"Of course I like you. But do you want to go head-first and break your neck?"

"I don't care."

"Nonsense. Where's your life-jacket?"

"I don't know. I left it somewhere."

As he looked back at her, he saw her mood change. Her eyes, faintly streaked with red round the blue pupil, began to blaze. The drooping wrinkles went down still more past the drooping mouth. She lifted her handbag as though to throw it.

"You are an old stick in the mud," she said.

"Maybe so. But—"

"You don't need to think you're so grand," she shrilled at him, half getting up. "I know lots of people a l-lot grander than you are. I'm going to see one. In the Adm—you go to

33

hell! I don't need you to buy me drinks. I've got my information. I've got my proofs. I've got my—"

"Steady. Here's your brandy."

She was working up steam, and seemed half frantic. Her outburst went almost unheard in the long crash and roar of water outside, which rattled the furniture and seemed even to rattle her teeth. Suddenly she seemed rather dizzy.

"Here, I'll hold these. Sit down."

"Maxie!" said Estelle tearfully, and sat down in his lap and put her head on his shoulder.

This was the point at which Miss Valerie Chatford walked into the Long Gallery.

To be found sprawled back in the public room of a liner, holding a glass of brandy at arm's length in each hand to keep it from spilling, and with a drunken woman strangling you at the same time, may be called embarrassing whoever sees you. But after the first moment—curiously enough—Max was not embarrassed at all.

He was furious. And this was caused by the look bestowed on him by Valerie Chatford.

She entered from the other end of the Long Gallery: that is, from the lounge. Max did not know who she was. It is not even certain that he noticed any detail about this girl except the look she gave him.

She had one of those cold, half-supercilious, washed-out faces which are usually called patrician. She trod the earth as though she owned it. Even in repose such faces often arouse ire. You can almost hear the voice: "Oh, really? How stupidly tiresome!" That was the sort of bored look she gave Max. Then even this faint flicker of interest died out.

Max had a hazy impression of a short white fur coat, and of small brown curls. Then she was gone, steadying herself with one hand on a chattering bookcase. And he realized what a human and likable sort of person Estelle was, after all.

"Max-ie."

"Yes?"

"Where's my brandy?"

"Here. Sit up and take it." He was filled with a sort of soothing despair. "Listen!" he said, adjusting that none-too-light weight on his lap. "There's only one thing to be done. Give me a little time, and I'll get blotto too. Then we'll both feel the same."

"Maxie, how awfully nice of you!"

"But in the meantime, what do you say to getting a little air on deck? Can you make it?"

"Max, don't be nasty. Of course I can make it!"

"Come on, then. Easy."

She seemed subdued and a trifle dazed. Toward her he now felt intensely protective. She was a good scout who only wanted looking after. They went through the lounge, digging their heels in as the furniture cracked and jumped and tilted up at them. They emerged into the hall beside the main stair-case.

"The last drink did me good," whispered Estelle, in a hoarse voice. "Just let me go down to my cabin and get a wrap and powder my nose; and I'll be with you in half a tick."

"Sure you can manage? Would you like me to go down with you?"

"Of course I can. You wait here. I'll be back in a minute."

He steadied her as she clutched the handrail of the stair-case, and watched her go down, holding her handbag to her breast.

On the wall over the two lifts opposite the staircase, there was a clock whose hands pointed to nine forty-five. In lulls of the roaring outside, you could hear the click as its hands jumped from one minute to the next.

And, while he waited, Max's heart warmed toward Estelle Zia Bey. She might have been only drunk, but she had seemed forlorn and rather pitiful as she stumbled down those stairs. This was (no doubt) a maudlin mood on Max's part, produced by loneliness or other causes. But she was the most heartening and human thing aboard this ship; you had only to contrast her with the frozen-faced girl who sailed through the Long Gallery.

He tried to remember what Estelle had told him about herself. She volunteered information in pounces. Her mind was like a railway yard, full of bewildering points and switches. But over every track ran a sort of bumpy good nature. She spoke highly of her second husband, Mr. Zia Bey, from whom she had been divorced some six months. She had two children, now at school in Switzerland: her husband had been awarded the custody of the children.

The hand of the clock kept on clicking. Five minutes.

Max, his life-jacket hung over his shoulder, was finding it increasingly difficult to stand up even with the aid of the cane. The deck under him seemed to slip from beneath his feet like a colossal chute, catching the breath in the pit of his stomach. It dived; halted, and climbed again, bobbing like a cork, before he could get his balance. Woodwork creaked in agony as the deck dropped.

He fell across to a pillar, held on to it, and lowered himself into the pillar-seat. A heavy draft was blowing: somewhere, a door kept on banging.

Maybe they hadn't better go out on deck, on a night like this. The sea was alive: it smote the *Edwardic's* plates like a fist. Anyway, he ought to have an overcoat. Estelle always announced firmly that her age was thirty-five. Where were all the other passengers? In the next room—the lounge—something heavy, which sounded like a potted palm, fell over with a crash and rolled. The lounge-steward should see to that. Every stick of furniture chattered there.

Ten minutes.

What was keeping the woman?

He was being dense, of course: she had passed out. She had gone down there with the best intentions in the world, but instead she had slid down on her berth into oblivion. Lathrop and Hooper must have given her a lot of liquor; though, of course, she had taken three or four cocktails before dinner.

He had waited several more minutes before apprehensions commenced to trouble him. Estelle was practically blind to the world. Suppose she had fallen down and hurt her head? Easy enough to do, in those cabins. The rubbery smell of the hall got into Max's nostrils, and wouldn't go out: he wondered whether he might not forfeit all his boasts by being seasick himself.

Better go down and see what had happened.

The steps were Max's most treacherous bit. Covered with brass bindings on the treads, they had a snaky movement of their own. But it seemed foolish to summon the lift just to go down one flight to B Deck.

He was breathing hard when he reached the bottom. The long alleyway on B Deck, gleaming white and shiny like a shoe-box, stretched away past the starboard cabins. It bowed steeply, and threw him forward. He turned into the alcove between his own and Estelle's cabins, and knocked at her closed door.

There was no reply. He knocked again.

36

"Want anything, sir?" asked his bedroom steward, instantly appearing from round the corner of the main alleyway.

"No, thanks. Go away."

After knocking a third time, he opened the door.

The cabin was in darkness. But a dim light burned in the small private bathroom on the right, whose door was open and hooked back. You could trace the outlines of shaking and banging objects which moved like shadows in the cabin.

It was square in shape. Against the wall opposite Max, at the extreme left, was the head of one berth. Then came a tiny bedside table. Then a porcelain wash-basin. Then a dressing-table, with a mirror over it. Then another bedside table, and the head of a second berth. All these were ranged in a line against the opposite wall.

Estelle Zia Bey, a mere dim shape in that light, had been sitting in front of the dressing-table with her back towards Max. She had now fallen face-forward, still sitting on a stool, and motionless except for the motion of the ship. It was as though she had slipped over unconscious while putting on lipstick. But there was a warm, sweet, acrid odor which stifled and sickened the nostrils in that overheated cabin.

Max switched on the light.

First of all he saw the blood-spots which spattered the mirror. Then he seemed to see blood everywhere. That was what he smelt, too.

*   *   *   *   *

He went outside and closed the door.

"Steward!" he called.

There was no answer.

"Steward!" bawled Max. His stomach seemed to be opening and shutting inside him; he closed his eyes, conquering nausea; and, when he opened them again, there was the steward in front of him.

"I want you to go and get the captain," said Max.

The enormity of this request appeared to stun his companion. In the half-light Max saw his shining, wide-open eyeballs, and his deprecating smirk.

"The captain, sir?"

"The captain."

"But *I* couldn't do that, sir. And anyway, you know, they wouldn't disturb the captain."

"Look here," said Max, fighting hard. Both he and the steward had to steady themselves before a pitch; but it carried them so lightly that they might have been flying. "I'm the captain's brother, do you understand? His brother. I've got orders from him to do exactly what I'm doing. You do just as I tell you, and take the message to him personally, or he'll murder you. Tell him I've got to see him at once in B-37, and say that he'll guess what I want to see him about. Now hop it."

After a pause the steward hopped it. Max went back into cabin B-37, and closed the door behind him.

5

Mrs. Zia Bey's throat had been cut.

This is one of the ugliest sights in the realm of violent death, and need not be fully described here. But Max had to look at it.

The frosted ceiling-bulb showed it with raw clearness. Fortunately her face was hidden; the arms, at either side of it, bent in at the elbows and cradled above her head. Her white silk gown was backless, so that he could see the long ridge of the backbone under the taut, brownish skin as she lay forward. The hair helped hide her face, too. There was so much blood that it would have been difficult to identify at first glance many of the toilet-articles on the dressing-table. Blood had spattered as far as the mirror when the artery was severed, and soaked the front and sides of her gown. When the ship's propellors shook out of water, the vibration through the whole cabin made her shiver as though she were crying. She slid, and would have fallen sideways if Max had not steadied her body.

This couldn't be real.

But it was.

Behind him, the door of the wardrobe kept swinging slowly open and shut—open and shut—with a maddening and monotonous *clack*. There were intervals of about twenty seconds between the clacks, and Max found himself jumping to them. He pushed the wardrobe door fast shut with his elbow. Then he forced himself to walk round and look at her from all sides.

Estelle's two trunks had been removed long ago, so that the cabin was comparatively clear. Her white purse, open, lay on a made-up bed. The sable coat lay beside it. There was even a speck or two of blood as far away as the white counterpane.

Died while she was drunk.

The silk wall-panel design of the cabin was blue and orange. It had become hot in here: sweating-hot, blinding-hot, choking-hot, and the rasping bulkheads squeaked interminably. But hardly five minutes passed before the door opened, and Commander Francis Matthews took a quick glance inside.

After that, he came in hastily and shut the door. For a time he said nothing. Max heard him breathe asthmatically.

"Done herself in?"

"No," said Max. "I don't think so, anyway."

"Why not?"

"Her throat's cut. I can't find anything she could have done it with. There's nothing here but a nail-file."

"Not murder?"

"Looks like it."

Commander Matthews turned his eyes round. *"You* didn't—?"

"No, no!"

"Bolt the door."

While Max did so, Commander Matthews walked across to the far berth, under the porthole on the left-hand side of the cabin, and sat down on the edge of the berth. The message had found him in the act of shaving, and there was still a smell of witch-hazel round him. Max observed this because odors are the most noticeable thing to a man with a queasy stomach. Commander Matthews' stocky elbows were outthrust, and he still breathed hard. The gold oak-leaves on the peak of his cap looked heavy and authoritative.

"What happened?"

Max told him.

"She came down here at quarter to ten," said the captain. "And you followed at just on ten o'clock?"

"Yes."

"I expected something. But not this. This looks like—"

With the sliding of the ship, the dead woman slid gently off the dressing-table before anybody could catch her.

She fell on her back, but rolled over again on her face, upsetting the bathroom stool on which she had been sitting. Small toilet-articles—an eyebrow-tweezers, an orange-stick, and a small bottle of nail-varnish—were swept off and fell in blood-stained patches round her. As she lay with her face against the light blue carpet, they could see that she still held a big gold lipstick in her right hand.

Commander Matthews got up and went to examine her.

"Usually," he said, "they take a long time to die. What happened? Didn't she yell, or put up a fight, or anything like that?"

"I don't know. We might ask the steward if he heard anything."

"Bump on the back of her head," said the captain, feeling in the bedraggled yellow hair. "Probably came up behind. Bashed her with something, and stunned her. Then held her head up, and—" He made a cutting gesture, from left to right.

"You make it very vivid."

Commander Matthews glanced up.

"I've seen this sort of thing before," he said unexpectedly. "In the old *Heraldic*. It was a laundry-steward did it."

"Did what?"

"Killed a woman like this. Sex maniac. You know what I mean. Only, in this case there doesn't seem to be any sign of anybody trying to—"

"No."

"Hard to tell. The fellow might have got scared, and sheered off."

Max shook his head. "I've got a feeling that there's more to it than that."

"So have I. Only, it might be. These things happen, I tell you." The captain paused. For the first time his gruff voice betrayed excitement. He examined the body more closely, and then took several quick looks round him. "My God, Max, we've got him! Look there. And there. And there. We've got him!"

"Where? What is it?"

"Finger-prints," said Commander Matthews.

Once pointed out, the traces became blatantly obvious. On the right-hand shoulder-strap of Estelle's white gown, a little

40

way down the back, they could see the clear print in blood of what looked like a thumb. Another, more smudged, was at her waist on the left side.

Commander Matthews got up from his squatting position, breathing hard through his nose. He looked closely at the two shallow drawers in the mahogany front of the dressing-table. Taking a box of matches out of his trousers' pocket, he struck a match and held it close to the stained mahogany surface. Just under the ledge of the glass top—in a place formerly hidden by the dead woman's body—they saw a half-print which looked like the narrower one of a finger.

The captain craned his neck round. He glanced at the wash-basin, which also had a mirror over it, at the left of the dressing-table. Two folded face-towels should have hung on a small rail at the side of it. Only one towel hung there now. Commander Matthews found the second towel, crumpled and blood-stained, in the wastepaper basket under the dress-ing-table.

He flung the towel back into the basket.

"That's it," he said calmly. "Killed her. Lost his head, wiped his hands, and bolted. Crazy fool."

Commander Matthews sounded almost relieved.

"Looks like it," admitted Max.

"Don't you agree?"

"I suppose so."

"Then what's the matter with you? Why have you got that funny look on your face?"

"Oh, you're probably right. I'm not denying it. Only—"

"Well? Well?"

"Only, it sounds almost too easy, that's all. 'The Bloody Thumb.' All done up into a parcel for us. Finger-prints where we couldn't miss 'em."

There was a silence, while the *Edwardic*'s engines throbbed and churned far below. Commander Matthews permitted himself a bleak smile.

"Don't get funny ideas, my lad," he warned. "You always were the one of the family for funny ideas."

"Yes."

"Now take a look at what really happens. I've seen this sort of thing before. I know. At this minute, the fellow's prob-ably shivering and sweating under the bed-clothes in his cabin, wondering why he did it and whether he's left any clues. Clues!" His face darkened. "Not that it isn't bad

41

enough. Just when I was worried about—other things. Fine business. We've got a maniac aboard."

"I agree. We've got a maniac aboard, all right."

"Yes. Now, see here, Max. I won't have this thing spread round," pursued the captain calmly. "No good alarming everybody. Easy does it; *and* we get our man. We'll take the finger-prints of every single person aboard this ship. Easy enough to find an excuse for that without giving the show away. Then we lock the fellow up until we get to the other side."

"That seems reasonable. Do you know anything about finger-prints? How to identify them, and the rest of it?"

For a moment this made the captain hesitate.

"No, but I think the purser does. Yes, I'm pretty certain Griswold does. Hold on!"

He reflected.

"Didn't that chap What's-his-name—Lathrop—didn't Lathrop tell me he was by way of being an authority on finger-prints?"

"I imagine he did. He's been telling the rest of us so, anyway."

"Good idea," muttered the captain, nodding emphatically as the plan unfolded in his mind. "We'll co-opt him, that's what. He's a policeman and he'll know how to keep his mouth shut."

"He's a lawyer. But it probably amounts to the same thing, as far as your purpose goes."

Commander Matthews was not listening.

"You can keep your mouth shut, I hope?"

"Yes. How many people are you going to let into the secret?"

Again the captain reflected.

"As few as possible. The purser, of course. And the photographer'll have to know, because we need pictures of those finger-prints. And the doctor . . ."

"You mean Dr. Archer?"

"Dr. Archer? No, I mean the ship's doctor. Who the devil said anything about Dr. Archer? Why tell him?"

"Because," replied Max, "somebody was practicing knife-throwing at a drawing of a woman's face outside Dr. Archer's door last night." And he repeated the story.

"I'm not trying to pester you, Frank," he went on, while the captain stood with fists on hips and turned down the corners of his mouth into a grim arc. "I know you've got too much on your mind as it is—"

"Nonsense. It's only my job."

"—but this idea of a sex-maniac doesn't sound very convincing. And you're worried about it yourself. What is all the mystery you were hinting about to me last night? What is it you suspect about one of your passengers? Because there is something. Furthermore, who is your ninth passenger? I'll swear there are nine passengers aboard; and that you know it, and for some reason you're hiding one of 'em."

Commander Matthews did not reply. He only made a contemptuous gesture.

"You see, Frank, it can't be a coincidence or an unrelated incident that this woman gets herself killed at this time. Finally, I suspect those finger-prints."

"But, damn it, man, there *are* the finger-prints. They're real. What do you suspect about them?"

"I don't know."

"Rats," said his brother shortly.

"All right. Maybe."

"Well, why do you say she was killed? You were going about with her, in spite of my advice. Why do you think she was killed?"

"I don't know."

"Good. Then let's get on with it and nab the murderer. Now, look here. I want you to go and find Mr. Lathrop, and ask him to come here immediately. The sooner we get started, the better. In the meantime, I'll have a word with the cabin steward. He may have seen somebody going in or out. Also, it might be a good idea to talk to the stewardess who attended to Mrs. Zia Bey. Not that questioning matters a curse in this case, because we've got the finger-prints. But I was wondering . . ."

His gaze strayed across to the berth on the right-hand side of the cabin. On the counterpane of this berth lay Estelle Zia Bey's white handbag, open; and her fur coat. Max again noticed what he had noticed before, the two tiny spots of blood on the side of the counterpane which overhung the berth. It seemed a very long distance for blood to have splashed.

"Whether she'd been robbed," concluded Commander Matthews thoughtfully.

43

"I was wondering," said Max, "just the same thing."

"Why?"

"She kept nursing that handbag like a baby, all this evening." Max stopped. Other vivid pictures came crowding and flashing back into his mind. "Come to think of it, I've never seen her without a handbag: white, black, or snakeskin. It's never been out of her hand, except when she kept it in her lap. And in each case the handbag has bulged as though she were carrying something clumsy inside."

They both moved across to the berth. Commander Matthews picked up the open handbag, shook it wide, and turned it upside down. A cascade of small articles tumbled out on the counterpane: another lipstick, a powder-compact, a small bunch of keys, some notes and coins, a comb, and a book of stamps. But what drew their attention was the largish-sized object which thudded down on the counterpane among the other things. Max stared at his brother, who made a noise like a man hit in the stomach. They saw now what Estelle Zia Bey seemed to have been carrying, and what made the unsightly bulge in the handbag.

It was a bottle of ink.

6

So he went up to find Lathrop, to fetch him to Mrs. Zia Bey's cabin.

He stayed in cabin B-37 only long enough to assure himself that there was no secret about the bottle or the ink. It was an ordinary bottle of blue-black writing ink, of a familiar American brand, such as you could buy anywhere for ten or fifteen cents. It was full, and did not seem to have been opened. He and Commander Matthews poured a little of the ink out in the wash-basin to have a look at it.

The time was now twenty-five minutes past ten o'clock. Wind and sea had fallen a good deal: and, though the *Edwardic* still pitched, it was a slow and ghostly motion done in almost complete silence. The silence seemed as oppressive as the noise had been half an hour before.

But it allowed Max to find Lathrop without difficulty. Lathrop was playing the grand piano in the lounge, and having a private sing-song all on his own.

Lathrop was a great stylist and poseur at the piano, making sweeping gestures which brought the cuffs clear out of the sleeves of his dinner-jacket.

"Oh, the moonlight's fair to-night along the Waaabash,
From the fields there comes the scent of new-mown hay—"

Then Lathrop broke off, still riffling the keys of the piano, to address Max.

"Sit down," he said. "And settle a late argument between Hooper and me. Do French officers always wear their hats indoors? Detectives do, I know. And Jews sometimes. But why French officers? I've got a theory about that fellow Benoit. He's really a ghost. He—

"Through the sycamores the candle-lights are gleaming,
On the banks of the Wabash, far away."

Thus Lathrop concluded, interrupting himself. His strong voice, and the tinkle of the piano, reached away into the dim recesses of the lounge. It sounded blattering and almost obscene. But Max found a way of stopping it.

"Can you come down to B-37 at once? Somebody has killed Mrs. Zia Bey."

There was dead silence.

Lathrop's hands rested motionless on the keys of the piano. But he turned his head round, the wrinkles climbing up his leathery neck. His face now looked as old as his well-brushed white hair.

"So there was something in that knife-throwing business," he said.

"Evidently."

"Killed? Murdered? Great—!" He checked himself. "How?"

"Her throat was cut. We haven't been able to find any weapon so far."

"I don't want any part of it," said Lathrop, and struck his little finger on a treble key of the piano.

"But the captain particularly wants you to go. He's waiting there now."

"Me? But why me? What can I do? Jumping Jupiter, haven't I got enough on my hands already?"

45

"Sh-h!"

"Yes, but I ask you!"

"It was true, wasn't it: what you told us this morning? About your knowing all about finger-prints?"

"Yes, that's true enough." Lathrop whistled. "You mean you've got some finger-prints? I don't mind helping with that."

Max ignored this.

"Mr. Lathrop, I'd like you to answer me one question. It may sound like a foolish question. It's probably just a wool-gathering notion of mine. Anyway, here you are. Is it possible to forge finger-prints?"

"No," answered Lathrop, after a slight pause.

"Are you sure of that? They're always doing it in the detective stories, to implicate innocent persons."

"I know they are. But here's the truth, if you're interested. It's possible to reproduce a print, of course; yes, and reproduce it very well. But it wouldn't deceive an expert, even aside from the fact that the mark would never stand chemical analysis. If you don't believe me, look it up in Gross. He's the final court of appeal. And Gross (if my memory's got it straight) says that no case has ever been brought to light anywhere in the world in which forged finger-prints have been used."*

Lathrop paused.

"Now, young man, I want to know why you asked me that," he added.

Max gave him a short sketch of the facts. "You're supposed to keep this dark," he warned. "The fewer people who know, the better. Consequently—"

"Sh-h!" hissed Lathrop.

A faint gurgling snore, followed by a grunt and mutter as of someone half-roused out of a doze, made Max swing round.

Mr. Hooper, of Bristol, slept in a tall brocaded wing-chair. The rays of one dim lamp just touched him. His short, stout body was tucked well back into the chair, whose back towered over his head. Mr. Hooper's chin had fallen forward into his collar. His stubbly iron-gray hair, cropped close against a round head, was of a darker color than the curving mustache which blew out with each bubbling movement of his

* Hans Gross, *Criminal Investigation* (Third Edition: London, Sweet & Maxwell, 1934) p. 192.

lips. There was a pink flush on his cheeks, as of pleasant after-dinner brandies. His closed eyelids had an almost child-like look. His hands were folded over his paunch, beatifically; and sleep was a beatitude.

"Keep your voice down," said Lathrop. "The old boy's not feeling very well. Did I tell you his son was very ill? That's why he's hurrying back. And yet—"

"And yet, what?"

"Somebody killed that woman," said Lathrop.

This was when Max first realized that they were moving toward terror, as surely as the ship was moving toward the submarine zone.

But he tried to fight this feeling off.

"Well?" he said. "Are you going down to B-37?"

"Naturally. Anything I can do. You're coming along, aren't you?"

"Not for a minute. I've got to rout out the purser, and he's got to find the photographer. You go on down ahead. But, between ourselves, what do you think of the finger-print situation?"

Lathrop got up from the piano. He seemed disturbed.

"I'm inclined to agree with your brother. Some nut who . . . you know. We ought to get him. All the same, I suppose now they'll be tearing around asking everybody, 'Where were you at such-and-such a time?' "

"There shouldn't be much of that. Not with the finger-prints to go by."

"And *I* can't prove any alibi, for one," said Lathrop humorously. "I was out on deck most of that time. Mean weather, too. The only person I remember talking to, and early in the evening at that, was that curly-haired girl who's been laid up. Chatford, the steward told me her name is."

"Not the fish-faced female in the white fur?"

Lathrop stared at him.

"Here! What do you mean, fish-faced?" he demanded. "She's a good-looker. Got class, too. I didn't get a chance to have a long talk with her, but she struck me as being the real goods and no mistake."

"She's the world's worst pain in the neck."

Again Lathrop stared at him, surprised at his tone. Max was surprised at it himself. But he could not help himself: his tongue ran away with him: and, as though for an outlet of his feelings, he put into the words all the concentrated venom which swelled up from other causes than this.

In fact, he almost yelled at Lathrop.

"All right, all right," said the latter. "I don't know what you've got against the poor girl, but let it go. I'll hop down and see your brother."

Max gave a surly assent.

As he went down in the lift to the purser's office on C Deck, the words "poor girl" rankled. He found the purser's office closed, its wooden blind drawn down. But, when he knocked at a door beside the desk, the purser's clerk—sitting in a fog of cigarette-smoke before a pile of passports and official forms—gave directions.

"He's not here," the clerk said. "If he's not in the lounge or the smoking-room, you'll probably find him in Mr. Kenworthy's cabin. B-70, on the port side."

It was in the last-named place that Max found him. The purser's uproarious laughter, followed by weak and sardonic mirth from another person, could be heard from behind the closed door of B-70. Max's knock produced a reply of anguish from the weaker voice.

"If that's Walsingham," it howled, "go away. I don't want any more scrambled eggs. I can't stand the sight of a scrambled egg. By cripes, Walsingham, if you bring just one more scrambled egg into this place, I'll rub your face in it."

Max opened the door.

Mr. Griswold, the purser, was a stout hearty-looking man with big spectacles and a grin from ear to ear. He sat back comfortably in an easy chair near the invalid's berth, and smoked a cigar.

"Come in," he invited. "Don't mind Mr. Kenworthy. He's a little upset."

"Upset?" said the Hon. Jerome Kenworthy. "Devil burn you, I'm dying. And what do you care?" He blinked at Max. "Look here, I'm sorry. I thought you were the evil-hearted Walsingham. Walsingham is a steward who suffers from the delusion that a constant diet of scrambled eggs, forcibly administered if necessary, can cure any thing from simple indigestion to the black plague. Don't keep the door open. Come in and witness the passing of my spirit."

Max later learned from the purser that to pester Jerome Kenworthy was a sport to which he looked forward. But this young man was genuinely ill. He had been able to hold no food on his stomach for twenty-four hours; and he looked it.

He occupied in grandeur a big three-berth cabin. Lying sideways with his head propped a little up on squashed pillows, he peered weakly at the door. Jerome Kenworthy was a thin, gangling youth whose pallor and prematurely lined mouth were only partly due to illness. His loose fair hair shaded one eye. He wore octagonal rimless spectacles which gave him a deceptively serious look. But his mouth and eyes had humor, even if this quality were now in abeyance.

The purser blew cigar-smoke in his direction.

"Griswold," said the young man, "I'm not kidding. I can't stand it."

The purser's grin faded.

"Do you mean that?"

"I'm dying, I tell you," whispered Kenworthy, with every evidence of earnestness. "I tried to stand up a while ago, and went over flop. That was when you tried to play your asinine joke . . ."

"Nonsense. I haven't been playing any jokes."

Kenworthy flopped over on his back and closed his eyes.

"Griswold," he said to the ceiling, "I admit you owe me one or two for that crossing in August. But not now. Wait till I can fight back. This is exactly like the worst hangover I ever had, only ten times worse."

Suddenly he remembered a duty.

"I beg your pardon," he added, rolling over and opening one eye at Max. "Er—can I do anything for you?"

"Sorry to butt in," said Max. "I was looking for the purser. The captain wants him."

Griswold sat up.

"The old man wants me?" he asked incredulously. "What is it?"

"I don't know, but it seems to be pretty serious. Can you come straightaway?"

"Somebody must have got his throat cut," observed the purser in an offhand tone. "Right! I'm at your service." He got up, spilling cigar-ash. Then he hesitated.

"See here," he said to Kenworthy. "I don't want anybody to think I'm putting the passengers off their feed. I don't want to get in bad. And, word of honor, I don't know what you're talking about. I haven't been playing any jokes on you."

Kenworthy closed his eyes.

"Get out," he said with weak malevolence. "I've got Walsingham trained, and now I'll train you. Get out, and don't come back ever again. I mean that. We are not amused."

"Yes, but what am I supposed to have *done?*"

Kenworthy opened one eye.

"Some people," he whispered, "might think it was funny to wait until this old tub was rolling its worst a little while ago; and make sure most of the lights were off in here, and I was feeling my worst. Then some people might think it was funny to put on a gas-mask, and suddenly pop the door open and look in at me with it."

The purser blinked at him.

"A gas-mask?"

"A gas-mask. Gaa!" said Kenworthy, and kicked out his heels and rattled all over like a skeleton. "I never saw anythink like it since I had D.T.'s in Miami. That damned swine-snouted thing standing still as death, looking in at me, and not moving when I spoke to it."

"Are you serious?"

"Oh, blimey. Am I serious? Get out."

"Old man, on my solemn word of honor, I never—!"

"Listen," quavered the other. "When I took passage in this hell-ship, I carefully chose a cabin just across the alleyway from all the lavatories. Now follow me. In just about one minute—" he extended a long hand, palm vertical—"I am going out that door at a speed of three hundred and eighty-five m.p.h. Chuck my dressing-gown on the bed. And keep out of my way. In other words, if you can't hear a hint, take pity on a strong man's dying agony, and buzz off about your business."

"But—"

"Out!"

"Sorry, old chap. I'll send the doctor to you."

"You do and I'll throw scrambled eggs at him. I want to be alone."

Motioning Max before him, the purser turned out the lights, went out into the alleyway, and closed the door behind them.

"He's always like that," the purser confided, with an air of apology, as they went up the passage. "Cruikshank and I used to have a great time kidding him."

"You mean he usually sees people in gas-masks opening his door and looking in at him?"

There was a pause in the breezy, deserted passage.

The purser frowned.

"Oh, he was probably trying to get back at me. Do you ever read detective stories?"

"Frequently."

The purser chuckled. "I was kidding him about it on the other trip. I said: Suppose you wanted to poison somebody? Well, do it aboard a liner. Wait until your victim starts to get seasick. Then feed him poison. He'll get worse and worse, while the doctor only smiles and prescribes a dry biscuit; so nobody can prevent it, and he's dead before anyone knows there's something wrong with him. Mr. Kenworthy turned green when I told him that."

The ingenuity of this made Max blink. Abruptly Griswold checked himself. He seemed to realize that he was talking to the brother of the *Edwardic*'s commander. His chuckle turned into a cough.

"But I don't want you to think . . ." he began hastily.

"No, no."

"And I was forgetting. What does the old man want with me? Where is he?"

All the easy-going air was wiped off his face as Max explained.

"Right!" he said, with curt efficiency. "I've got an ink-roll for finger-prints in my office. We'll take the prints on place-cards. The photographer's got just the apparatus for this, too. Tell the old man we'll be with him in five minutes. Excuse me."

And he clattered off down the stairs towards his office.

Max was left standing in the open space of B Deck before the staircase. The *Edwardic*'s "shop"—opposite the head of these stairs—glowed yellow with concealed lights behind its glass sides, though it had been closed long ago. Behind it was the barber's, also closed. Max stood and stared at rows of souvenir desk-lighters, dolls, paper-knives, and ornaments tumbled together in the windows. Like Kenworthy, he was not amused when someone unexpectedly touched him on the shoulder from behind.

"Good evening," observed Dr. Reginald Archer. "Interested in the shop? Thinking of some lady?"

"Yes."

"I hope I didn't startle you?"

"No."

Dr. Archer had evidently come up the stairs. He was muffled up in a bathrobe of thick white towelling. His thinning hair fluffed up in damp spikes, and he scrubbed at it with a towel. His bare feet were thrust into slippers. but he conscientiously carried a life-jacket.

"Just been having a turn in the swimming-pool," explained the doctor. "Down on E Deck, you'll find it. Good Lord! It's a quarter to eleven! I've been down there over an hour."

"Have a good swim?"

"Splendid!" said the doctor. His face, scrubbed down to the sandy eyebrows, radiated sly good-nature. He continued to rub his head with the towel. "It was a bit rough at first, but the ship steadied. I feel a new man. Nothing like a bit of exercise. And nothing like a shower for getting one's self really clean, either. I shall sleep tonight."

(I wish *I* could. Looking at the open edges of the throat was the worst.)

"No more knife-throwings tonight?"

"Eh? Oh! No, I hope not." Dr. Archer paused, and peered round him. "Hullo! This is B Deck, isn't it?"

"Yes."

"Then I've come up one too far. My cabin's on C. Idiotic thing to do. I'm very careless sometimes." He yawned hugely; and immediately apologized. "Ah, well. Time to turn in. Not a bad day. See you tomorrow. Good night."

"Good night."

Small night-noises crept out to take possession of the *Edwardic*. The rise and fall of her bows had become as drowsy as the motion of a cradle. The sea sang whisperingly; hardly a loose chair stirred. Max turned round, and walked aft along the starboard passage toward his own cabin.

Voices, low and indistinguishable, argued behind the closed door of B-37. A scared cabin-steward, and a still more scared stewardess, hung about near the two cabins and pretended not to be listening.

Max thought: I am rather tired. The purser and the photographer are on their way. I have done all I can do for the moment. I will just go into the peace and quiet and cleanness of my own cabin for a few minutes, and sit down, and close my eyes. Frank can spare me for those few minutes, anyway.

He opened the door. Despite his own untidiness, all things

were placed in order by a phantom steward whom you never
saw at work. His berth, its linen fresh and crisp, had been
turned down for the night. A dim light burned over the wash-
stand. He sat down on the edge of the berth, unslinging his
life-jacket from his shoulder and propping up his cane
against the wardrobe. He put his hands to his aching head.
The berth looked very inviting. It would do no harm if he
merely stretched out for a minute or two, to relax. He
stretched out. In thirty seconds he was asleep.

7

"You're a fine one, you are!" said a voice.

He was roused to wakefulness by a hand shaking his
shoulder. He sat bolt upright, the mists dispelling. He was
conscious of a sense of refreshment and well-being such as
he would not have believed possible.

The lights were full on, though, with a perpetually blacked-
out room, that might have meant any time at all. Lathrop
stood at his bedside, glowering at him.

"Here," continued Lathrop. "As a matter of form, write
your John Hancock across the top of this card. Then we'll
use this ink-roller, and get your left and right thumb-prints
on the card. Your brother wanted to let you sleep; but, if I
have to lose sleep over this thing, I'm going to see that
somebody else does too."

"What time is it?"

"Two o'clock in the morning."

"Two o'clock? That's better! I was afraid I'd slept—"

"That's better, is it?" inquired Lathrop, whose bitterness
was not without justification. "We've just finished across the
way. Argue, argue, argue; yammer, yammer, yammer. You
ought to be glad you missed it. No offense intended; but of
all the pig-headed people I ever did see, your brother and
his ship's surgeon take the cake."

"Have you been taking finger-prints?"

"I don't know. The purser and the third officer went out
three hours ago, with another roller—they bagged the best
one. We haven't seen 'em since. They've probably turned in

long ago. Their orders were that if they found any passenger still up, to get his prints; but, if he'd gone to sleep, to let it wait until morning. The big job will be the crew. The excuse is that the captain's just had Admiralty orders to finger-print everybody before landing in England. With all the red tape there already is, they ought to swallow that one easy."

Max sat up on the edge of the berth.

His head felt cool, and his nerves were steady; it was as though he had come out from under a drug or a fever.

"The skipper, the doctor, and I," pursued Lathrop, deftly taking the impressions of left and right thumbs after Max had signed the card, "have been detecting. And debating. And measuring. And taking each other's finger-prints. Hours of it."

"Look. I ought to apologize."

"For what?"

"For going to sleep, or passing out, or whatever you want to call it. I don't know why it happened. I'd hate to hear what a psychiatrist might say about it."

Lathrop gave him a keen glance from under dark eye-brows that contrasted with white hair. Numbering the card, he put it away in an envelope and put the envelope in his pocket. He screwed on the cap of his fountain-pen, put the ink-roller on its tray, and sat down in a wicker chair.

"What's wrong?" he asked quietly. "Couldn't you take it?"

"I've had," said Max, "some pretty tough assignments in my time. I tested that Robertson submarine-escape appara-tus in two hundred feet of water: the thing that was supposed to be defective. I was the last man who talked to Greaser Steinmetz before the Feds shot him. It seems funny now. Ever since that fire—"

Lathrop nodded.

"Yes. What is it you're really afraid of?"

"Fire. And things blowing up. It was a chemical factory fire, you understand."

"Fire, and things blowing up," repeated Lathrop, with his eye on the carpet.

"Forget it!" he added with sudden briskness, and slapped the arms of the chair and got up. "What we all need, young fellow, is a good night's sleep. I've got a sweet job ahead of me tomorrow: going over seven or eight hundred sets of finger-prints. But it's better than some things. I'd hate to stand in the shoes of the man who left that corpse next door. Lord pity his dreams tonight! Well, I'll be seeing you."

The *Edwardic* shouldered on.

Cabin B-37 was now empty, for they had removed the body. Max glanced into a blood-spattered shell before he closed his door after Lathrop. He yawned, undressed slowly, and put on his dressing-gown. What he wanted was a warm shower to induce real sleep. So he opened the door of his private bathroom—and came face to face with Miss Valerie Chatford.

He stopped dead, and they stared at each other.

She was sitting on the rim of the bathtub, facing him. She did not appear so aloof now. Perhaps this was caused by the fact that she looked physically exhausted. Her cramped fingers unclenched from the rim of the tub; she got to her feet as though her legs were cramped too. She was wearing a gray evening-gown with a string of pearls round her neck. Her white fur wrap and her life-jacket lay in a heap on the floor. Gray eyes, of the same color as the dress but with a more luminous quality like the pearls, regarded him in defiant anger.

Distantly, he heard his own voice speak.

"How long have *you* been in there?"

"Since ten o'clock."

"Since—"

"How else could I get out?" she cried pettishly, and massaged her wrists. "Without being caught, anyway? There was always somebody in front of your cabin door."

"You have been sitting in my bathroom for four hours?"

"Yes. And now will you please, please stand aside and let me out of this horrible place?"

It is an unchivalrous fact to record, but Max roared with laughter. She looked so fiercely disdainful that he could not help it. Also, the stiffness of her legs compelled her to waddle a little when she walked. He picked up her coat and life-jacket as she passed him, her chin in the air.

"But what did you want in my bathroom? Couldn't you have—?"

"Kindly don't be disgusting."

"I was going to say," continued Max, twisting the knife, "couldn't you have walked out whenever you liked?"

"No."

"I am sorry. You look tired, all right. May I offer you—er—a more comfortable seat?"

"Thanks. I will stay a moment, if I may."

He had to admire the casual coolness with which she took advantage of this. She even grew less disdainful. When he saw her close at hand, Max admitted that perhaps "washed-out" was not quite the right word to describe her complexion. It was of that quality which is called milky and yet seems ethereal. The short curls, in shining brown hair brushed back from her forehead, made her look even younger than her twenty-two or three years. She was distinctly pretty; with any sort of animation, she might even have been attractive.

Miss Chatford spoke unexpectedly.

"The captain of a ship is all-powerful at sea, isn't he?"

"I beg your pardon?"

"The captain can do anything he likes. I mean, even if he ordered somebody to be keel-hauled, or whatever else it is they do, they'd have to do it?"

"I think you're confusing Captain Matthews of the *Edwardic* with Captain Bligh of the *Bounty*. But go on."

"And they tell me," said Miss Chatford, "that you're the captain's brother."

Max thought: Young lady, you are being almost conciliating. You want to get something out of me. And it is a source of satisfaction to reflect that, whatever it is you want, you won't get it.

Besides, the vision of old Frank ordering somebody to be keel-hauled could not be viewed without gravity-removing results.

"Who told you that?"

"Mr.—Mr. Lathrop, I think it was. The man who was talking to you in here a few minutes ago. So you must have a lot of influence with him, mustn't you?"

"With Lathrop?"

"Please don't misunderstand me," said Miss Chatford. "With your brother."

"About as much as I have with the Lord Chancellor."

"Don't fence," said Miss Chatford suddenly. "I know that Mrs. What'shername was murdered in the cabin opposite. I know you discovered her body. I know you sent for the captain, and he came down, and you found a bottle of ink in her handbag."

56

"How do you know that?"

Miss Chatford hesitated.

"I was watching. And listening. As a matter of fact, I came down here to see Mrs. Zia Bey myself. At about ten minutes to ten. But I heard her talking to some man in her cabin, so I slipped in here to wait until he went. After a little while, he did go."

"You saw the murderer leave?"

"No, I didn't see him. I had the door closed. But I heard him. After a minute I opened this door to look out—and you came along. I saw you open her door, and look in, and I saw what you saw.

"I tried to get away when you sent the steward for the captain. But, just as I slipped out, there was the stewardess coming along the passage. So I had to come back in here again. And there's been no chance to get away all this time, because of all the people. I even had to stay in that bathroom while you slept, because they were still there."

Max stood and studied her.

"You knew Mrs. Zia Bey?"

"No. I never spoke to her in my life."

"Then why did you want to see her? And have you any idea who did kill her? And why should she be carrying a bottle of ink in her handbag?"

"She wasn't carrying a bottle of ink in her handbag," returned Valerie Chatford, after a slight pause.

"I beg your pardon: she was. We found it."

"You will persist in misunderstanding me! I mean, she wasn't carrying it originally. She was carrying a big thick envelope stuffed with letters or papers or something; that's what made the handbag bulge. Whoever killed her took away the envelope, and put a bottle of ink into the handbag instead."

"But why in blazes should he do that?"

"I don't know. But I'm *sure* that's what must have happened. There's where I want you to help me."

"Help you?"

"Yes. You see, what she had in that handbag wasn't everything. She left a big envelope with the purser as well. You know what I mean, don't you? If you have any valuables, you put them into an envelope the purser gives you, and seal it up and write your name across it; and he puts it in his

57

safe until the end of the trip. I'm sure she left an envelope with the purser on the first day out."

"Well?"

"Well, if the captain says so—and the captain's word is law, isn't it?—you can get that envelope from the purser. And you can give it to me."

Again there was a silence.

The calm cheek of this request was so staggering as to inspire a kind of admiration. Max did not say anything for a time. He shaded his eyes against the overhead light, and studied her again.

"And of course," he suggested, "without saying anything about your part in it?"

"Yes."

"Or mentioning what you were doing here tonight?"

"That's it."

"Or, in fact, even asking for any explanation from you at all?"

"I can't explain! I can't explain anything. But you do understand? You will trust me, won't you?"

Max said:

"Candidly, I will not. I have come across this sort of thing in books and films; but, by all the gods, I never imagined it could happen in real life. Do you seriously imagine that you, or any other woman outside a story, can get away with that? Do you think you can tell what you choose to tell, and keep back what doesn't suit your purpose; and then look like a martyr and say you're sure some poor goop will trust you? They ruddy well won't. _I_ won't. It's too late to wake everybody up tonight. But tomorrow morning this information will be passed on to Frank. Then you can talk to him. It's out of my province."

The long, drowsy swish of water rolled and curled past the ship's side, falling back in a hiss of recoiling waves. It was intensified in the hush of early morning, where every light seemed to take on a harder brightness.

Valerie Chatford sat back in her chair. She had long eyelashes, whose shadows moved on her cheeks as the eyelids winked up and down. The breast of her gray gown rose and fell with rapid breathing. As usual, she hardly seemed to open her lips when she spoke.

"So you're going to tell the captain?"

"Naturally."

"If you do, you know, I shall simply deny it."

"Very well."

"I shall say I was never here at all."

"You've got to make up your own mind about that."

"Why," she asked, "have you made up your mind to be such a beast to me? Please don't deny it. When I saw you sitting half drunk in the Long Gallery tonight, with that trollop in your lap—"

"Miss Chatford, it's getting late. Anyway, why bother to talk about her like that? I liked her very much. She was worth ten of—"

"Of me?"

"Of anybody else aboard this ship."

"I daresay you would think so. I've noticed you're only gallant to the sort of women you think you have no need to be gallant to," said Valerie. She got up. She put on her white fur wrap, and slung the cords of the life-jacket across her arm. "And, anyway," she added from the door, "if *I* were a full-grown man, I should be ashamed to admit I was afraid of fire. I heard you talking to Mr. Lathrop, you know. Go-ood night, Mr. Max Matthews."

With that poisoned thrust she left him; and, though she stepped across the sill calmly enough, she spoiled the effect of it by slamming the door with a crash which must have been audible on A Deck. When Max turned in to bed, he addressed angry speeches to her even in sleep.

On Sunday morning, January twenty-first, he awoke to a late breakfast and a stroll on deck. Thoughts of Valerie Chatford were overshadowed by his knowledge of the finger-print census which must now be buzzing through the ship. There was nobody in the dining-room except Dr. Archer, who nodded genially on his way out, but did not stop to speak.

A Sunday quiet existed even here. (They always locked up the dart-board and hid the table-tennis equipment, as a gesture, until after lunch.) He went out on deck into an intensely cold morning, with a light wind and a pale sun shining on the lead-colored sea. The *Edwardic* was now steering a zigzag track; far away aft, you could follow the pattern in the white froth of the wake until it faded away into black water. They had set watches along the rails of the boat-deck, as well as a man in the crow's nest. But after half a dozen circuits of B Deck, Max encountered nobody except George A. Hooper dozing under a rug in a deck-chair.

59

And he did not see his brother until the religious service in the lounge at eleven o'clock.

This was conducted by Commander Matthews, who looked rather like a Puritan father, and held the Bible clumsily. He read the Twenty-third Psalm; and read it, Max thought, very well for old Frank. A small orchestra played two hymns. There was no prayer. The only persons present were Dr. Archer, Hooper, Max and Valerie Chatford—who did not look at him.

When the service broke up, Max drew Commander Matthews aside.

"Well? How about it? Have they got the finger-prints?"

"Sh-h!" urged the captain, glancing round quickly. He seemed, this morning, heavy and thoughtful. "I saw the purser for a few minutes. They got Hooper's and the Frenchman's prints last night; and yours and Lathrop's, of course. They're tackling Dr. Archer, Miss Chatford, and young Kenworthy this morning. They've begun to take the crew in relays of—"

"How long will it be before we know?"

"Now don't be impatient," said Commander Matthews, with the maddening tolerance of one who is patient by nature. "We'll get the swine. He can't get away, you know."

"Yes; but how long before we find out?"

"Lathrop says it may take all day. Just cool off and keep quiet. I'll send you word as soon as we hear anything."

It was not until half an hour later that Max remembered he had said nothing about Valerie Chatford. Never mind: that could wait. If those finger-prints nailed the murderer, such information as she might have (unless the whole thing were a lie, as he rather suspected) would be only additional details.

Lunch, and still no word.

Dr. Archer, Captain Benoit, Hooper, and Max alone went in to lunch. Talk at the captain's table was sluggish. It chiefly concerned the wireless news posted on the bulletin-board; the prospect of their being convoyed; and their probable port of destination. Dr. Archer thought Southampton. Hooper plumped for Liverpool. The table-steward, consulted as to his opinion, confidently predicted Glasgow.

Tea, and still no word.

Max was getting into a fever. He searched the ship over without finding either Lathrop or the purser. Lathrop's cabin number, he ascertained, was C-42, but Lathrop was not there; the purser's window remained closed, and repeated knockings on the door beside it drew no reply.

The wind had freshened at sundown. Prowling through lounge, Long Gallery, and smoking-room, Max found in one corner of the smoking-room a copy of *Gone with the Wind*, which had the imposing names *Pierre Marie Celestin Benoit* impressed on the fly-leaf with a rubber stamp. He had not been able to find the library-steward (you never could) and get any books from the Long Gallery. So he sat down and tried to read, but even this failed to charm. Despairing, he went on deck. It was here, in the dim red glow between the lights, that the purser found him.

"I've been looking for you," said Mr. Griswold, clearing his throat. "Cruikshank's just gone up to the bridge after the old man. Come down to my office."

"Have you got it?"

"Oh, ah. Yes. We've got it."

Despite the cold wind, Max felt his skin crawl under the thick overcoat. It may have been his imagination, but Griswold's face between the lights looked muddy with nerves.

"Well? Who killed her?"

"Come *on*," said the purser.

The office on C Deck, whose door Griswold had to unlock, was full of bright lights and a haze of cigarette-smoke. Lathrop, sweating in that close atmosphere, sat in his shirt-sleeves at the desk against one wall. Photographic enlargements—giant's thumb-prints, richly black, and pierced with numbered lines—lay in front of him. There was a magnifying glass almost the size of a saucer. There was a sheaf of notes at his elbow. Behind him the purser's clerk was stacking improvised cardboard files on top of the safe.

"Come in, Commander," Lathrop invited, creaking back in his swivel chair as the door opened again in a hurry, and the captain pushed past Max.

"Cruikshank says—"

"Yes," said Lathrop, rubbing his knuckles into hollowed eyes, and spreading his arms hugely. "You want to know whose finger-prints those are. I can tell you short and sweet. I don't know."

He added:

"They are not the finger-prints of anybody aboard this ship."

61

After that bald pronouncement, four voices began to speak at once. It was Commander Matthews who silenced the rest.

"Is this a joke?"

"No. No, no, no, no," groaned Lathrop. "I don't go half blind to play jokes." He pressed his eyes again. "Neither does Griswold. You can take it from me here and now. We have here"—he held up the enlargements—"the prints of a left and right thumb, found on the body. We have here"—he pointed to the improvised filing-cases—"the left and right thumb-prints of every living soul on this ship. And the two originals don't belong to anybody."

"It's true, sir," the purser agreed glumly.

"But that's impossible!"

"You're telling me?" inquired Lathrop. "It's true just the same."

"Some mistake . . ."

"There's no mistake, sir," said the purser, who had begun to swell like a bullfrog. "Mr. Lathrop and I have each been over the whole lot twice. There's no possibility of a mistake. If you don't mind my saying so, there's not much I don't know about finger-prints myself. It's part of my job."

Commander Matthews shouldered his way across the white-painted office. He leaned his back against the safe, planted his feet, and folded his arms.

"This wants thinking out," he declared, with such authority that nobody spoke for some seconds while he ruminated. "The prints," he presently added, peering up from under shaggy eyebrows and the brim of his cap, "the prints must have been forged."

"No," said Lathrop.

"Won't do, sir," said the purser.

"Why not? Tell me that? With a rubber stamp or something . . ." Commander Matthews ruminated again. "Stop a bit! Haven't we got a passenger whose business is manufacturing rubber stamps?"

Lathrop stopped him.

"Oddly enough, your brother"—he blinked at Max—"was asking me about forged finger-prints only last night. So Griswold and I took it up. We ourselves are willing to swear these finger-prints aren't phoney." He tapped the enlargement. "But we had to be sure. Now, it seems you've got quite a handy crowd aboard this ship. The surgeon's assistant (Banks? That's it!) is a qualified analytical chemist. So we had him make a chemical anlysis."

"A chemical analysis?" repeated Commander Matthews. "How do you mean? You can't make a chemical analysis of a photograph on a sheet of paper."

"No. But you can analyze the blood-marks themselves, from the woman's dress," said Lathrop. "That's the final test, Commander. The one thing no forger could ever get round is the oil from the sweat-glands in the human fingers."

He paused.

"We got the report hours ago," he went on. "The two thumb-prints weren't forged in any way. They were made by living fingers. You can take that as established."

For a time nobody spoke. The smoke-haze in the purser's office got into their lungs, but no one made a move to turn on the electric fan.

"This wants thinking out," insisted the captain, shaking his head from side to side. "This wants thinking out."

"Commander," said Lathrop hesitantly, "I don't want to harp on this. But are you sure you haven't got a stowaway? Wait! I don't mean the official stowaway, I don't mean the stowaway you know all about, the ninth passenger whom you're keeping in a cabin on the boat-deck. We've got *his* prints all right. And he didn't make the marks either."

Max turned round and glanced at his brother. So he had been right after all! There was a ninth passenger, whom Frank was carefully keeping from the public eye. But who? And why?

"What I mean is," pursued Lathrop, "have you maybe got a person hiding himself away, that none of us knows anything about? That's the only other explanation. Are you *sure* you haven't got a stowaway?"

"Dead certain," replied the captain.

And, when Frank Matthews spoke like that, he meant it.

"Then, sir, the thing's impossible!" said the purser. "It can't have happened."

Commander Matthews was very formal with his officers. "What's the good of talking like that, Mr. Griswold? It did happen. And, consequently, there's an explanation for it. But there's only one explanation I can see. You or someone else must have mixed up the cards, or made an error somewhere. I'm sorry, Mr. Griswold; but I'm afraid you'll have to take all the finger-prints all over again."

Lathrop uttered a howl of despair, but the purser merely nodded. He seemed a very different person from the double-chinned and sleepy-eyed joker who had chuckled over Jerome Kenworthy's sea-sickness the night before.

"Very good, sir. But I'm just as certain there was no mistake as you are certain that there's no stowaway."

Commander Matthews brooded. "No chance of somebody flum-diddling you, was there? Playing games with the cards, or getting the wrong prints to you?"

"No."

"Sure?"

"Cruikshank and I," returned the purser, "took all the prints ourselves, with the exception of four sets—your own, sir; Mr. Lathrop's; the ship's surgeon's; and Mr. Max Matthews'. Both Cruikshank and I can testify that no funny business was put up on us by our group, if Mr. Lathrop can testify the same about his group?"

"I can, definitely," swore Lathrop. "And you might tell him, Griswold, that I took yours and Cruikshank's; while you re-took my prints as a double-check."

"That's right, sir."

There was a long silence.

The purser stepped across and touched the button of the electric fan. It twirled slowly, and then began to hum with a vehemence that sounded sardonic. It blew ashes wide from several ashtrays, but nobody noticed.

"And to knock the last prop out from under you, sir," the purser added, not without malice, "I can tell you they weren't the dead woman's prints either. Not that it was likely she'd have her own thumb-prints in those places. But we thought of it; and made sure."

Commander Matthews, still cradling his folded arms, spoke with toiling lucidity.

"Let me get this quite clear. As I see it, there are three points we've got here.

"One! The finger-prints on the scene of the crime were not forged. They were made by the hands of a living person.

"Two! There is no stowaway, or any person hiding on board whose prints we haven't got.

"Three! There was no flummery or mistake about the taking or testing of the prints taken for comparison. That is, each person made his proper prints on the proper card, handing it in without trickery; and each card was honestly and accurately compared with a photograph of the original blood-marks.—Is all that correct?"*

"Right," agreed Lathrop.

Commander Matthews straightened up. He removed his cap, which left a tight reddish band in the skin of his forehead. Taking out a handkerchief, he mopped his forehead and rubbed the handkerchief up over his wiry black hair.

"But, damn it all," he shouted, *"somebody* made the prints!"

"Evidently not."

"You don't think the woman was murdered by a ghost?"

"I don't know," muttered Lathrop.

Commander Matthews put his cap back on again. "It's a murder case," he said. "We've got to be detectives. Funny. Well—let's leave the thumb-prints and try to think back for other clues."

The purser was the first to volunteer. "There was one funny thing that happened last night, sir. With that Frenchman."

They all glanced at him sharply.

"Captain Benoit?"

"Yes, sir. Cruikshank and I started our round at a little past eleven o'clock. We'd orders, you remember, to get the prints of any passengers who were still up. Well, the Frenchman was still up. He's in cabin B-71, on the starboard side. And, the minute I stuck my head in that cabin, I thought, 'By jing, we've got him!' For a guiltier-looking bloke I never saw in my life."

(Interest had grown intense.)

"He was sitting in front of his berth, using it as a kind of

* It is only fair to state here that all three of Commander Matthew's points were perfectly correct, as was later to be discovered—C.D.

65

table. Spread out on the berth were four or five rubber stamps and an ink-pad."

"Rubber stamps again!" groaned Lathrop.

"Anyway, he was printing his address on some big sheets of paper. Now, the Frenchman doesn't speak any English: not more than a couple of words, anyway. And I don't speak much French myself. Cruikshank *claims* to be able to speak French; but mostly it consists of saying, 'Ah, oui,' and looking wise; so I shouldn't rely too much on his version of the conversation. Cruikshank said, 'Monsieur, nous voulons votre print de pouce,' which didn't seem to mean much to the bloke. He fired back about fifty sentences, very much excited, and Cruikshank said, 'Ah, oui.' When finally he did seem to understand what we were after, he started to sweat and twisted his moustache and looked like death. When we insisted, he reached out and was going to press his thumb on the ink-pad—his own ink-pad—to make the impression with.

"Now, there was no earthly reason why he shouldn't use his own ink-pad. Ink's ink, however you look at it. But we were so suspicious we wouldn't let him. I was getting pretty certain we'd nailed our man. Cruikshank grabbed his wrist, and said, 'Nong, nong, monsieur, il faut se servir de notre roller.' So we held his wrists and got good, careful prints with the roller. All the time the bloke was talking away twenty to the dozen, and Cruikshank was saying, 'Ah, oui,' which seemed to surprise him. When we went away the Frenchman was looking at us with a peculiar kind of look—I don't know how to describe it—"

"Guilty?" suggested Lathrop.

The purser scratched his head.

"N-no. Not guilty. As I say, hanged if I know how to describe it. I asked Cruikshank what he was palavering about, but Cruikshank wasn't sure. We went tearing down to the photographer's. I said, 'Teddy, get those pictures out in a hurry, because I think we've got our man.' And he did. And," added the purser morosely, "the bloody thumb-prints—you know what I mean, sir—weren't Benoit's. Whoever made 'em, he didn't."

The silence of anti-climax hung heavily in the office.

"But that doesn't help us, Mr. Griswold," said the captain in some exasperation.

"I know, sir. But it seemed queer. What did he want to act so funny for?"

"It may be worth finding out. Max, you used to speak good French?"

"Passable."

"We'll turn him over to you, then," said Commander Matthews. "No other incidents of any kind, Mr. Griswold?"

"No, sir. All the rest agreed as gently as lambs." Again the purser hesitated. "But there's one or two things I'd like to ask, if I may. What evidence have you got about the murder? Were there any witnesses hanging about? Did the steward or the stewardess see anything?"

Commander Matthews shook his head.

"Not a thing. Or so they claim." He glanced at Lathrop. "But there's one point we might release, if it helps any. According to the stewardess, Mrs. Zia Bey wasn't carrying a bottle of ink in her handbag. She was carrying an envelope stuffed with letters or papers: the stewardess claims to have seen it once when Mrs. Zia Bey was dressing. Oh, and one other thing! There was no bottle of ink among the lady's possessions. The stewardess helped unpack her trunk, and swears to it."

"Ink!" said the purser. "Ink! . . . Which means, sir, that the murderer deliberately took along a bottle of ink to her cabin?"

"So it seems."

"And substituted it for the envelope?"

"Evidently."

"But why," asked the purser unanswerably, "ink?"

"Speaking for myself," grunted Lathrop, adjusting his tie and reaching for his coat, "all I want now is food. But, if you ask me, this whole case is screwy. It sounds like Nick Carter. First the bloody thumb-mark, and now the packet of papers. If you can only dig up a hypodermic full of strange Indian arrow-poison . . . Which reminds me. You'd better have your surgeon do a regular autopsy: what you call a post-mortem. Yes, I know the woman died of having her throat cut! But that's exactly the sort of point which plays the devil at trials, unless you've taken every precaution; and, as a lawyer, I warn you. Have we any other information?"

"Yes," responded Max—and proceeded to tell the whole adventure of Miss Valerie Chatford.

"Jupiter!" whistled Lathrop. "You do get in with the women, don't you?"

"Not with that one, I'm glad to say."

67

Commander Matthews's face was a picture of heavy doubt and indecision. "A little thing like that?" he said, evidently referring to the physical presence of Valerie Chatford. "You don't think she could have . . . ?" He made the gesture of one cutting a throat.

"I don't know," admitted Max. "Perhaps, or perhaps not. There wasn't any blood on her: I noticed that. And the murderer must have got a good deal of blood on him, I think."

"Hold on!" interposed Lathrop querulously. "I hope this isn't going to turn into another of those cases in which it's claimed that the murderer ran around naked—and, consequently, had no blood-stains on any clothes. The Courvoisier case. The Borden case. The Wallace case." He ticked them off on his fingers. "In each case that was suggested. And in each case there wasn't a scrap of evidence to support it. All the cases did seem to prove is that a murderer doesn't get nearly as messed up with blood as people seem to think."

"Mr. Matthews didn't say anything about Miss Chatford running around naked," the purser pointed out. His eyes seemed to turn inward, speculatively. "Though (Lordy!) what a sight that would be, wouldn't it?"

"Mr. Griswold!"

"Sorry, sir. Although"—disregarding the captain's frown, he went on with drowsy happiness—"you remember the time that Yugoslavian countess wandered into the lounge without a stitch on when the priest was conducting six o'clock mass. Not that I think Miss Chatford would, mind!"

"Mr. Griswold," said the captain, with muffled thunder echoing under his tone, "we'll have no more of that, if you please. The question isn't what the murderer wore or didn't wear. The question is how in holy blue blazes two thumb-prints—real, honest thumb-prints—were left on the scene of the crime by a ghost! By somebody who isn't aboard this ship at all! By . . ."

After holding up his own thumbs to illustrate, Commander Matthews let his arms fall and made a hopeless gesture.

"I don't believe it!" he added. "It's impossible. And the question is, what are we going to do?"

"I know what I'd do, if I were in your place," said Lathrop.

"Well?"

"I'd put it up to Sir Henry Merrivale," answered Lathrop. "I've never met him, but I hear he's the real goods at untangling impossibilities."

Max stared at Lathrop's calm face.

"Sir Henry Merrivale?" Max shouted, with a feeling that the world was going still more mad. "I used to know him seven or eight years ago, when I was in Fleet Street. But he's two thousand miles away! He's——"

"No, he's not," returned Lathrop practically. "He's up in a cabin next to the Commander's on the boat deck."

"Old H.M. aboard this ship?"

Lathrop looked surprised. "Didn't your brother tell you? No, I see he didn't. That's the ninth passenger. I don't know why they're being so hush-hush about it, or what all the mystery is about. But the Commander had to produce him when it was a question of taking everybody's finger-prints."

"Old H.M.! Good Lord, he's the very man for our money! Where is he now?"

Commander Matthews consulted his watch.

"Nearly dinner-time. At the moment, I expect he's up in the barber's shop getting a shave. I told him most people would be out of the way by this time." The captain permitted himself a bleak grin. "You say you know him pretty well, Max?"

"He used to kick me out of his office about twice a week."

"Then go up and see him. He won't listen to *me*. Rummiest blighter I ever dropped across," declared Commander Matthews, shaking his head. "Tell him the story. And see what happens. I'll be rather interested to hear what he says to this one."

9

"Looky here," howled an irate voice. "Burn me, you don't have to be tactful about it. I know I'm as bald as Julius Caesar. *But I don't want any hair-restorer!* I want a shave. S-h-a-v-e, shave. That's all I want. For the love of Esau will you stop gabblin' about hair-restorer and get on with it?"

"Very good stuff, sir," hissed the tempter. "Grow whiskers on billiard-balls, this preparation would. Why, my uncle—my own uncle, mind you, sir——"

Max peered round the corner of the barber's door.

The sight he saw was sufficiently impressive.

H.M., weight two hundred pounds, was tilted back in the barber's chair at such a perilous angle that you momentarily expected him to slide out backwards when the ship pitched. A voluminous white cloth covered him to the chin, and almost covered the chair as well. All you could see of him, projecting out of this, was his head. His face was set in an expression of malevolence beyond description as, wooden and martyred, he glared at the ceiling from behind his big spectacles.

The barber, a trim little man in a white jacket, was stropping a razor with long and loving sweeps like Sweeny Todd.

"And mind you, sir, he was as bald as you are, if you'll allow me to say. Balder! After all, you have got a little bit here," declared the barber, pulling down one of H.M.'s ears and peering behind it.

"And he said to me, 'Jack,' he said, 'where did you get that wonderful stuff you gave me? It's marvelous.' And I said, 'I'm glad to hear it, Uncle William: was it efficacious?' 'Efficacious?' he said, 'I tell you, Jack, without a word of a lie, twenty-four hours after I put the first batch on, me 'air started coming up like one of those nature-study motion pictures where they show a flower coming up whingo overnight. Black 'air, too, and I'm sixty-three if I'm a day.' Now what might your age be, sir; if I may make so bold?"

"Looky here, son. *I don't want any hair-restorer!* I got—"

"Just as you like, sir. It's your look-out," said the barber, putting down the razor, touching a lever with his foot, and sending the chair still further backwards in a way that brought a howl of apprehension from its occupant. "Could I interest you in a nice false nose, now?"

"I don't want a false nose," said H.M. "What's the matter, son? Are you goin' to cut off the one I've got already? And mind you be careful with that hot towel. I got a sensitive skin. I got—"

"Oh, dear, no, sir!" said the barber. "I won't hurt you. I once shaved fourteen customers in a hundred-mile gale, and never even nicked one of 'em. No: I was meaning for the fancy-dress party. I don't know as they'll have a fancy-dress party this time, what with so few passengers; but what I always say is, there's nothing like a good fancy-dress party. I could turn you into a fine brigand, sir. Or you could stick out your chin and wear a little hat and go as Mussolini."

"For the love of Mike be careful with that towel! Be careful with—"

"Coming straightaway, sir," said the barber, deftly flicking off H.M.'s spectacles and swathing his face with a smoking towel. Then the barber caught sight of Max. "Come right in, sir! Have a seat. You're next."

"Nothing for me, thanks," said Max. "I want to talk to that gentleman there."

As he spoke, the figure in the chair appeared galvanized. A minor convulsion afflicted the white robe. A hand groped from beneath the robe and plucked off the towel. H.M.'s face, heated lobster-red, rolled round as malignant as the evil one's, and glared at Max.

"Reporters!" he howled. "Still reporters! Just when I thought I was goin' to get a little peace and quiet at last, the place starts to rain reporters again. Oh, my eye. Gimme my glasses."

"But, sir—" began the barber.

"Gimme my glasses," insisted H.M. "I've changed my mind. I don't want a shave. I'm goin' to grow whiskers clear down to here." The length of his projected beard, as illustrated by him, appeared improbable. He rolled out of the chair, thrust money at the barber, and put on his spectacles. His corporation, preceding him in splendor like the figurehead of a man-o'-war, was now decorated (in addition to the gold watch-chain) with an enormous elk's tooth which somebody had given him in New York.

Lumbering over to the hat-pegs, he put on a raincoat and a big tweed cap, which he pulled down as far as his ears: a sight which would have to be seen to be believed.

"But, look here—!" protested Max.

With enormous dignity H.M. waddled out of the room. Max followed him. He went as far as the doll-and-souvenir-stuffed shop. Then H.M.'s manner thawed a little.

"Now say what you got to say," he growled, sniffing querulously. "If you'd 'a' said it in there, it'd be whistlin' all over this ship in ten minutes."

A wave of relief flooded through Max.

"I'm glad to see you again after all these years, H.M.," he said. "You don't look a day older. But what in blazes are you doing aboard this ship? And why the secrecy?"

"I *am* older, though," said H.M. darkly. "I got indigestion, too. See?" From the pocket of his raincoat he produced a

71

Gargantuan bottle of white pellets, and sniffed at it. "I'm probably not long for this world, son, but I'll do the best I can while I'm here. When I'm gone"—he gave Max a prophetic and sinister look, which boded the worst—"maybe they'll think more of the old man than they do now. And never you mind what I'm doin' here. I got my reasons."

"How long were you in America?"

"Five days."

Max forebore to question further. What H.M.'s position at Whitehall had become, since the war, he did not know; but he believed that the old man still had twice the brains of any person who was apt to succeed him as chief of the Military Intelligence Department. Still, it seemed discreet not to throw out any hints—yet.

Instead he took another tack. It was past the dinner hour, but for the first time on this voyage he did not feel in the least hungry.

"Do you know," he asked, "what's been happening aboard this ship?"

As H.M. only growled, he began to sketch out a brief account. H.M. listened with his sharp little eyes growing wider behind the spectacles.

"Oh, my eye!" he breathed. "Shades of Masters! Shades of—" Tortured and persecuted by fiends, he raised his big fists. "Not another impossibility?"

"I'm afraid so. And as bad as any you've ever encountered. If I remember some of your other cases, all you had to explain was how a murderer got out of a locked room,* or went across snow without leaving foot-prints.† Here you've got to explain fingerprints—real, living prints—left by a murderer who doesn't exist. You see how it is, H.M. It would be a great help if you could look into it. Frank has enough responsibilities on his mind as it is."

"Don't you think I got any responsiblities on *my* mind?"

"Yes, I know. But then you thrive on being persecuted. Frank doesn't."

For a moment he thought he had said too much. H.M. eyed him with a glare of such awful and Jovian power, one eye squinted shut and the other wide open, that he searched his mind for a compliment to deflect the thunderbolt.

---

* *The Judas Window,* William Morrow & Co., 1938.
† *The White Priory Murders,* William Morrow & Co., 1934.

However, H.M. concluded by turning down the corners of his mouth with sour dignity.

"I want air," he announced. "Plenty of it. Come on out on deck and tell me the whole story."

They groped out through the black-out compartments which were set up at nightfall. If there can be degrees of blackness—as opposed to mere darkness—the third night at sea was perhaps a little lighter than the other two. It was just possible to discern your hand before your face, but no more.

They were on the lee side of B Deck, unprotected by canvas screens. A few stars, looking unsteady with the slow rise and fall of the decks, glittered in tiny bitter points. The air, a degree or so above freezing, crawled under Max's shirt; it numbed his chest, and made his scalp and hands tingle; but he liked its clean chill.

Standing by the rail, they could look down into luminousness. Where everything else was black, the wash past the ship's side glowed faintly white and phosphorescent. It threw back no reflection. It was dead light, a corpse's candle at sea. It curled and wove in small veins and lines, spreading like disentangled lace in the midst of a vast seething noise which filled the ears to the exclusion of all other sound. It held the eye hypnotically, while that seething dulled the brain to drowsiness.

"Now, son," said a voice from the darkness beside him.

Staring at the wake and beyond—at black, oily-looking water which made up their world—Max told the full story. He left out nothing. As it afterwards proved, that was just as well.

When he had concluded, H.M.'s silence was a little ominous. Max had lost all sense of time. They seemed to be talking in a cold void, which was not sea or earth or sky. The seething of the wash droned eternally in his ears.

"So!" muttered the distant-sounding voice. "Not the pleasantest kind of doings. Hey?"

"No."

"And it's your idea," rumbled H.M.'s voice out of the dark, "that the murderer is the same feller who was throwing knives at a picture of a woman—presumably Mrs. Zia Bey—outside Dr. Archer's door on Friday night?"

"I should think so."

"Also, that it's the same feller who put on a gas mask and

73

either by accident or design stuck his head into young Kenworthy's cabin?"

Max hesitated. "That doesn't necessarily follow. Kenworthy seems to be a target for that sort of thing. It may have been a joke of the purser's."

"Uh-huh. Sure. It may have been. This purser, y'see, strikes me as being . . . never mind. Still, you do think the gas-mask incident was connected with this."

"Maybe, or maybe not. All I can tell you is that it struck me as being particularly ugly. Why, I don't know."

"I can tell you why," growled the voice, with an air of knowing more than anybody else in the world. "Because it's the infantile mind, that's why. It's the infantile mind that planned this murder, and every detail of the business. That's what you're dealin' with, son: arrested development in an adult. What makes it worse is that it seems to be an adult of caution and brains as well; and that's an awful bad combination. Tell me. Have you people been doin' any detective work? Have you tried to find out, for instance, where all the passengers were between nine-forty-five and ten last night?"

"You think the murderer was a passenger?"

"I dunno, son. It may have been a passenger. Or a ship's officer. Or anybody down to the cook's cat. But we got to make a beginning somewhere. Have you questioned 'em? Or found out where they were?"

"No." Max reflected. "I can tell you what a few of them say. Valerie Chatford was in my cabin. Dr. Archer was having a turn in the swimming-pool down below. Lathrop was out on deck. I don't know about any of the others."

"The Frenchman?"

"No information. He was in his own cabin at shortly past eleven o'clock, but that means nothing at all."

"Besides," argued H.M., "a French officer wouldn't be wearing . . ." He paused, while the hissing of the water filled a dead world. A hollow, incredulous note had come into H.M.'s voice. There was a sound as though he were hammering his fist on the wooden rail. "Oh, Lord love a duck! Is there anything in *that,* now? I was just thinkin' about Saturday morning."

"You think the Frenchman's tied up in this somehow?"

"I think he knows something, son," answered H.M. seriously. "And I'd dearly love to know what he was tryin' to

74

tell the two finger-print hounds when they nailed him in his cabin last night. I also think—"

"Yes?"

There was no reply. H.M. remained silent for so long that Max wondered whether he had gone to sleep with his elbows on the rail. But, by straining his eyes in the gloom, Max could just make out a faint reflection on big spectacles set malignantly, and a rain-coated figure which might have been an over-stout gargoyle leaning out from a cathedral roof.

Then his voice rose querulously. "I can't be bothered with this!" he growled. (Which meant that he had struck a snag, and wouldn't admit it.) "Burn me, ain't I got enough on my mind as it is? Has every twiddlin' crime in the world got to be heaped on me?"

Max said quietly: "This could concern your department, H.M."

"Meaning what?"

"It could be espionage."

Again H.M. was silent. It need hardly be said that Max could not read his expression. In the first place, it was so dark that he could not be seen at all. In the second place, poker-players at the Diogenes Club have found this a very unprofitable proceeding even in full light.

The *Edwardic* rolled slowly, so that the small, keen stars in a blue-black sky swayed and shifted up past the hood of the deck. Even with eyes growing used to these conditions, you could discern little more than that the sea seemed vaster and more oily-black, polished with white-veined waves.

"It could be," H.M. admitted at length. His voice sounded heavy, not very sure of itself. "Espionage, son, is far from being a joke in these days. It's wide and it's deep and it sinks under your feet—like that water out there. It runs much deeper than it ever did twenty-five years ago. Not picturesque like all the legends have made it, or always dealin' with very important issues. The proper enemy agent is an ordinary insignificant sort of person. The clerk, the small professional man, the young girl, the middle-aged woman. Not askin' for rewards, or even very brainy: but all fanatical idealists. You could shoot the lot of 'em without causing much of a flurry to G.H.Q. But each one of those little mites, individually, is a potential death's head.

"Take this ship, for instance. Suppose somebody left a porthole open all night on a lighted room. You wouldn't need to be very clever to do that. You wouldn't need to be deep in the enemy's councils. But, considering that light can be seen for five miles at sea, the general result might be disconcertin' to many of us."

"You think a person would do that? And take the chance of being blown to glory along with the rest of us?"

H.M. sighed gustily.

"Oh, son! If you're a fanatical idealist, you know the submarine captain'll be too gentlemanly to open fire before he's seen everybody safely into the boats."

"Do you?"

"Sure you do."

"And, anyway, they've posted watches along the boat-deck. Wouldn't the light be seen from here?"

"It probably would," conceded H.M. with the same off-handedness of manner. "Still, no harm in trying. Before we left New York, I had information that one of the women aboard this ship was an enemy agent. I dunno whether it's reliable information or not. And I'm givin' nothing away. *I* wanted to broadcast the news far and wide; post it on the bulletin-board, if necessary, like a warning against card-sharpers. But your brother said no, and he's the skipper." H.M.'s voice grew bitter. "Still, I'm only an old cloth-head. See anybody in Whitehall."

Max stared down at the phosphorescent mist boiling and flickering forty feet below.

"A woman. You don't mean Estelle Zia Bey?"

"I dunno who was meant. Neither does the captain: he got the information, not me. It doesn't sound like Mrs. Zia Bey to me, even if it's true. More probably some stewardess. Some dream-fed zealot who quite honestly thinks she's serving a great cause, and who'd be better served with the back of a hair-brush than with a firin'-squad. Phooey."

"And that's why you're aboard this ship?"

"Ho ho!" said H.M., with ghoulish amusement. "No, son. I'm glad to say I've got other fish to fry. Whoever this would-be spy may be, she's no Mademoiselle Docteur. She's just a fool. But we do get murder on top of it, which (to say the least) is rather a rummy coincidence."

His big voice sharpened. He was disturbed. He played with ideas, slapping at them, like a heavy-pawed cat with a ball of wool.

"Y'see, that murder was planned very skillfully. That's

what bothers me like blazes. The mentality behind it may be infantile; but it was also efficient and swift as *that*"—he snapped his fingers—"for getting results. I hope there's no more fun and games in store for us."

"How so?"

"Well, look here. Suppose I pitched you over the rail this minute. Suppose I got my hands under your arms, takin' you off guard, and gave you a strong heave. Son, you'd be a goner as soon as your feet left this deck."

Max hunched his shoulders uneasily. In this darkness it seemed impossible to tell who was friend or foe. You might look round, and see the wrong face behind you.

"Don't go trying it," he warned. "I'd be fairly hefty to handle. I have powerful lung power in the water. And I'm a good swimmer."

"I doubt if it would help you," said H.M. calmly. "That's what I meant by sayin' you'd be a goner if your feet left this deck. The point is, they wouldn't be able to find you. They wouldn't be able to see you. Look out there! Black as the underside of Tartarus! Not a shine, not a gleam. You'd drown in a smother, or be left behind to freeze to death, while six hundred people heard you call and couldn't save you—because they don't dare turn on a searchlight. Oh, my eye. These black-out conditions were made to order for the convenience of a murderer."

Max shivered.

"Do you mean to say," he demanded, "that even if they knew where and when you went over, they wouldn't show a light?"

"They daren't, son. It's orders. Your own brother couldn't disobey. Where other lives would be put in danger, the one life would have to go. That's war."

For the first time Max realized something of the cruelty of a black sea, and a blind ship trying to grope without success in the direction of a vague shout.

"I'm not tryin' to play bogey-man," said H.M., with an unmirthful chuckle. "But there it is. A rope couldn't be seen, and they daren't launch a boat. So it's a possibility to be considered. And—"

"Listen!" said Max.

Sweepingly, their ears were filled with the myriad small noises which make up the clamor of the sea. You did not

77

realize how loud they were until the wind blew them at you.

From the pitch blackness far up ahead in the forepart of B Deck, Max heard the scuffle. He saw the flash and heard the explosion of a revolver-shot. It was followed less by a scream than by a harsh, hoarse release of breath, merging afterwards into a heavy splash which brought the feet of the look-outs on the boat-deck scurrying like rats. There were no more identifiable sounds; relentlessly the strong waves smoothed out over them.

10

Shortly before these events took place, Valerie Chatford was going up the main stairs to the lounge.

She contemplated her image, as she passed, in the big mirrors fronting each landing. Her problem was how to make two evening-gowns seem like half a dozen on a voyage of eight (or more) days. Her problem, moreover, was to get on with the job she had to do. On the first night, she had been uncompromisingly seasick. On the second night, she had still been so unsteady inside that as a defense she had put on an air of haughtiness which surprised even herself. But it had been of great assistance when she saw that body sprawled in B-37.

Tonight there was color in her cheeks. She turned her head left and right, tilting the chin, to examine the smooth face and thick curly hair. She smiled—a smile which would have astonished Max Matthews, for it brought animation to her features like a lamp turned on. She was wearing her pink dress.

Valerie wavered between determination and excitement. She had almost bungled everything last night. She mustn't bungle again, or the people at home wouldn't like it. They would hardly be as proud of her as she wanted them to be.

But how to get at the man?

That was her difficulty.

Following an announcement on the bulletin-board that the ship's orchestra would play in the lounge at nine o'clock, the orchestra had begun only a few minutes ago. Its strains floated down the stairs with defiant lightness. Valerie walked into the lounge, sank down in one of the deep chairs, and saw her opportunity.

For chance or accident—which Sir Henry Merrivale called, simply, the blinkin' awful cussedness of things in general—flew over the *Edwardic* with the usual malice in its beak.

It decreed that at this moment the Hon. Jerome Kenworthy should come crawling up on deck for his first public appearance in proper clothes. The ship had now been steady for nearly twenty-four hours. That was enough. Kenworthy was headed in a bee-line for the bar in the smoking-room. But, lulled by a siren orchestra, and reflecting that healing liquids could be brought here just as well, he flopped down in a chair in the lounge.

And Valerie saw her chance.

She saw a lean, wiry, fair-haired young man with a worried crease across his high forehead, and several short wrinkles, like commas, round the corners of his mouth. His face also was long in more senses than one, decorated by octagonal spectacles with gold wires to the ears. He had put on a dinner-jacket without any dinner to pad it out. He opened and shut his mouth like a fish. He gave his order to a steward. Stretching out his arms to lean back in the chair, he closed his eyes.

Valerie glanced round the lounge. Except for the orchestra and Kenworthy, it was empty.

She had long debated exactly the course she would take with this young man. This was the first time she had ever set eyes on him, but his character had been fully reported to her. And he looked rather nice, which made it easier.

Nevertheless, Valerie's heart was pounding with excitement. Even her eyesight seemed to jump. She waited a few minutes more. Then she gathered up the skirts of her gown, pink satin inside pink lace; she slipped across to the felt-topped mahogany table beside which he sat; she slipped into a chair opposite him, and put her plump elbows on the table.

"Don't worry," she said, looking into his eyes. "I'll save you, cousin."

Jerome Kenworthy, just raising to his mouth his first whisky-and-soda in three days, started violently.

From that mouth there escaped a long, shuddering noise

like, *"A-a-a-a-h!"* with which even strong natures, on certain occasions, will greet the sudden ringing of a telephone. His bones shook inside him. He stared back at her, getting a firm grip on himself.

"I am, madam," he said, "much obliged to you. But who—er—?"

"It's all right," she assured him. "I'm Valerie."

Kenworthy searched his memory.

"To the best of my knowledge," he said truthfully, "I never set eyes on you before. Valerie who?"

"Valerie Chatford. But that's not the point." Her voice was urgent. "You don't need to worry about You-Know getting her throat cut last night. The murderer got all the letters. I am absolutely sure of that."

Jerome Kenworthy gave her a long look, and then put down his glass carefully on the table.

He said: "Is this another rib?"

It was Valerie's turn to be puzzled.

"Rib?"

"I beg your pardon. I will shed the sinister Yankee influence. Is this some more of Griswold's tomfoolery? Like the gas-mask? Or routing me out to get my fingerprints for no good reason on God's earth?"

"Who is Griswold?"

"Ha ha ha," observed Kenworthy. "My head aches, and a drowsy numbness pains, as though of scented hemlock I had drunk. Hemlock. That reminds me. Just one moment." He picked up his glass, drained it, became for a moment a man in agony, and settled back. "I have a strong presentiment that you and I are talking at cross-purposes. Before we go any further, will you tell me just who you think I am?"

"But you're Jerome Kenworthy!" she cried, while waltz-music filled the dimly lighted lounge. "Your father is Lord Abbsdale; he's something at Whitehall now; I don't know what—"

"Admiralty. That's right."

"And you live, or used to live, at Thetlands Park in Oxfordshire. I used to visit you there. Your mother is my Aunt Molly. My mother, your Aunt Ellen—"

Light came to Jerome Kenworthy. He remembered, twelve or fifteen years ago, a dim little girl in braids playing on the green lawns at Thetlands; and fierce arguments, and a swing by the Dutch garden.

The whisky flowed softly to his head and made him sentimental. After the three days he had been through, he thought
with affection of Thetlands and even of his father, that old
pain in the neck. If this accursed war were ever over, he
would settle there cushily as master of broad acres.

"Great Scott," he said, "of course I remember you! Valerie
. . . What did you say your married name was?"

"I'm not married."

"No, I mean Aunt Ellen's married name. Chatford, that's
it! This is something in the nature of a celebration. Won't
you join me in a drink?"

"I'd love to. May I have a Grand Marnier?"

Kenworthy gave the orders. "But, I say! Where are you all
now? And how are you? And where have you been keeping
yourselves?"

Valerie clasped her hands loosely. Her eyes, gray and
dark-fringed and set rather wide apart, she kept fixed on the
top of the table. Her face, which Max Matthews had thought
over-bred, had that look only in its delicate formation and the
expression of the thin, smooth-shining lips.

"Oh, everywhere," she answered. "Mother and Daddy and
I moved out to Bermuda. . . . You remember?"

"Yes, I knew it was something like that."

"And then, a year or so ago, we moved to upstate New
York. But, when the war came along, I—well, I thought I'd
like to do my bit to help, that's all." She lifted her eyes,
smiled, and lowered them. "I even hoped your father—sorry:
Uncle Fred—might get me something to do. But I hardly liked
to write, because you know the horrible row he had with both
my mother and my father. And you know what he's like."

Kenworthy eagerly welcomed his second whisky.

"I do know. But that, light of my elder days, is unqualified
ancient history. I can assure you with certainty that the old
man *will* find something for you to do. You won't be able to
avoid it. He had already, I deeply regret to say, snaffled me."

Kenworthy drank.

Valerie plucked at the edge of the table. "And there's another thing too . . ."

"Continue, star of my bosom. Prosit!"

"What did you say?"

"I said prosit. Mud in your eye!"

"Oh! Awfully good luck, Jerome." She picked up the small
glass. "Do you mind if I'm perfectly shameless? But I can't

help telling you." She moved the glass back and forth on the table. "Ever since I was a little girl, I've been rather a hero-worshiper of yours." She laughed a little. "It's true. Aunt Molly used to send us your school magazine. I know about all the prizes you won. I know you were trained for the Diplomatic, and—well, left it."

"Yes," said Kenworthy.

Dull red crept up his face.

"I've kept hearing about you. I even knew you were in New York. First from seeing it in the Society bits in the papers, and then in the gossip-columns, once or twice. And, when I heard you were tied up with that horrible woman . . ."

"Which particular woman?"

Valerie leaned across the table, even her pink dress seeming to swish with earnestness. She lowered her voice.

"But that's what I was trying to tell you. That woman—you know—was murdered last night down in B-37. We're not supposed to know about it. She was, Jerome. Her throat was cut. It was awful. I saw it."

"But, my God!—what's her name?"

"Sh-h! Keep your voice down!"

"What's her name?"

"Estelle Zia Bey. In her handbag she had a stack of letters—oh, that thick!" said Valerie, illustrating with her hands. "Blackmailing letters. There must have been heaps of other letters besides yours, but yours were all I was interested in."

Kenworthy reflected, his wits whirling. "Look here, Valerie. Believe it or not, and so help me Harry, I don't know any woman named Estelle Zia Bey!"

"Jerome, please!"

"It's true."

She had not expected this.

Now, one thing must be made clear. The girl who called herself Valerie Chatford was not, according to her lights, dishonest. She followed a certain course because she believed she must. She was something of a complex character, in which shrewdness, naïveté, loyalty, zeal, passion, imaginativeness, and a certain weakness were all intermingled in cool blood. So far she had been safe. And his denial baffled her.

She knew that Jerome Kenworthy was not the murderer. For (if the truth must be told) she had seen the murderer at work. That knowledge of hers she meant to use, presently, as a part of her plan. But—up to now—all her second-hand information about Kenworthy had been correct.

She spoke in a pleading voice.

"B-but it must be!" she stammered. "You know Trimalchio's Bar, don't you? On East Sixty-Fifth Street?"

"I know Trimalchio's, and well I wot it! My sage friends from this ship advised me to go there as soon as I set foot on American soil."

"It was—what's that disgusting word they use?—a hang-out of hers. In the afternoon."

Kenworthy stared at the past.

"If she hung out at Trimalchio's, I fail to see how I could have avoided meeting her. My acquaintance with the females infesting that place was extensive and peculiar. Could she have used another name? All I wish to point out, with some fervency, is that I never wrote an incriminating letter in my life. Our family lawyer told me the facts of life about that when I was fifteen; and I have been a temperate correspondent ever since. So I don't—" He broke off. "Look here, how do you happen to know about Trimalchio's?"

Valerie turned her eyes away from him.

"I'm sorry," she said in a low voice. "I was only trying to help you."

"Yes; but . . ."

"Perhaps it was foolish of me to go down and try to t-tackle her," said Valerie. "Like a silly school-girl with a favorite elder brother. And it's landed me in a dreadful mess, I'm afraid."

"A mess?"

"I have friends who go to Trimalchio's. They told me about you. And mother always said you could be *redeemed*. I thought perhaps if I could argue with Mrs. Zia Bey, and persuade her to give up the letters—or even steal them—"

"Dash it all, I tell you I never wrote any letters!"

Valerie grew curt. "That, if I did something like that, you might like me a little better when I introduced myself to you. That even Uncle Fred might like me a little better, and perhaps help me in war-work. Please forget it. I see now it was a silly romantic notion, like most of my notions."

He was instantly all contrition.

One part of her mind exulted with glee in her ability to be so smoothly and undetectably tough. The other part said that

83

this was a decent fellow who was being taken for a ride. She only wished fervently that, instead of Jerome Kenworthy, the person in his place were that black-avised limping young man who spoke in short syllables and seemed to have the weight of the earth on his shoulders. She detested the ape Matthews, who was afraid of fire.

"Valerie my ancient of days," said Kenworthy, "you are a brick. Sit down again. Allow me to buy you another drink. And if it's a chance to help your country you want—"

"I don't think I'm really interested."

"A chance to help this home of majesty, this sceptered isle, this England," pursued Kenworthy, with the whisky singing on an empty stomach; "well, let me tell you the sort of work *I've* been assigned to do."

"Oh? What's that?"

"But, before we proceed to it, let me inform you that I feel guilty as the very devil. What is this mess you're in?"

"It's nothing, Jerome. Really it isn't."

"Probably not. Still, what is it?"

"I'd rather not say."

"Ne'er tilt that proud chin at me, my pet. So far as I can see, some exceedingly dirty work must be going on hereabouts." Kenworthy's eyes narrowed behind the octagonal spectacles. The small comma-wrinkles deepened round his mouth as he stared at his empty glass. "Murder! Suffering cats, murder; I'd better see if I've ever met the woman, by the way. Griswold can probably arrange that. He might have said something about it, confound him. Have they any idea who did it?"

"I don't think so."

"Just what is your part in it?"

"I—I was hiding in a cabin opposite. And a foul beast named Matthews, a brother of the captain, went and told the captain all about it." Evidently on the verge of tears, she outlined the story. It was only what she had told Max Matthews: no more.

Kenworthy was shaken.

"And you did all that for me? Devil burn my body!"

"It was nothing, Jerome. It was only stupid and silly and romantic, and it may make dreadful trouble for me when the captain comes to question me about it. What on earth am I to do?"

"Do?"

"Yes. You see, that's not all. Mrs.—Mrs. Zia Bey left a sealed envelope with the purser, in his office. I thought it might contain more letters. So I asked this man Matthews to get it for me, but he wouldn't. The captain probably knows all about it by now."

Kenworthy blinked at her.

"My dear Valerie, there is only one thing you can possibly do. Griswold, the purser, is a great friend of mine. He'll understand. Tell him the truth. Tell the captain the truth."

"Of course, I thought of that the first thing. But mightn't that make it awfully difficult for you?"

"Valerie, I keep telling you—there aren't any letters. On my solemn word of honor there aren't."

She drew a deep breath. Her clear gray eyes, which had been turned sideways to contemplate a mahogany pillar, now moved back to his face.

"Yes, Jerome. But suppose they *thought* there were?"

"Suppose what?"

"Suppose they *thought* there were letters. I should have to explain about the letters, you know, in telling why I went to Mrs. Zia Bey's cabin. And it was common gossip at Trimalchio's that you had been about with her and had written her letters. If it was the ship's officers who introduced you to Trimalchio's, they'll probably have heard it. In any case they'll have to question you. You'll be dragged into this. Jerome, Jerome"—her eyebrows were pinched together over the short, straight nose; her face was passionate with earnestness, and her voice almost a moan—"I'm thinking of *you*. Think of the publicity of a murder investigation, when we get to England! And your father."

(Checkmate.)

Throughout the latter part of this conversation, when both persons had experienced strong emotions of different kinds, the orchestra had been hurtling through to a grand finale of popular airs. It made a sort of musical explosion under the glass roof, and fell away in dead silence.

This was broken by the sound of one pair of hands applauding loudly and hollowly. Both Valerie and Kenworthy jumped. The applause proceeded from John E. Lathrop, who had slipped in unseen and was sitting some distance away from them, smoking a cigar. He winked at Valerie. His enthusiasm was followed by a milder, more man-of-the-

85

worldly pat of clapping from Dr. Reginald Archer, still further away in the pale-lit gloom.

Valerie and Kenworthy joined in. The orchestra-leader bowed as gravely as though the room had been full of people, after which his men began to pack up their instruments. The applause hung briefly in the air, and died. It was as though music had never been. The small night-noises of the lounge crept out: it began to creak and quiver like a shaky floor.

The time was thirty-seven minutes past nine o'clock.

Kenworthy, who had started to speak with some loudness, checked himself.

"I have begun to feel," he complained, "that I am getting deeper and deeper into something without quite knowing what it is. O hand of hymning angel! If you don't propose to tell the captain and the purser the truth, what do you propose to tell them?"

Valerie shrugged her shoulders.

"I shall deny the man Matthews' story. I warned him I meant to, last night."

"And then?"

"I shall say I was with you."

He stared at her. "But you can't do that! When did this cavalcade of dirty work occur? Nine-forty-five to ten o'clock. In that case you'd have to say you were in my cabin, holding my head over the basin. And that won't do."

"Why not? Who knows where you were?"

"The purser," retorted Kenworthy unanswerably. He peered up. "And hold on to your hat, my lady. Here comes Griswold now."

The purser tried to sidle in unobtrusively. But every person who saw him enter, through the door to the main hall, felt a change in the atmosphere. He passed Dr. Archer, and nodded. Once he saw he was observed, Griswold walked with briskness. He came straight toward Valerie and Kenworthy. Even at a distance they could see that though the purser's fleshy face was composed, a faint rash stood out against the pallor of his forehead, and he breathed hard through the nostrils.

Valerie almost guessed the sort of news he brought.

Valerie, always sensitive to atmospheres, felt her muscles stiffen and a breath of pure panic through her body. She tried to hold Kenworthy's eye. She sensed that her original advantage over him might be slipping away. And she wanted to rouse no suspicions. But she tried again.

"The purser was in your cabin between nine-forty-five and ten last night?"

Kenworthy thought back. "I don't know what time it was. Zounds, woman. No, wait. I think he came in later than ten o'clock. Yes, I'm sure of it. Unless he was that bloke in the gas-mask: *that* was earlier. What I am trying to get at is that he knows I was in no shape to entertain female visitors, however char—"

"Sh-h! Please!"

"Good evening, Miss Chatford," intoned the purser, looming over their table. His jowl was down in his collar, and his expression frightened Valerie. But he spoke with a sort of buckled-in friendliness and ease. "Good evening, Mr. Kenworthy," he added formally. "Glad to see you're up and about again."

"Thanks. Have a drink."

"Not just now. I'd like to have a word in private with Miss Chatford, if I may."

They could hear him breathe. Out of the corner of her eye, Valerie saw Lathrop get up across the room and stroll over to the piano. The thud of the ship's engines was loud in her ears.

"But, Mr. Griswold!" she protested. "Anything you have to say, you can say in front of my cousin."

"Your *what?*"

"My cousin. Mr. Kenworthy is my cousin."

"This is no time for joking," said the purser, after a pause.

"It's true, so help me!" cried Kenworthy, and quite honestly believed this. "I've known her since she was so high. Valerie Chatford. She used to have braids and ride on a sheepdog."

The purser sat down.

"You never told me you had a cousin," he said, somewhat reproachfully.

"Nor," Kenworthy pointed out, "have I ever heard you sit down and recite a long list of your own relatives like the catalogue of ships in Homer. Don't be an ass, Griswold."

"I mean," said the purser, taking no notice of this, "that I had a long talk with you last night, and you never mentioned anything about having a relative aboard. Particularly an attractive young lady like this. That's not like you, young fellow."

Kenworthy started to answer; but the purser cut him short, which was just as well.

"Just a minute. I don't know what you're up to, but I've got to tell you frankly that this is no time for any of your usual funny business. We'll come back to that." He paused, and slapped his knee. "Miss Chatford, I represent the captain. By his orders, I want to ask you a few questions. Also by his orders, we've decided it's no good keeping from the passengers any longer"—he looked at Kenworthy—"the fact that there was a murder last night. That stewardess has blabbed. It's all over the ship." He looked back at Valerie. "But then I suppose you'd heard about it?"

"Yes. I've heard about it," said Valerie, and shivered.

"Ah? Had you?"

From his pocket, leisurely, the purser took a broad buff envelope eight or ten inches long. Its contents made the sides bulge. The top was slit open, but across the still-sealed flap had been written the name, "Estelle Zia Bey."

"This evening," he went on, "Mr. Max Matthews told us a lot of things. Among other things, he mentioned this envelope. You mentioned it to him, Miss Chatford. It was deposited at my office. Acting on the captain's orders, I opened it. Valuable contents? Here's your valuable contents!"

He twisted round.

Turning the envelope upside down, he shook it out on the table. All it contained were some wadded strips of newspaper, evidently cut out with a big pair of scissors.

"Dummies," said the purser. "Now, Miss Chatford, the captain would like to know why you wanted this envelope. He'd like to know why you asked Mr. Max Matthews to get it for you."

Valerie could hear the blood beating in her ear-drums.

She might be playing things too far. It would shortly be time to do what she had planned all along—confess certain facts—but not yet. Not, she thought to herself, just yet.

"I don't understand what you're talking about."

"The captain would like to know," pursued Griswold, "where you got the idea that Mrs. Zia Bey was hiding a bundle of letters in her handbag, and that the murderer stole them."

"I still don't understand what you're talking about."

"The captain would like to know what you were doing in Mr. Matthews' cabin last night."

"But I wasn't in Mr. Matthews' cabin!"

"No? Where were you?"

"I was with my cousin, Mr. Kenworthy."

All three had been speaking in whispers. All three had been leaning forward confidentially, Griswold with his elbow on his knee. Now the purser sat back. His bristly black eyebrows rose in a furrowed forehead: there was about him a suggestion of George Robey. But he exuded rich satisfaction, as of one who says, 'I knew it!'

"Is that so, Miss Chatford? You were with Mr. Kenworthy?"

"Yes."

"The captain would like to know what time you were with Mr. Kenworthy?"

"I think I went round to his cabin about half-past nine. I left about ten o'clock."

"You're sure of that, now? You're sure of those times?"

"More or less, yes."

The purser's expression said, 'Oh, stow it!' But he did not comment on this; his bull-frog jowl continued to move in and out. He peered at Kenworthy instead. "What," he asked, "do you have to say to that?"

"*Stop,*" said Kenworthy, in such a loud voice that Lathrop at the piano glanced up. The piano tinkled in the distance.

After drawing a deep breath, Kenworthy went on: "Before I get into this third degree, there is some information I must have. From you, Griswold. I am not trying to evade your questions. I'll do what I think is right. What—I—think—is—right. Tell me. Could I have a look at this Mrs. Zia Bey who was murdered? At the body?"

Again the purser's eyebrows went up.

"Certainly. Don't tell me she was a pal of yours?"

"No. Not under that name, anyhow. What I'm really getting at is this. You are familiar (I can swear) with a dive called Trimalchio's, in New York?"

The other looked puzzled.

"I know it, yes. Haven't been there for a long time. It's a sort of English club. Plenty of Royal Navy and R.N.R. men used to drop in there." He laughed shortly. "And lousy with spies, I hear. What's all this? What's the idea?"

"Did you know Mrs. Zia Bey?"

The purser shrugged his shoulders. "I've heard of her. Most people have. Vaguely. A bad lot, but nice-natured."

"Where did you hear about her? At Trimalchio's?"

"I don't remember. *Why?*"

"What I'm getting at," persisted Kenworthy, opening and shutting his hands, "is this. Did you ever hear any gossip about Mrs. Zia Bey and . . ."

"Jerome!" cried Valerie, but not a muscle moved in his thin, donnish face.

". . . and any man in particular?" he concluded.

"I shouldn't expect to hear any other kind of gossip about her." Griswold frowned. "No, I don't remember. It seems to me I once heard she was going about with a fashionable professional man, architect or doctor or something of the sort." His frown grew deeper. "I repeat, why?"

"It was only—What," said Kenworthy, "was that noise?"

He broke off and held up his hand. A slight but abrupt roll of the ship intensified the rattle and creak of the lounge. All three of them moved to the roll.

"It sounded," said Valerie, "like a woman screaming."

"It was a woman screaming," agreed Kenworthy. "Not Mrs. Zia Bey's ghost, I trust."

"Don't talk like that," said the purser. His forehead shone like butter where the light from a pillar struck it. He was back again in the mood with which he had entered a few minutes ago. "Look here at me. I was sent to ask questions, and I mean to ask 'em. You say that sounded like a woman screaming."

"Yes, it did," said Valerie. "From downstairs."

"Miss Chatford, how long have you been here in the lounge? Since when?"

"I—I don't remember."

"Since when, please?"

"Well, I came up here and sat down only a minute or so

90

after the orchestra started playing. It was their first number. I can tell you that, if it helps any."

"Where had you been before then?"

"In my cabin, brushing up after dinner."

"What about you, Mr. Kenworthy?"

Kenworthy rubbed his jaw. "I can't do much better than that myself," he answered. "It wasn't a great length of time after the orchestra started. I got dressed and came up to get a drink. I was going on into the bar, but I stopped here."

"The orchestra began at nine o'clock," said the purser. "You put it at a few minutes past? All right. All right. All right." He consulted his watch. "You say you heard someone screaming just now. When you were coming up here to the lounge at a little past nine, did you hear anybody yell then? Any commotion at all?"

"No," said two voices together.

"Sure of that? No row—from out on B-Deck?"

"No."

A tall shadow reared up over the back of Valerie's tall chair, two hands, one holding a cigar, appeared over her head. She turned round, to see the homely face of Lathrop grinning down at her. Though she rather liked Lathrop, she had an intense contempt for him. He seemed to her to have the reactions of a schoolboy in the body of a grown and white-haired man. Valerie was perhaps too frantically serious-minded.

Lathrop's shambling figure draped itself over the back of the chair. Cigar-smoke blew down at her. He dissipated the smoke by leaning over and fanning a big knuckly hand under her nose.

"What's this about a row?" he asked.

"Nothing, sir," said the purser.

"Glad to hear it. I was hoping nothing had happened to poor old Hooper."

"Hooper?" repeated the purser sharply.

"Yes; good old G.A. He promised to meet me here and listen to the orchestra, but he didn't show up." Lathrop was staring straight back at the purser, and staring hard. "I hope he hasn't fallen overboard or anything. He's going to teach me how to play a game called Nap. If he's as good at that as he is at throwing darts, I'm practically ruined. He's taken me for a dollar sixty-five already, and laughs to high heaven whenever he thinks of it. Good night, all."

"Mr. Lathrop!" said the purser. And the emotional heat of the room went up several degrees.

Lathrop did not go far. He turned round, slowly, on the soles of his feet.

"Yes?"

"As a matter of form, sir, the captain would like to know what you were doing about nine o'clock this evening."

"Nine?" said Lathrop, without commenting. "I was in my cabin."

"You too?"

"Me too. Whatever that means. I came up here about ten past nine to listen to the music. Something else," Lathrop stated rather than asked, "has happened."

"Yes," admitted the purser. He got to his feet. "Dr. Archer!" he called across the lounge.

At the far end, near some palms, a lounging figure stirred beside the door. The doctor, a book carried over his arm and a finger between its pages, walked down the strip of gray carpet which constituted the aisle at one side. His tread was jaunty and purposeful; but his lips, in a scrubbed face, looked so dry as to be cracked. He was still pleasant, the kindly physician lending an ear in the consulting-room. His light eyes smiled at Valerie, with an individual nod in greeting to each other person. But his plump hand held the book tightly.

"Yes, purser?" he invited.

Griswold was apologetic. "Captain's orders, Doctor. We're checking up. Do you happen to remember where you were round about nine o'clock to-night?"

"I do."

"Well?"

"In my cabin," replied Dr. Archer. "Why do you close your eyes? Have I said anything so very extraordinary? Most people go to their cabins immediately after dinner. To get a coat. To pick up a book." He held up his own. "I came up from there about a quarter past nine, drifted into the smoking-room, had a drink, and finally wandered in here to hear the orchestra. You will forgive me: but there is very little else aboard this ship to do."

Without any change of voice or expression he added:

"Go on and tell us what's happened now. Everybody aboard this ship knows what happened last night. Spit it out. Get it over with. Is anything else wrong?"

The purser drew a deep breath.

"Yes," he acknowledged. "There's been another—unfortunate accident. Now, there's nothing to be alarmed about! I assure you you can trust the captain. And he thinks you'll feel better if you face it fairly and squarely, and know all about it."

"Another murder?" the doctor asked sharply.

"I'm afraid so. But there's nothing to be alarmed about."

Lathrop breathed hard. His voice was incredulous. "Do you mean to tell me," he said, "that what I said—just joking—about poor old Hooper . . ."

But the purser turned on him.

"Hooper?" he repeated. "Who said anything about Hooper? Hooper's all right. It's that Frenchman, Captain Benoit. He was shot through the back of the head on B Deck three-quarters of an hour ago." Griswold's face grew suffused with dark blood. "If we'd known what he was talking about last night, we might have saved his life."

12

When Max and H.M. heard that shot, from their position by the rail on the starboard side, the time was just one minute to nine o'clock.

H.M. owns a big gun-metal watch with luminous figures painted on the dial. In that epic darkness, Max saw the watch emerge from under jacket and raincoat, and turn over bodilessly in the air, like an effect of trick photography. As they both began to run towards the place where the shot had been fired, he saw the watch disappear again, presumably into a waistcoat pocket.

"That means business, son," said H.M.'s voice hoarsely. "For the love of Esau, watch your step. Watch your step!"

Groping and poking ahead of him with his cane, Max slithered on his bad leg. Darkness was a wall which you might strike palpably with your face. He lost H.M., and failed to find him again. He could just distinguish the black solidity of the rail, and of the steel pillars supporting the deck above, when they moved with the rolling of the ship.

He was at a point, he judged, well towards the bows when

a yellow light curled and flickered up ahead. It was only the light of a match, and yet it seemed to have the power of a dark lantern. It even seemed to defy the icy wind.

"Douse that light!" shouted a voice.

The voice bawled almost directly in Max's ear. He had not realized he was in the midst of a small crowd, until the bitter air was agitated by a dozen movements. Something hard, a shoulder or a hand, struck him hard under the left shoulder-blade, pitching him forward. His knees were stiff with cold, and the cane clattered out of his hand. He knew a second of panic as the rail rushed at him, tilting over deeply to show him the phosphorescent wash boiling below.

Just ahead of him, somebody reached out of the darkness and struck at the hand that was holding the match. Its light went out. But not before Max, flung back from the rail again with the port-roll of the deck, had seen every detail of the scene picked out in shadow and gleam.

The match was being held by George A. Hooper. He held it at about the level of his ear. His back was hunched and his shoulders, so that you could see the gray stubbly hair on the round scalp, and the shine of the rolling eyes. Standing a little way back from the rail, Hooper peered at it, and then down to the deck, as though he had seen a snake at his feet. The match went out.

"Don't you know better than to show a light on deck?" demanded the voice of Mr. Cruikshank, the third officer. "Don't you know better than—"

Hooper did not reply. He struck another match.

"Sir, are you crazy? Give me those matches!"

There was a scuffle. Either the wind blew the match out, or the third officer put it out. Hooper's protest rose plaintively. He did not seem alarmed: only absorbed and fascinated, with a rapidly mounting excitement.

"There's a man overboard," he managed to stutter out. "Spang down he went, splash bang, with a bullet in the back of his head. For God's sake don't stand there and fuss about matches. There's a man *overboard.*"

"Steady. Sure?"

"That's right, sir," panted another voice out of the dark. "I'm number four look-out. We saw him fall from up on the boat-deck. I gave the hail and heard the telegraph ring; but we don't seem to be more than slowing down?"

The tone of the last voice held a question.

"If you're number four look-out," said the third officer, "what the devil are you doing down here? Go back to your post!"

"Orders to find out where he fell from. Number three, and Mr. Billings, said they thought he had—"

"Had what?"

"Shot himself, sir. Done himself in. You could see his face turn over in that phosphorescent stuff before he went under. The revolver fell along with him."

"Dead?"

"Ah, that he was!" interposed Hooper, with a sudden excited burst. "Shot slap bang through the back of the head, poor chap. Dead as mutton. It was the French officer with the uniform: lovely uniform. Shot slap bang through the back of the head; saw it done myself. But he didn't do it himself, no fear! I even saw the chap who shot him. And then dash my buttons if he didn't pitch him slap bang overboard—"

"Just a moment," interrupted the third officer sharply. "You're sure he was dead?"

"Slap bang through the—"

"Take that message to the bridge," said the third officer to number four look-out. His voice in the blackness seemed to have a note of relief. "No, stop; I'll take it myself. You stay here, Mr. Hooper. I'll keep your matches. *Who's that?*"

Heavy footsteps had pounded up and seemed to mix into the scramble.

"It's Griswold," replied the purser's throaty voice. "What's up?"

"Ah! Our friend Benoit's been shot and chucked overboard, Griswold. We're for it. This is Mr. Hooper here somewhere. Take charge of him. I'm going up to the bridge."

"Think the old man'll stop?"

"No. Not a chance in a million to pick him up, even if the Frenchman's alive. And it's too dangerous."

"Right. I'll stand by. Who's that over there?"

"Picked him up like a sack," continued Hooper with wildly accelerating excitement, as though the novelty of his having seen this were slowly dawning on him, "and dash my buttons if he didn't pitch him slap bang *overboard*."

The purser's voice was gruff.

"Here, sir, steady! Keep your feet! Not fainting on me, are you?"

Hooper's tones shrank to thinness and hard-breathing.

"It's me 'eart," he complained. "The excitement and all. Can't stand it. It's me 'eart.'

"Let me give you a hand, then. Like to go inside?"

"Ah! That I would! Wait till I pick up my lifejacket. It's in the deck-chair over there somewhere."

Again the purser spoke sharply. "Who's that behind me?"

Max had been listening to all this with a kind of wild abstraction like Hooper's. He groped round on the deck for his cane, and, by a miracle, found it. In doing so he happened to touch someone's trouser-leg, causing the legs to leap into the air with a jerk which showed the state of all their rattling nerves. But it was H.M.'s voice which answered the purser.

"It's only me, son."

"Sir Henry?"

"Uh-huh. Sort of nice weather we're havin' for the time of year."

"Will you take Mr. Hooper inside? Here's his arm. Now feel round with your feet, and you'll find a kind of narrow iron plate running across the deck. Wherever you feel one of those, it leads across to a door. Follow the iron band and it'll take you inside. Excuse me."

Max caught hold of someone's coat, whether H.M.'s or Hooper's he could not be sure, and brought up behind the other two. They shuffled across, found a door, and emerged through another black-out compartment into soft light which nevertheless dazzled their eyes.

They were in a narrow white-painted passage at the end of which, and at right angles to it, ran the main alleyway of cabins on the starboard side. The red rubber floor felt more reassuring than ever the open deck had been. On their right was a cabin door, closed, which bore the neat black number B-71. Memory returned to Max. That was the number of Captain Benoit's cabin.

"This," growled H.M., "has got to stop. Listen, son. Tell me. What happened out there, exactly? How'd you come to see it?"

Hooper seemed not unwilling to tell his story. But he took some time before he spoke.

He was leaning up against the white wall with his back to it, and his feet thrust out far as though he were going to slide down. Slow breathing animated his tubby little figure. He stared at the floor. His right hand was thrust under his jacket over the heart, patting it; a life-jacket dangled from the limp fingers of his left hand. There was a flush on his waxy cheeks above the iron-gray mustache.

"This'll be something to tell 'em at home," he breathed, still continuing to pat his heart. "Me, George Hooper, saw a poor chap get himself shot and pitched overboard. His cap had a red and gold top on it."

"Yes, sure. But what did you *see?*"

"I," said Hooper, suddenly looking up out of pale bluish eyes, "takes myself out for a breath of fresh air. I've got a deck-chair just outside there, outside that door."

(It was true, Max remembered. He had seen Hooper dozing in that deck-chair during his walk round B Deck in the morning.)

"I sits down in the chair," pursued Hooper, controlling his breath, "and pulls the rug over me. I sits there maybe ten or fifteen minutes, and I thinks to myself I'll go inside again, when the door opens. That door there. I could hear it open. And people came out on deck."

"How many people?"

"Two," replied Hooper after reflection. "You could hear them walk, if you couldn't see. They went over to the rail. You could just barely"—a born story-teller, he pressed his thumb and forefinger together, holding them up dramatically —"you could just barely see their heads and shoulders. Well, what did I think? Nothing! Until it started. I hear a noise like fighting. I hear a kind of big blaze and bang like Bonfire Night. And there's the end of a gun pointing at the poor chap's 'air under the cap, and somebody behind him firing it. And up I jumps out of my chair."

Here Hooper jumped again. In moments of strong excitement, he reverted to broad Somerset. His tone was injured.

"I said, *'Here, me-son! what's-thee-doing?'* God, I thought, this won't do! There wasn't anything except a kind of screech from the poor chap. Over I goes to the rail, just in time to see his boots go over the edge. Leather boots, they were. I touched one. But over he went, and somebody else started to run away very soft on his feet when I looked down over the edge to see where the poor chap went.

"He landed head first in that white frothy stuff that's got lights in it, and turned over on his back, and started to slip along backward as fast as a beetle down a drain. You couldn't see him longer nor two seconds before there was

97

nothing but frothy water again. Poor chap. I reckon it's a shame."

Hooper broke off.

Once more patting his waistcoat over the heart, and slowing down his panting breath, he appealed to them about the shame of this. But he still seemed lost in wonder that he had been the person to see it.

Throughout the recital H.M. had remained heavy and thoughtful, the corners of his mouth drawn down, peering at Hooper over spectacles pulled down on his broad nose. He removed his cap, which gave him a more human appearance. He sniffed. Putting his fists on his hips, he contemplated his companions with a surprising mildness.

"So," he murmured. "It looks as though we've been done in the eye again. Could you see the person who fired the shot? Could you identify him if you saw him again?"

"Oh, lad, lad! Don't ask for miracles!"

(It was a new experience for H.M. to be addressed as "lad," and the corners of his mouth went still further down. But he persisted.)

"Well, was he tall or short? Fat or thin?"

"I don't know."

"You say he started to run away. Which direction did he go? Fore or aft? Or back through this door?"

"Blest if *I* can tell you. I was thinking about that poor chap—"

The black-out doors at the end of the passage banged and shook. Commander Matthews, wearing a light oilskin, groped through from the deck. His face was without expression; he nodded to them, and glanced at the door of B-71.

"So Benoit's gone," he observed.

"Another of us," said Max.

"I wanted to tell you something," the captain went on crisply. "Benoit shot himself. It's very unfortunate."

Hooper bounced upright.

"For the benefit of the crew," said Commander Matthews, "and until we get to the other side, Benoit shot himself. Do you understand? Two witnesses on the boat-deck saw the revolver fall into the water along with him. The fellow was probably mad. He killed Mrs. Zia Bey and then took his own life. There is no more danger. Is that clear?"

He paused, and glanced round, as the third officer pushed through the black-out doors behind him.

"My job," said Commander Matthews, "is to get this ship safely to port. I'll see it's done. But I won't run the risk of panic. Is that clear?"

Hooper nodded slowly. His pale blue eye, unexpectedly shrewd, rolled round and then surveyed the floor.

"In my cloth-headed way," observed H.M., "I think you're doin' the right thing. What about the passengers?"

"The passengers are to be told the truth," said the captain. "In fact, it's to be crammed down their throats. I understand they all know about Mrs. Zia Bey now, anyway; the crew know, I can tell you. But there's a special reason. Since this morning, there's been a special and mutual watch-system instituted among the crew. I ordered it. Five minutes after Benoit went overboard, I had reports from all the officers in charge. Every member of this ship's crew was at his post, or can produce an alibi, for the time of the shooting."

Commander Matthews did not raise his voice. But the atmosphere of the passage had grown as cold as the deck outside.

"You see what that means, don't you? If you don't I'll tell you. This murdering maniac must be one of the seven remaining passengers. Or else it's one of my own officers, which I tell you frankly I rule out. Very well."

Without apparent emotion, Commander Matthews lifted his open right hand and struck it so heavily on the white wall of the passage that the door of B-71 rattled in its frame.

"This passenger who's guilty won't get away with it. None of them will get away with anything. They'll be questioned, they'll be watched, they'll be surrounded, they'll be deviled, until we weed out the man we want. That's all. Mr. Cruikshank!"

"Sir?"

"Go and get the purser, and ask him if he will join us here. Sir Henry Merrivale, I ask you straight. I'm no detective. It's out of my line. Will you take over?"

H.M., a big somnolent bulk, had been leaning his back against the closed door of the cabin. From the pocket of his raincoat he took out a black pipe, so caked that there would be hardly room for a lead-pencil to go into the bowl, and stuck it in one corner of his mouth. His usual expression of cynicism, as of one smelling a bad breakfast-egg, had deserted him. He sucked at the pipe-stem. His narrow eyes moved sideways behind the big spectacles.

"Son," he said, "I'd be proud to."

"And land this swine before we get to the other side?"

"I promise nothin'," said H.M. unexpectedly. "I only promise things when I get mad. I'm not mad now. Just sort of—tightenin' my belt and spittin' on my hands. Like you."

"Have you got any ideas about this? Who's doing it? And why? And how those damned finger-prints were made?"

"Well . . . now, I wouldn't say an *idea*," argued H.M., as though carefully defining his terms. The pipe shifted from one side of his mouth to the other. "One or two things did strike me as fishy, when I heard young Max's story. And I'd like very much to see this feller Benoit's belongings. I'd like to take a good look at his cabin. Could we go there, son? Where is it?"

"Just behind you," said the captain, nodding. "Any assistance you want is yours. Just ask for it."

Grunting, H.M. turned round. The back of his bald head shone even in that dim light; and above the leathery creases in the neck at the base of his skull stuck out a fringe of grayish black hair which the barber seemed to have missed. He hunched his shoulders and grunted again. Then he opened the door.

13

The roof-light was burning in B-71. With true French thriftiness, Captain Benoit had booked one of the smallest single cabins aboard the ship.

In shape it was a narrowish oblong, with the door on the narrow side. You looked into a kind of white-painted cell. Along the left-hand wall stood the berth, set long-ways with its head against the wall opposite the door. In this wall opposite the door, there was room for a dressing-table and a wash-basin. The wall to the right had a deep alcove, terminating in a sealed porthole. The glass-faced wardrobe stood to the right of the door. There was one chair.

Since there could be little room in the cabin for anybody except H.M., the others remained outside. H.M. lumbered in, glowering. The more he poked and probed about the cabin, the more dissatisfied he appeared to become.

A wool dressing-gown hung from a wall-peg, with a pair of slippers under it. On the chair, neatly piled, lay a life-jacket, a gas-mask box, and a blanket. H.M. examined them, and then turned his attention to the dressing-table.

On this stood a folding leather traveling-frame, containing two old photographs, one of an elderly French military man with a fierce brushed-up mustache, the other of a good-humored middle-aged woman—presumably Benoit's parents—which lent a homely, domestic touch to a dead man's room. Comb, brushes, and scissors were set out in an even line. There was a tin of Kleen-O for buttons, of tan polish for boots. Clothes-brush and boot-brush hung on hooks beside the wash-stand, on whose rack had been ranged shaving-tackle, tooth-brush, and tooth-powder.

H.M. opened the dressing-table drawers. He peered into the alcove of the porthole. With infinite labor he got down on his knees and pawed under the bed, dragging out a flat cabin trunk which proved to be empty except for some soiled linen.

He pushed it back, and opened the door of the wardrobe. Here he discovered a spare uniform, with the three gold stripes of a captain on the shoulder-epaulettes, two lounge suits of civilian clothes, some ties on the hanger-rack, a spare pair of knee-length boots, and two pairs of shoes. After adjusting his spectacles so that apparently he could not see at all, H.M. peered at the sleeve of the uniform. As a last resort, he reached up and groped round without success on the top of the wardrobe.

"Oh, my eye!" he muttered.

Throughout this he continued to chew at the empty pipe, and his expression grew more disconsolate each minute.

"What is it?" Max asked from the doorway. "What are you looking for?"

H.M. sat down on the edge of the berth.

The third officer had arrived back with the purser. To both of them Commander Matthews gave low-voiced instructions, after which he excused himself and disappeared on his own duties. In the absence of the skipper, the absorbed third officer ventured an indiscreet whisper to the purser.

"Looks like a boiled owl," he said.

"I was cogitatin', damn you," said H.M., opening one wrathful eye. "That's the way I cogitate. Lemme see, now."

101

Again he hauled himself to his feet, and again attacked the dressing-table. From on top of a neat pile of shirts and socks in the upper drawer, he took out a small cardboard box. This he shook out on the bed. It contained five rubber stamps with wooden handles, and an ink-pad in its tin container.

"You two bloodhounds," pursued H.M., waving a rubber stamp malevolently at the third officer and the purser, "were in here last night. Hey? You came to get Captain Benoit's finger-prints?"

"That's right, sir," admitted the third officer, shifting uncomfortably.

"And Captain Benoit was sittin' here (I'm told) amusing himself with a lot of rubber stamps and an ink-pad?"

"Yes, sir."

"Are these the same rubber stamps?"

The third officer stepped gingerly into the cabin. He picked up two or three of the stamps and turned them over. "They look like the same ones, anyway. I didn't examine 'em."

"When you finally made him understand you wanted his finger-prints, he offered to give you samples by pressing his thumb on this ink-pad here. That is, he started to. But you prevented him before he could do it, and got his prints from your own ink-roller. Is that right? Hey?"

The third officer nodded.

"That's right, sir."

"Excuse me!" interposed a new and interested voice.

It was Hooper, whom everybody had forgotten. He had kept in the background, at times wrapped in profound meditation over his adventure, and at other times gazing with fascinated eyes into the cabin. The rubber stamps drew him. He wandered into the cabin, adding to its congestion. He picked up the stamps one after another, and examined them with a professional scrutiny. His air of the expert about to pronounce an authoritative opinion was so overwhelming that nobody else spoke.

"Make these myself," he explained. "Hooper's, Broad Mead, Bristol."

The general verdict, it appeared, was favorable until he opened the ink-pad with the intention of pressing one of the stamps on it. Then he stopped. It was the ink-pad which interested him, not the stamp. He studied it, touched it with his finger, and held it up horizontally to his eye. An expression of wonder crept across his small features.

"Here's a funny thing," he said. "The poor chap must have been daft! Would there be a bottle of ink among his things, now?"

"*Ink?*" roared H.M., galvanized.

"Yes. About half a bottle of ink," agreed Hooper, eyeing the pad. "You wouldn't see anything wrong with this pad, I'd like to bet?"

"No. What about it?"

Hooper chuckled. "Ah! But I would. This is a new pad. Brand new! And yet do you know what the poor chap's gone and done? He's poured about half a bottle of ordinary writing ink smack down on top of the ink that's already in the pad! Spoils the pad; of course it does. Squelchy as glue. Look. People do do some soft things, don't they?"

With this profound observation, he put the pad down on the berth. The third officer, the purser, and Max looked at each other.

"But why should he do that?" the third officer wanted to know.

"Ah!" said Hooper. "Don't ask me!"

He dusted his hands.

"Oo-er!" he added, consulting his watch. "Nearly half-past nine. I'll bet a fiver I've missed that concert. Clean forgot about it. But who wouldn't forget about it, seeing a poor chap dropped smack bang overboard like that? Do you want me for anything else?"

"Just a minute, son," said H.M., whose expression was wooden. He addressed the purser. "You get any orders from the captain?"

"Only to take orders from you."

"Uh-huh. Well. Did the late Mrs. Zia Bey deposit any sealed envelope at your office?"

The purser snapped his fingers. "I nearly forgot. Yes, sir, she did. At the old man—sorry, the captain's orders I opened it. Here it is." He drew the buff envelope out of his pocket. "There's nothing in it but squashed newspapers, as you can see for yourself."

H.M. took the envelope and emptied its contents part way out. He weighed it in his hand, sniffing. He did not speak for so long a time that the others shifted and coughed. Finally he handed the envelope back.

"All right. Tell me, son. Are you any good at scarin' people?"

The purser contracted his George Robey eyebrows and looked sinister.

"All right. Then I got a commission for you. I'm not goin' to appear in this thing myself any more than I need. I want you to find this Chatford girl. Show her that envelope. Yell blue thunder at her. Try to find out what she was really doin' in Max Matthews's cabin last night. You won't; but you start the demoralization process and I'll complete it. If you see any of the other passengers, you can ask 'em—be more tactful there, though—what they were doin' about nine o'clock to-night. Got that?"

"Yes."

"That's all, then. Hop it. *You*," H.M. said to the third officer, "stay here. And you too, Mr. . . . . harrum . . ."

"Hooper."

"Hooper. You stay here too, if you got nothing very pressin' to do. Now we can settle down comfortably."

After drawing at the empty pipe for some time, H.M. at last began to fill it from an oilskin pouch. He lifted the skirts of his raincoat, whisked a large American kitchen-match across the seat of his trousers, and lit the pipe. Sniffing contentedly, he got into the berth and sat propped up in it with his back against the pillows like a convalescent. The smoke was vile. But he puffed with drowsy relish for another interval. Then he pointed the pipe-stem at Cruikshank.

"You and the purser," he said, "spoke French to Benoit last night. Tell me the honest-Injun truth. How much did you understand?"

"Sorry. Not much, I'm afraid."

"That's the kind of truth I want, anyway. What do you think he was trying to tell you?"

The other hesitated.

"It's like this," he said in a rush. "In understanding French, you can do well enough if you get off in the right groove. That is, if you know at the start what the conversation is supposed to be about; if you pick up some words, you get clues to the rest. But when it's not clear at the start, the thing only gets more incomprehensible as it goes along." Again he hesitated. "To tell you the truth, he seemed to be talking about some woman."

"So?"

"Yes. It was 'elle' this, and 'elle' that. For a minute I thought he was confessing to the murder. I wanted to question him about it, but I didn't want to show off my ignorance in front of Griswold. And does the word traître mean what I think it does?"

H.M.'s eyes narrowed.

"It means traitor, yes. Are you sure that's what he said? For Lord's sake, son, be careful! Could it have been traite? Or traité? Or traiteur?"

The third officer's dark complexion went still darker.

"That's beyond me." He brooded. "No, look here! I'm almost certain it was traître; somebody was a traître. One thing more, sir." His jaw hardened. "Can I make a suggestion without being laughed at? Griswold thinks it's very funny, but I'm not so sure. I think Benoit may have been a member of the French Intelligence."

H.M. showed no disposition to laugh. He blew a large smoke-ring, and watched it distend and dissolve towards the white roof. He looked even more bothered.

"I've been thinkin' of that," he replied with an air of apology. The sharp little eyes fastened on Cruikshank. "But I say, son. Let's have your views. Don't you think a member of the French Intelligence would be likely to know English?"

"Thinking back on it," said Cruikshank, "I'm not so sure he didn't know some English, at least"—and the pipe came out of H.M.'s mouth in a hurry.

"So? What makes you believe that?"

"Nothing I could swear to in court. It's an afterthought, I admit. Only—well, like this. Now I look back on it, I remember something I said to Griswold. I said: 'What do you suppose the fellow wants with all those rubber stamps?' I spoke out of the side of my mouth, and in more or less a mumble."

"Uh-huh. Well?"

"I could almost swear, by the look of the fellow's eyes, that he'd understood me. He started to stretch out his hand, as though to pick up the stamps, and then thought better of it. This is all hind-sight, mind you! Griswold and I were pretty excited at the time. Still, if he spoke so little English, what was he doing in America? I'd hate to go up and down Broadway asking my way in French."

"Another point. Do me a favor, son. Just pull out that trunk from under the berth again, will you?"

The third officer did so; and at H.M.'s direction, turned it over. On the under-side, in addition to *Edwardic* and *B* labels, there were pasted on it the labels of the Pennsylvania Hotel in New York and the Willard Hotel in Washington.

"Washington," repeated H.M., relaxing as Cruikshank pushed the trunk back. "I was coming to this identity business, and the traveling. But you got his passport, haven't you?"

The other showed a gleam of relief.

"Yes; I don't think the passports have been returned yet," he conceded. "They're still down in Griswold's office. They—" He broke off. "Hullo! Where's Mr. Hooper?"

The inconspicuous manufacturer of rubber stamps had disappeared. Even Max, standing by the door, had not noticed him go. H.M., with a roar, poured himself out of the berth and stood upright.

"I hope he understands the skipper's orders," H.M. said. "Burn me, how in blazes did he get out of here? He's burstin' with his great adventure. I hope he won't go confidin' it to a friendly steward or stewardess."

The third officer was alert.

"Shall I go after him?"

"You'd better. Hammer it through his head that he's to keep quiet. If we get a panic started aboard this tub, there'd be trouble for fair."

As Cruikshank left the cabin, H.M. appeared to have reached the last stage of despondency. He blundered about in the confined space, picking things up and putting them down. He picked up a comb. He absent-mindedly juggled a dry shaving-brush. He noted that Benoit had been reared in the Spartan tradition of those who use straight-bladed razors; and, with an abrupt growl of interest, he caught up the razor and opened it. Its polished blade glittered wickedly under the light.

Max Matthews felt somewhat queasy about the stomach.

"Were you thinking," said Max, "that it would be an ideal weapon for cutting a throat?"

"I was."

"But we know Benoit didn't do it."

"Oh, sure," acknowledged H.M., making a slow and suggestive sweep in the air with the razor. "We know Benoit didn't do it. We also know—"

A startled exclamation from the door almost made him slice his left thumb off. He glared, his shoulders hunching up to his ears, as the head of Benoit's cabin-steward appeared behind Max. But the steward pulled himself together. He was a delicate-faced, soft-voiced elderly man, who resembled a retired parson.

"Did you ring, sir?"

"No," said H.M., and waited.

There was a long, delicately balanced pause, while H.M. swept the razor in the air once more, and the ship's engines thudded far below. The creaking of the bulkheads sounded like a creaking of bone and sinew as the steward appeared to brace himself.

"I beg your pardon, sir. May I ask a question?"

"Sure. What is it?"

"Is it true what I hear? That Captain Benoit has shot himself?"

"I'm afraid it is. Why?"

The steward moistened his lips. "Then I'm very sorry. I think I must have burnt his suicide-note."

Dead silence.

H.M. shut up the razor and replaced it in the rack over the wash-basin.

"But it was in the waste-paper basket!" the steward protested, with more excitement in his gentle voice. "I tidied up the cabin and made up the berth during dinner, and there it was in the waste-paper basket." He pointed to the usual basket beside the dressing-table. "It wasn't torn. But what else could I do except throw it out, when it was in the waste-paper basket?"

"Just a minute, son!" urged H.M., with powerful restraint. He took the now-dead pipe out of his mouth and put it in his pocket. *"What* was in the waste-paper basket?"

"A note, sir. On ship's stationery. Signed by Captain Benoit."

"And you found this note?"

"Yes, sir, but I couldn't read it. It was written in French. All I can tell you was that it was addressed to the captain—I mean the commander, that is. Anyway, it was just a sheet of paper headed 'Monsoor lee Capitann' of the *Edwardic* in big letters across the top."

"And it was in the waste-paper bas . . ."

H.M. remained wooden of expression, though his big chest rose and fell. He stopped. His eyes wandered round the cabin, and fixed on a point beside the door. He lumbered over and touched the button of the electric-fan.

Softly, insistently, the drone of the fan raised to a thick singing in that small place. It began to swing in measured movements from side to side, sweeping the cabin. There were a few sheets of paper in the box which had held Benoit's rubber stamps. H.M. put one of the sheets down near the edge of the dressing-table. As the strong breeze raked the table-top, moved away, and swung back again, the paper began to flutter. Sixty seconds later—an eternity of time by heart-beat or watch-tick—they saw it slide off. It hung in the air, gently touched the rim of the waste-paper basket, and came to rest on the carpet.

"I see," muttered the steward. They had all been standing as stiff as dummies, staring at the scratching paper. "If it'd done then what it did now, you'd have had the poor gentleman's suicide-note."

"Suicide-note!" said H.M. with contempt; but he checked himself and grunted. "Where is that paper now, son?"

"In the incinerator, I'm afraid."

Outside, far down the white-painted alley of cabins, a woman began to scream.

H.M.'s expression was not pleasant. "I dunno what that is," he said to Max. "But if I wanted to wrap myself up in the mantle of prophecy, I'd have a thunderin' good shot at it. I told you our pal Hooper was burstin' with his adventure. If he's started to spread the story among the crew—" He paused, and turned to the steward. "That's all, son. No, it wasn't your fault! You don't have to keep quiet about it. The Frenchman left a note, shot himself, and the note was destroyed. No secret there. You can go."

He beckoned Max into the cabin.

They listened, but the screams were not repeated. The sea had begun to rise, and the ship's rolling was heavier. Gay-colored curtains at the porthole stood out with the motion, taut as flags in a breeze, and sank gently with the roll to the other side, while Cabin B-71 chattered like teeth.

"The truth," snarled H.M., pointing to the waste-paper basket. "Maybe the whole truth. Carefully written out by the cautious Benoit. Put down for our lovin' hands to find. And snatched away from us by the fraction of an inch when . . . What was that book Benoit was reading?"

"*Gone with the Wind,*" said Max; and began to laugh for the first time since he had set foot aboard.

The *Edwardic* shouldered on.

14

Two nights later, they entered the submarine zone.

Since the early hours of Monday morning, the weather had been wicked. Squalls gradually congealing into a sleet-storm whistled from the north-east. The life-boats had to be hauled in and sealed with canvas; they would have been swamped or smashed by the drive of thirty-foot waves. Griswold, totting up the damage done to broken crockery, had his swivel-chair break under him. No passenger was unaffected by it, to some extent at least, and on Monday night only Lathrop and Max staggered into the dining-saloon. On Tuesday night it was deserted.

Toward Wednesday morning the gale subsided. It was even possible to walk with some degree of balance, if anybody were abroad in the passages. Wednesday dawned dark and very cold on a slow-rolling sea. The gulls screamed again. Towards eight o'clock they were overhauled and passed, a mile or so away, by another liner going in the same direction. She was as gray and featureless as a ghost-ship against the darker gray sea; she might have been transparent. A bright white light, winking and flashing from the side of the bridge, signalled in Morse that she was the *Andalusia,* one of the White Planet's crack liners. Stewards at the rail, with binoculars, could see that she was carrying a six-inch gun aft. The *Edwardic* carried no arms except the captain's revolver, and a .22 rifle belonging to the second engineer.

During those bad two days, all thoughts even of murder had been flooded out of Max Matthews's mind. He doubted if anybody else worried about it. His thoughts during the last part of the storm were as elementary as a dog's; and he felt as sick as one. Everything else had grown remote.

Lying in his berth, wedged there with pillows against the plungings of the cabin, he sometimes dozed and sometimes reviewed his life. He remembered every opportunity lost, every drink too many, every wrong judgment. The great ghostly ship, with its hundreds of shrouded cabins, had become his universe. And sometimes he thought of Valerie Chatford.

Valerie Chatford.

When he first began definitely to suspect her he could not afterwards remember.

Tracing it back, he thought it originated in a chance remark from Jerome Kenworthy. This was on Monday morning, just when the weather was getting bad, and just before Kenworthy (as well as nearly everyone else) had hurried away to seclusion. He and Kenworthy and Dr. Archer and Lathrop had been trying to play shuffle-board on the boat-deck. Kenworthy had quoted Valerie as saying that, to give the devil his due, Hitler was a brilliant man and you couldn't blame the Germans for following him.

This, of course, was nothing. Max completely forgot it, until bad dreams accompanied the first touch of seasickness on Monday night. Aided by certain remarks of Sir Henry Merrivale, his subconscious mind got to work. It gave him a particularly vivid dream of Valerie Chatford, a swastika band on her arm, marching in the midst of a crowd of women.

He awoke in a fever; for the next dream, to tell the truth, had been of Valerie Chatford in next to nothing at all, and himself about to put his arms round her.

His waking mind said to him: You know where that started. It is an echo of that conversation in the purser's office, where they were discussing legends of people committing murders without any clothes, and so crept into the dream. His vague instincts said: That girl attracts you intensely, so much so that in your mentally crocked-up state you shy away from her and think you dislike her.

The swastika image followed him into real sickness throughout Tuesday.

On Wednesday morning, with the sea running more calmly, he got up to find with surprise that he felt as fit as he had ever been: though very empty, and somewhat weak. It was a pleasure to walk. He even felt hearty, and sang in his bath. This diminished a good deal after breakfast, though he confined himself cautiously to toast and coffee.

What he did realize, with ugly post-dream clearness, was that they had come back to murder. For two days the *Edwardic* had been a dead ship. Now they must pick up again. His suspicions of Valerie Chatford—not necessarily as a murderess, but for certain as a slippery character of some kind—angered him once more. Of course, you can't suspect a girl of anything just because you dream about her with a swastika sleeve-band. But there were facts. Her claim to be Kenworthy's cousin, as told to the purser, was infuriating rubbish; though Kenworthy corroborated it, and this shook Max's nerve. Her claim to be with Kenworthy between nine-forty-five and ten o'clock on Saturday night, also as told to the purser and also corroborated by Kenworthy, he knew to be an outright lie.

Damn the girl.

She was the first person he saw when he went up on deck shortly before noon. He found her in the big open space aft on A Deck, where the huge hatch-cover was piled with sandbags, and a few deck-chairs had hopefully been set out. She wore a tan coat with the collar turned up; the wind blew her curly hair. Her back was towards him, and she stood looking at the white zigzag track of the wake.

"Good morning," he said. On an idiotic but irresistible impulse he added: "Heil Hitler!"

The words rattled against the cold morning air. They startled as he said them. For a second or two Valerie did not move. Then she turned round.

"Good morning," she answered through tightened lips. "Is that your idea of a joke?"

(He wished he hadn't said those words. It was as though he had been talking treason himself.)

"Every time we meet," said Max, "it seems to consist in you asking me, in one way or another, whether that is my idea of a joke."

"If we didn't meet . . ." Valerie suggested pointedly.

(She was attractive, though. You couldn't deny that. It had given him a shock when she turned round. All her washed-out airs had gone. Though there were shadows under her eyes, the sea air had given her color; she seemed possessed by a quiet inner excitement, though she instantly became glacial when she faced him.)

"If we *didn't* meet . . . ?" she repeated.

"Now that you've gained a cousin, don't you think you can afford to be generous?"

"Are you suggesting that Jerome isn't my cousin?"

"I'm saying, at least, that you weren't in his cabin between a quarter to ten and ten on Saturday night."

Her eyes were maliciously innocent. "How do you know where I was then, Mr. Matthews? You didn't see me until two o'clock."

This was true.

It brought him up with a start to realize its truth. But, as usual, she was twisting words.

"You told me—"

"Oh, no, Mr. Matthews! No! I couldn't have told you anything. I didn't see you at all then. At least, that's my story to the captain and the purser. And you haven't disproved it."

Max had realized several times before, of course, that there are occasions on which even the most easy-going man feels impelled to place an exasperating female across his knee and wallop her with a strap. But he had never experienced the wish so strongly as now. What exasperated him worst was a feeling that Valerie might be making mysteries where there were no mysteries. She had him on the hip now. She was winning this exchange, when she spoiled it by adding:

"Why did you say, 'Heil Hitler'?"

"You appear to think he's worthy of heiling."

"I don't think anything of the sort, *Mr.* Matthews. But I do think it's stupid and silly to underestimate your opponent; and regard him only as a funny little man with a mustache."

"Agreed. But I doubt if anybody in France or England does underestimate him."

"And," said Valerie, her color going up like a flag, "if the Germans really get started, our side will jolly soon find out differently."

Max was unperturbed.

"Anything you say. This is, so to speak, English soil. You can say what you please when you please. Why don't *you* heil Hitler? Or climb up in the crow's nest and sing the Horst Wessel? We'd all like that aboard a munitions ship."

Valerie flared out at him. "I jolly well *will* say what I like!" she cried. "I'll say—"

Here they were interrupted by the calm, drawling voice of Lathrop. The doors of the smoking-room, aft, stood open on this part of the deck. Two of the port-hole-windows were also open. Lathrop's head appeared in one of these windows.

"Oi! Sh-h! For the love of Pete remember where you are!" Lathrop cautioned.

The head disappeared, and he came out to join them.

"I've just been having half a pint of champagne," he went

112

on, his hands dug into the pockets of a blowing topcoat, and his white hair windblown. He breathed deeply. "What we used to call, forty years ago, The Boy. Nothing like it for a rocky stomach." He glanced at Valerie, and his eye twinkled. "My professional advice to you is: don't go heiling Hitler here; or, free speech or no free speech, you'll get yourself beaned with a marlin-spike. And I'll tell you what your trouble is, young lady. You're too serious-minded."

"All the best things in life are serious," said Valerie.

Lathrop gestured comfortably. "We-el, that depends on how you look at it. What I think you mean is, all the serious things in life are best. And that's wrong, young lady. That's wrong. You need relaxation. So I'll tell you what we'll do. Let's all go up on the boat-deck and have some deck-tennis or shuffleboard."

Valerie searched for words.

"I won't play shuffle-board," she said, "with that *rattle-snake*."

"You mean this fellow?" inquired Lathrop, jerking his thumb toward Max without surprise. "Oh, he's all right. No alibis, now. Come along."

Valerie spoke unexpectedly.

"I suppose you'd say," she began, "that Drink wasn't serious."

"I think," observed Max, while they looked at her in surprise, "Miss Chatford is now going to preach us a sermon on temperance. And, speaking of alibis—"

A cold, unpleasant silence gathered round them, while Valerie went red. Lathrop broke it. "I'm going to see that you two make it up," he said grimly, "if it's the last thing I ever do." He gripped an arm of each of them. "You're getting some exercise. No arguments, if you like the word better. Come with me."

On the boat-deck, at the top of a tall companionway, the full force of the wind whipped at them. It stung water to their eyes, and made them more conscious of the ship's roll. In a big cleared space, well aft of the camouflaged bombing-planes, were two nets for deck-tennis and a shuffle-board run-way. Lines of benches ran to port and starboard. Sitting alone on the edge of one of these benches was Sir Henry Merrivale.

His big shoes were planted wide apart, and his tweed cap pulled down behind his ears. Some six feet in front of him

113

stood a peg in a wooden base; and he was trying, with a handful of quoits made out of rope, to throw one so as to ring the peg. Utterly absorbed in this, he talked to himself in a stream of malignant mutterings, with comments, each time he threw a quoit. He was conscious of nobody. He might have been on another planet.

"If the feller could understand English, why not say so? Too far to the right . . . Then there's the question of the razor-strop. Humph. Too high . . . And the inky, inky ink. Missed the goddamned thing again."

"H.M.!"

"Why so many stamps, all about the same? Ship keeps rollin' . . . If there could only be a good *reason*—"

Max went close and uttered a piercing whistle.

Roused out of his reverie, H.M. jerked back, glared, and accepted the situation.

"So it's you, is it?" he grumbled. "About time you got up off your bed and walked."

"You weren't seasick, I suppose?"

"Me?" scoffed H.M., with hollow-voiced and incredulous astonishment. "Never been seasick a day in my life. It's your imagination, son, that's all it is. Why, take me, for instance. When I went round Cape Hatteras—"

"Yes. Are you busy?"

"Oh, I was just sittin' and thinkin'," said H.M., scratching the side of his nose. "And a ghostly murderer, that leaves ghost's finger-prints, wants a lot of cogitation."

"I don't think you've met Miss Chatford or Mr. Lathrop? Or have you?"

Lathrop, impressed, shook hands with an obvious respect which soothed and pleased the old man. Valerie remained cold and very much on the prickly side. H.M., after getting up to duck her a grave bow, gathered up the quoits from the deck and returned to his bench.

"We've heard a lot about you in the States, Sir Henry," said Lathrop. "I'm only sorry I didn't know you were there this time. The boys at City Hall would have given you a rip-roaring reception."

"I know," said H.M. apologetically. "That's one of the reasons why I sort of sneaked in and out. I love America. It's the most hospitable country there is. But it's so goddam hospitable that every time I spend a fortnight there they have to carry me aboard ship pickled in alcohol. I'm an old man. I can't stand the racket any more."

"Besides," pursued Lathrop, with one eye cocked at him, "you'd hardly expect—at a time like this—finding you away from home—"

"H'mf. So," said H.M., and tossed a quoit.

"And then, if I remember rightly, it was in the papers that you were going to be given a peerage and go into the House of Lords."

"It's a lie!" said H.M., galvanized. "Don't you believe a word of it. They tried to, yes. They're still skulkin' in ambush, just aching for an excuse to grab me and stick me in the House of Lords. But I fooled 'em twice, and I can still fool 'em again. Phooey." He threw another quoit, which landed several feet wide of the peg. "I say. I suppose the purser told you we were having a little meeting here to discuss murder?"

He nodded toward the companion-way. Hooper and Dr. Archer, still a trifle pale round the gills, were clambering up, followed by the third officer and the purser.

And, though not a word was spoken, Max sensed a new atmosphere.

The purser was uneasy. He wore his cap jauntily, but he was uneasy.

"Good morning," said Griswold, his expression stolid. "Is everybody here?"

"Not exactly, son," said H.M. "Where's the Commander?"

There was a slight pause. "The captain won't be able to be with us this morning," Griswold answered casually. "Er—maybe for all day."

H.M. paused with a quoit lifted. His sharp little eyes searched the purser's face. With the roll of the ship, his bench moved up and down against a gray sea stung with white-caps. Wind whipped the boat-deck.

"Oh," observed H.M., and threw the quoit again wide of the mark. He did not pursue the subject, but everybody knew what it meant. Studying the boat-deck, Max realized why its aspect seemed different this morning.

The look-outs at the rails had been doubled. They were in the zone.

Valerie cried out: "So you wanted to play shuffle-board, did you?" she asked Lathrop. "You knew there was going to be another inquisition!"

H.M. cut her off, and turned to the purser.

"Those eight little finger-print cards," he said. "You've got 'em where they can't be tampered with?"

"They're locked in my safe. Houdini himself couldn't get at 'em. I didn't lock up the umpty-umph hundred others, since all the crew have got alibis for Sunday night. They're not much good to us."

H.M. took careful aim with still another quoit. The corners of his mouth were drawn down; over this whole group hung a heavy, deadly air which was getting on Max's nerves.

"Tell me, son," pursued H.M., closing one eye and lazily sighting with the quoit, while the deck rose and made their legs feel light. "Suppose we did snaffle the murderer, or someone we could prove was mixed up in the murder. What would you do with him? Lock him up in the brig?"

The third officer laughed, without much amusement.

"No, sir. That's another idea out of the story-books. I've been asked about it before. The brig is only used when an A.B. goes on the spree in port, and has to be suppressed. It's not for passengers."

H.M. persisted.

"Well, what would you do with him, then? A suspected murderer?"

The third officer shrugged his shoulders.

"The captain would probably just confine him to his cabin, until he could be handed over to the authorities in port."

"Confine him under guard?"

"Locked in, more like. After all, he couldn't get away. There's only one way of escaping from this ship when you couldn't get a boat. Straight down."

"Uh-huh. Like Benoit," agreed H.M.

After carefully sighting again, he tossed the quoit, and it landed two feet beyond the peg. His face smoothed itself out. His manner was heavy and quiet, but Max liked it even less. After drawing a deep, gusty breath, he looked straight at Valerie Chatford.

"We'd better get on with it, then," he said. "You lock up the gal there. I'll be responsible for handin' her over to the authorities when we get to the other side."

15

There was a silence.

Valerie had backed away. She balanced herself lightly, not without grace, on the moving deck. Wind brushed her curly hair behind the ears, forcing her to lower her eyelids. But her face was one of stark terror.

"I don't know what you're talking about!" she cried in a high-pitched voice, which the wind choked back. *"Me?"*

"You," said H.M. "Looky here. The captain, and the chief engineer, and the officers on the bridge, and these fellers here" —he indicated Cruikshank and Griswold—"can't afford to fool about. They're on the spot. In case you didn't know it, carryin' munitions in a gale, such as we've had for the past two days, is no ruddy picnic. There's enough on everybody's mind as it is. They can't let you go on throwin' spanners into the machinery just for fun."

The very quietness of his voice made her draw back still further.

"Just a minute before you answer," resumed H.M. "There's no proper 'gray powder' aboard for developin' finger-print impressions. But French chalk, powdered very fine and used with a soft brush, does almost as well. Your finger-prints were all over the metal part of the light-switch in Mrs. Zia Bey's cabin. They were also on a powder-bowl on the dressing-table. Cruikshank got 'em last night, and Griswold compared 'em. Is that right, son?"

The third officer nodded grimly.

The purser glowered at the deck.

Not a sound came from any of the others, except that Hooper, dropping his life-jacket with a thud, flopped down on the bench beside H.M. Dr. Archer put one hand on the back of the bench, gripping it hard.

"I want you to stop actin' the fool," continued H.M., calmly sighting with another quoit, "and take back all the ghost stories you've been telling us. Now I warn you. This is your last chance."

"Do you deny," cried Valerie, "that I am—"

Again H.M. stopped her. "I'm not denyin' that your name may be Valerie Chatford, and that you may really be Kenworthy's cousin. I thought that name Kenworthy was familiar. He's old Abbsdale's son, of course. I knew Abbsdale when he was an r.a. at Falklands. As a matter of fact, the skipper and I have been in touch with him this morning."

"In touch with him?" repeated Lathrop. "But how in thunderation did you manage that? You can't send a radiogram from this ship. They won't let you. We're cut off from everybody."

"I sort of thought," said H.M., "that it might qualify as official business. We used the radio telephone." Again his eyes fastened on Valerie. "Abbsdale's got a sister, Ellen Kenworthy. Her first husband was Jossy Bernard, of the Foreign Office; and they had one daughter—Valerie—before Jossy died about eighteen years ago. Later on, Ellen married a schoolmaster named Chatford. There was blue blazes to pay over that. First, because Chatford wasn't quite out of the top drawer. Second and more important, because Abbsdale's a holy terror and Chatford had been thought to be living with his housekeeper, a woman called Vogel. But Ellen married him, took the child, and went out to Bermuda. Abbsdale refused to speak to her again. Right, young feller?"

In the act of throwing a quoit, he craned his neck round again.

Jerome Kenworthy, an itinerant specter muffled up to the ears in a big tweed coat, wabbled up the companion-way with his life-jacket bumping behind him. He got to the bench, pushing Hooper over, and sat down.

"This young feller," pursued H.M., "talked to his father on the radio telephone, and *he* says the gal is genuine. Right! We'll let it go at that. What we won't let go is the spankin' lie that she was with young Kenworthy for fifteen minutes on Saturday night. Now, my wench, are you goin' to admit you were in Mrs. Zia Bey's cabin or not?"

Valerie's jaw had grown hard under the soft skin. She was frightened. But she also seemed bewildered. And there was another emotion which Max could neither define or quite put into words. Uncertainty, suspicion, what?

"Light of my life," murmured Kenworthy, contemplating his shoes with a kind of horror, "you had better own up. This morning they grilled me like a sole. And nothing would please me more than to be presented with a gratuitous alibi.

But it won't wash. At the moment I don't care what happens. I don't give a damn if the ship goes down. Have we got to sit out in all this wind? Couldn't we just all go down to the bar and die?"

Valerie, puckering up her eyes, spoke in a wondering voice.

"But—well, suppose I didn't tell *quite* the truth?" she cried. "What on earth are you making all the fuss about?"

H.M. was genuinely staggered. He remained holding the rope ring in the air like a man with paralysis, his mouth open and the peak of the cap sliding down over his eyes.

"Oh, Lord love a duck!" he breathed. "This is broad-mindedness for fair. Oh, my eye. Two murders in five days. A near-panic in submarine waters. A semi-lunatic goin' about with a razor and a revolver. And the girl wants to know what we're makin' all the fuss about."

"Nonsense!" said Valerie. Impatience began to mix with her fear, or at least so Max interpreted it. "You know who the murderer was."

"Do we, now?"

"Of course you do! It was Captain Benoit."

"Captain Benoit?"

"Naturally. You know that. You've known it since Sunday night."

"My dear, good wench . . . !"

"I don't care what sort of stories you put about, *I* heard the truth from my stewardess," continued Valerie. "Captain Benoit killed Mrs. Zia Bey. He couldn't face it afterwards, so he shot himself. My stewardess has a cousin who's one of the look-outs. She says he actually saw it happen; actually saw him put the gun to his head and pull the trigger. It was a crime of passion, as I could have told you. Frenchmen are like that anyway. He wrote her a lot of letters, and then he went ga-ga and killed her and got back the letters."

Hooper had jumped up and was shaking his head violently, but Valerie would not be interrupted.

"As I say, I could have told you that long ago," she fired at them. "I saw him on Saturday night."

"Half a minute," said H.M., in such a clear, sharp voice that it checked the girl's apparent hysteria. "You saw Captain Benoit kill Mrs. Zia Bey?"

Valerie corrected herself.

"I didn't exactly see him *kill* her. That would have been

119

too horrible. I couldn't have stood it. But I saw him—well, at work. I saw him come out of her cabin after she must have been dead."

H.M., still holding the quoit, stared at it as though he had never seen it before.

"Benoit's on the scene of the crime," H.M. muttered. "Benoit tries to tell 'em something, and is surprised when they say 'Ah, oui.' Benoit leaves a note. Benoit is polished off . . ." His voice trailed away, and then grew strong again. "And so the man who knew too much," he groaned, "gets it in the neck again. When did you see him come out of Mrs. Zia Bey's cabin?"

"A-about five minutes to ten. He was carrying a big bundle of papers, incriminating letters—oh, a bundle three or four inches thick!"

"Are you lying to us again?" thundered H.M.

Dr. Archer interposed. "If you'll allow me to say so," he smiled, "this young lady seems to have—er—almost a morbid fixation on the subject of incriminating letters. A pile of letters three or four inches thick is not a bundle. It's an archive."

"People do do some queer things, don't they?" ruminated Hooper. "Sounds like a film. That it do."

"Yes, I know it does," agreed Lathrop grimly. "Now that the cat's out of the bag, there are a few things I could bear to understand myself. Young Matthews told us your story about those mysterious letters long ago, Miss Chatford. What I wish you'd tell us is this: How did you know the woman had a bagful of letters to start with?"

H.M.'s powerful lungs quieted an incipient babble when everybody began to talk at once.

"Easy, now! Burn me, take it easy. Just tell us the story, my wench. What happened to you between nine-forty-five and ten o'clock on Saturday night? And this time, mind, we want the whole truth."

Valerie braced herself.

"I went down to Mrs. Zia Bey's cabin, to plead with her to give up poor Jerome's letters . . ."

"Devil take my body, I tell you I never wrote any let—"

"Sh-h! Go on, my wench."

"To do somebody a favor, then," retorted Valerie, and tears (considerably assisted by a stance facing the wind)

120

started into her eyes. "When I got outside the door, I heard her talking to some man inside."

"What man?" asked H.M. "Could you identify his voice?"

"No, I'm afraid not. It was rather a deep voice, but speaking low, and I couldn't hear any words. I went into Mr. Matthews's cabin across the passage (not knowing it was his cabin, or I wouldn't have gone); and waited for the man to go. In a little while I heard the door of B-37 open and close. I risked a little peek out. It was Captain Benoit, just turning into the main alleyway with his back to me. He had a long envelope full of letters in his hand."

"How'd you know they were letters?"

Valerie gestured. "Well, they were papers of some kind, so naturally they must have been letters."

"Uh-huh. And then?"

She swallowed hard. "I tapped on the door of Mrs. Zia Bey's cabin. There was no answer. So I opened the door. The light was on. I saw her lying on the dressing-table, all over blood—Ugh! I nearly fainted. I went close to make sure she was really what she seemed to be. I must have left my fingerprints on the powder-bowl then. Oh, and I turned out the light when I left the cabin.

"I didn't know what I was doing. I felt simply horrible. So I vaguely remember dodging back into Mr. Matthews's cabin, and wondering what I was to do *now*. I stayed there for maybe five minutes more with the door closed."

The purser interposed.

"You realize, don't you, Miss Chatford," he said, "that the real murderer must have been in B-37, probably hiding in the bathroom, when you went in to look at Mrs. Zia Bey's body?"

"H-how's that?"

"Unless," the purser scowled hideously, "unless Benoit killed Mrs. Zia Bey and somebody else killed Benoit. Which doesn't sound likely. Go on."

Again Valerie gestured.

"I'd been back in Mr. Matthews's cabin for perhaps five minutes . . ."

"Stop again," interrupted H.M. "During that time, did anybody leave B-37 after Captain Benoit? Did you hear anybody?"

Valerie shook her head.

"I'm sorry. I was much too upset to notice. I shouldn't have

121

heard it if anybody had. But it *must* have been Benoit, mustn't it? Surely it must! I never thought about anybody else. His shooting himself, everything else, all fits in. You're trying to b-bully me, and I won't be bullied!

"But that's all there is. In about five minutes, I heard some-one come along and tap at the door of B-37. I peeped out again, and there was Mr. Matthews. Presently he opened the door. Later I tried to get away, when he sent the steward to get the captain; but I almost walked straight into a stew-ardess, and I had to go back again. Everything else I told him was true. I stayed cooped up in his cabin, and later in the bathroom, for hours and hours and hours. Only to be in-sulted when Mr. Matthews did come in."

H.M. seemed slightly dazed.

"You've known this all the time, and thought Benoit was the murderer? Then why didn't you speak out?"

"I did it to save Jerome," cried the girl tragically. "I even thought I might get a word of t-thanks."

Now this was far overplaying her rôle, as she instinc-tively felt herself. She overplayed it still more as she pro-ceeded to tell them the same story, about the letters, as she had told Kenworthy himself. But the little devil of emotional acting had got into her Aryan soul, and called for sentimental drama. Max knew this. Kenworthy himself, having had sev-eral days for reflection, knew it too.

"So you were protectin' this feller's good name; is that it?" inquired H.M., tossing his last quoit.

"Yes."

H.M. opened one eye at Kenworthy. "Were there any let-ters, son?"

"For the last time," returned Kenworthy, "emphatically, *no!* Candidly, do I look the sort of bloke who would pour out his soul on paper? Orally, yes. At a night-club, without doubt. For the eyes of a solicitor, no. Don't think I'm not grateful, Valerie. I appreciate what you tried to do no end, and the governor will appreciate it too. But, without wanting to be unchivalrous, it seems to me that your best efforts to help me have done nothing but land me in the soup."

"Have you seen the woman's body, son?"

"I've seen it." The young man's long face, behind his oc-tagonal spectacles, turned slightly green. "In the ice-house or cold-storage room or whatever it is."

"And did you know her?"

"No. Except—" His eyebrows drew together. "I've got a hazy sort of idea that I saw her once before, under circumstances which struck me as being very comic, and with somebody whose face I'll swear I've seen aboard this ship."

"But where? And when? And who?"

"I can't remember!" groaned Kenworthy. "If this sea would steady down a bit, and give my innards time to take the pressure off my brain, maybe I could stir the old subconscious."

"You may have that opportunity," the third officer grinned, "if we run into fog. As we're apt to do."

"Many thanks for small consolations. All the same, sir"— Kenworthy appealed to H.M.—"see if you can't apply a consolation too. After all, is it so impossible that Benoit killed the woman and then committed suicide? It seems the most reasonable explanation to my enfeebled wits."

Dr. Archer interposed crisply.

"Ah!" he said, tapping with well-manicured fingers on the back of the bench. "Exactly the question I was about to ask. *Why* are you all so sure it was not suicide?"

"Because, son—"

"One moment!" said Dr. Archer, lifting a magisterial hand. "Accepting," he smiled and bowed, "accepting Miss Chatford's latest story, I can't see any other explanation. Is it likely, now, that still *another* person slipped out of Mrs. Zia Bey's cabin after Captain Benoit had gone? At least, without being heard by Miss Chatford? She heard the door open and close before. Surely she would have heard it again? Aren't you creating a straw-murderer for the pleasure of stumping yourself with a problem? Believe me, ladies and gentlemen, I've had some experience with these things. I insist that my experience ought to carry some weight."

H.M. rolled up his head. "Experience? What experience?"

The doctor's quizzical expression became a broad and twisted grin.

"I was for some years," he replied, "one of the acting police surgeons (it was a part-time job for several of us) of A Division of the Metropolitan Police. I've said little in this business so far. I wanted the mountain to come to Mahomet. Still"—he flipped finger and thumb together, as though he were flicking a bread-pellet—"there it is. Does the name of Chief Inspector Masters mean anything to you, Sir Henry?

Or Sergeant, now Inspector, Pollard? But never mind my bona fides. On Monday morning, at the request of the ship's surgeon (who had never done one) I performed a post-mortem on the body of Mrs. Zia Bey."

"Good!" said Lathrop, swinging round. "I kept insisting that somebody ought to do that. In law—"

Dr. Archer stopped him.

"As Mr. Lathrop says," he continued, "Mr. Lathrop's insistence on the point led to results. The result of that post-mortem might surprise you."

H.M. stared at him. "I say, son. You're not goin' to tell us the woman was poisoned or drowned?"

The doctor laughed. Max thought that his constant twingling, or laughing, or pointed innuendo, might have got on their nerves if they had not all been so determinedly cheerful. It was a part of the atmosphere they were pledged to establish among themselves.

"I only said," Dr. Archer pointed out smoothly, "that the result might surprise you. That's aside from the point. I must ask you, as a medical jurist: What evidence have you that Captain Benoit did not, in fact, shoot himself?"

Then up rose George A. Hooper, with his arms flapping, and again related his story.

"You actually saw all this?" persisted the doctor.

"Ah; I saw the murder. With my own eyes," added Hooper, pointing to them by way of emphasis.

"But, in pitch darkness, how could you be sure there was another person with him? Or be sure he was shot through the back of the head?"

"When the gun went off," answered Hooper simply, "I saw it."

"By the flash of the revolver-shot?"

"Ah."

"My dear sir, that's impossible."

Hooper changed color. "Are you," he inquired after reflection, "calling me a liar?"

"Not at all. I merely say—"

"If that," said Hooper, suddenly bouncing up like an indiarubber man, "is not calling me a liar—"

"S-h! Oi! Now, now," intervened Lathrop soothingly, while H.M. picked up the quoits and continued to toss them without comment. "It's all impossible," Lathrop went on, himself evidently at his wit's end. "Non-existent people who leave bloody fingerprints are impossible. When two and two don't make four, it's impossible, I tell you, Sir Henry, you've got to get us out of this, or we'll all go nuts. This can't go on much longer. Or can it?"

*   *   *   *   *

That night, the murderer struck again.

16

Wednesday evening. Wind fresh, N.N.E., barometer rising. Latitude and longitude deleted at request of censor. An air of tension growing, as though an echo from the muffled crackle of the wireless-key had crept down into the passengers' quarters.

No word was said about it. The officers went about their business as casually as ever. But you never saw them except at a distance. They appeared and vanished; and a door blew shut. A liner at sea is sensitive as a theater to emotional atmospheres, which is why everybody knew.

The passengers joked a good deal among themselves. It was announced that a film would be shown in the lounge after dinner, but that the bar would close at ten o'clock.

Max, killing time until it was a reasonably decent hour to think of dressing for dinner, lounged down to his cabin shortly before seven. He got no farther than the door past the shop on B Deck, when he was arrested by familiar tones.

"Looky here," howled an irate voice. "This is beginnin' to get on my nerves. I know your heart's secret about it. *But I still don't want any hair-restorer.* I want a shave, s-h-a-v-e, shave. For five days I been shavin' myself to keep out of your way. For the love of Esau will you stop gabblin' about hair-restorer and get on with it?"

" 'Air," said the barber, "is like grass. Now grass grows, don't it, sir? No thoughtful man can have any doubt about that. And there you are. *Why* does it grow?"

"I dunno. What I'm saying is—"

"Exactly my point, sir," said the barber triumphantly.

125

"It grows because the rain falls on it and waters it. We see that even grass, which is God's gift and a natural phenomenon, as you might say, requires something poured on it to make it sprout. Isn't that so?"

Max pushed back the curtain and put his head into the barber's shop.

Clean and white-tiled, with mirrors a-gleam, the place looked very trim except for H.M. His spectacles were down on his nose, and he peered at a neck-breaking angle behind the great swathing of white cloth. But he could not hold the barber's eye.

The barber, after opening a little glass door to inspect steaming towels, closed it with satisfaction and went on whipping up lather in a porcelain mug.

"So if even Dame Nature must be pampered in that way, what's the result? Come in, sir: you're next!"

The barber broke off, and stopped whisking up lather, as he recognized Max. A sinister suspicion appeared to cross his mind. He put down the mug. But as Max merely nodded, considering that he could do with a haircut anyway, drifted across to a chair, and picked up a copy of the *Tatler,* the barber was reassured. Though he continued to regard Max with the deepest misgiving out of the corner of his eye, he went on with his work.

"I'll tell you something else, sir," he continued in a loud voice. "I won't say, mind you, that I didn't feel just a little bit 'urt the other day. (Let me have your glasses, sir. That's it.)"

"Listen, son. Did you hear what I told you about the towel? Not too hot. I got a sensitive—"

"I have my pride, sir, same as anybody else," said the barber in an injured tone. "You were the first customer I'd had, too. (Now the hot towel, *if* you please. That's right. Not too hot, is it?)"

"Uh!"

"It is, sir, or it isn't?"

"Uh! Uh! *Uh!*"

"Then we'll just let it stay. Hold still, sir, while I wrap it round and make a little place for your nose to come out. Speaking of noses—but I'll come back to that. What I really wanted to say was, I have my pride the same as anybody else. Not that you didn't pay me my money, three times over. No! But it's very seldom that a gentleman sits down in my chair, and gets up again, when I've got the lather actually on the brush."

"Wha-ha?"

"I said, on the brush. However, no offense, I'm sure! They say the film tonight is Shirley Temple, and I'm sure you'll en— Is anything wrong, sir?"

There was so long a silence that Max, flipping over the pages of the magazine without seeing them, at last became conscious of it. He felt sick and disgusted with the whole mess. He knew Valerie Chatford was a crook. He had a creepy feeling that they were not done with trouble. As the effect of the silence reached him like a kind of explosion, he glanced up.

He saw H.M.'s face reflected in the big mirror on the wall. H.M., holding the hot towel in one hand, had struggled upright in the barber's chair. His red-heated face, the eyes wide and unblinking, was set in an expression which could not have been more curious if the barber had hit him across the back of the head with a bottle of the famous hairrestorer.

"Gimme my glasses!" he said suddenly.

"Sir?"

"Gimme my glasses," howled H.M., sliding out of the chair and fumbling with the cloth round his neck. "I'm sorry, but I haven't got time to get shaved now."

It was almost all up with the barber's artistic pride. For a moment it seemed touch and go whether he would not smash the shaving-mug on the floor, and dance on the pieces.

A minor convulsion afflicted the white robe.

"Get me out of this Appius Claudius get-up, can't you?" urged H.M. But, when the cover was removed, he changed his mind. He reached out and shook the barber's hand.

"Son," he said solemnly, "you don't know what you've done for me. When I think that I've been avoidin' this place, when all the time it was the fount and origin of inspiration, I could kick myself from here to the forepeak. I'm comin' back. Burn me, I'll even buy a bottle of your tonic! In the meantime, here's a quid to go on with. Come on, Max. We got business."

Two customers fled the barber's shop with such celerity that he had to run after them with their life-jackets. As they were going downstairs, H.M. imparted information.

"We've got to find the purser," he said. "I'm not sure, and I hate to make predictions; but I think I've got it."

Though the purser's window was open, Griswold himself was absent. His assistant, a pleasant freckled-faced young man with a serious manner, expressed regret.

"All I want," insisted H.M., "is a look at the passengers' finger-print cards. Just the passengers'. And a magnifying glass."

"I'm sorry, sir. Those cards are in the safe, and I don't know how to open it."

"Where's the purser?"

The young man hesitated. "At a conference in the captain's quarters, I think. I couldn't disturb him even for you."

H.M.'s face grew more sober. "Ho? Submarines about?"

"Couldn't say, sir. I should come back later, if I were you."

"How much later?"

"Probably a lot later. After dinner, anyhow."

"That's torn it," growled H.M., as the roll-top window rumbled down.

"Can't you go up and break in on them?"

"Well. Now. Not if it's as serious as all that. This looks," said H.M., "uncommonly like business. For cat's sake," he barked, himself the least patient of men, "can't you be patient for a while? This'll keep, won't it? And a spot of grub won't do us any harm."

The spot of grub, when it materialized, brought all the remaining passengers down to dinner. H.M., his napkin tucked into his collar, ate steadily and said nothing. Otherwise there was much subdued gaiety in the dining-room. Nobody made any reference to submarines. Hooper and Lathrop became involved in a long, complicated Biblical argument about the Israelites crossing the Jordan; they debated the width of the Jordan for some time before someone asked hesitantly whether they didn't mean the Red Sea.

Hooper, as stubborn as a whole Somersetshire regiment, tucked in his chin and refused to budge from his position that it was the Jordan. Lathrop, more nimble, contributed a gruesome anecdote about a flood in Pennsylvania. Dr. Archer capped this with another anecdote, still more gruesome, about the Spanish War. For some reason these stories were considered amusing, and everybody laughed at them.

(Waiting. And still more waiting. With a flash of insight

Max realized that war is nearly all waiting, and that is why it tears the nerves.)

After dinner they all trooped up to the lounge, where a motion picture screen had been set up. They gravely watched Shirley Temple reducing wicked rich men to tears and uniting true hearts: a spectacle which depressed the judicious but at least provided something to do. In the middle of it Max lost H.M.—and he did not reappear.

The *Edwardic's* lounge regained its night-time rattle. It started to pitch again; Kenworthy, to his mortification, left in a hurry. Dr. Archer suggested a swim in the pool, where Max half promised to join him. Then he deliberately followed Valerie Chatford into the smoking-room.

She sat down in the gloom which centered round the couch, far away from any light in that dim red place.

"Hello," said Max. "Join me in a drink?"

"No, thank you."

"Sorry. I forgot you didn't approve of Drink."

"If you put it like that," murmured Valerie, "I'll have a brandy."

The clock above the empty fireplace ticked loudly. He had not meant to sting her with that remark. As she left the lounge, he had thought she looked tired and lonely and low-spirited. She was again wearing the dove-gray evening gown, which had something vaguely loose and shabby about it; nothing you could define, yet evident the second time it was worn.

"Enjoy the picture?"

"Oh, so-so."

"Not feeling very fit?"

"I'm quite all right, thanks. Why this sudden friendliness, *Mr*. Matthews?"

(Oh, God! thought Max.)

He felt her eyes measuring him. Her bare shoulders were white, of a milky smoothness; they conveyed the impression of youth even more than her face. She kept opening and shutting the catch of her handbag.

"I shouldn't have said that," she told him. "I'm as bad as you are."

"Impossible."

"No, it isn't. You think I made a dreadful exhibition of myself up on the boat-deck this morning, don't you?"

He hesitated, and she was after it.

"Yes, you do. Anyway, one thing is a relief. You don't either like or respect me, so I don't have to pretend with you any more. I know what a show I made of myself as well as you do." Suddenly she began to beat her handbag against her thigh. Her voice broke, with almost shocking intensity. "Only I'm miserable, miserable, miserable! Nobody in hell is as miserable as I am!"

More acting?

It might be, and yet Max doubted it. Sincerity had rung in that as he had seldom heard it before.

"Steady," he said. "I don't think you made a show of yourself at all. Only you might have told them what you knew at the beginning, and not made such a mystery of it."

"Then the story I told," she went on, "about black-mailing letters in the woman's handbag . . ."

This was the point at which Valerie's own handbag, from having its catch snapped so often, fell open. The steward carrying their brandies loomed over them in the gloom. He set down the brandies on the low coffee-table in front of the couch. Max heard the clock tick loudly.

Both he and the steward saw what was in Valerie's hand-bag: a large nickelled electric torch with a big head and bulb. The steward hesitated before bending forward confidentially.

"I'm sure I beg your pardon, miss. But—"

"Yes?"

"That torch," said the other, smiling without offense. "You won't take it out on deck, will you? I just thought I'd warn you."

"No, of course not!" said Valerie. "I only got it in case we—you know. The electricity might go off. And it would be awfully dark and cold getting down into one of those boats."

"That's all right, miss," the steward assured her. He had a manner like a diplomat; he could mention the weather in tones of one imparting confidential information. "Only," he added in a lower voice, "I hear there was something last night. Someone leaving a port open, or maybe one of the look-outs smoking on deck. Anyway, they're getting pretty keen on it. It's calm tonight, you know."

"But," said Valerie, and stopped. "They wouldn't—well, do anything until we were in the boats?"

"No, of course not," the steward soothed, and smiled

again. "Nothing to worry about, miss." He directed a significant glance at Max. "Bar closes at ten tonight, sir. I shall have to turn the lights out. Any last orders?"

Max shook his head, and the steward faded away, leaving them alone.

"Cigarette?"

"No, thanks," said Valerie.

He lit a cigarette for himself, and finished his brandy at one go; he hesitated on the edge of making a comment.

"I'm sorry." Valerie spoke with such abruptness that he jumped. "I'm going to seem very rude again. And I don't mean it this time. But would you finish the brandy for me?" She got to her feet, sweeping up the life-jacket. "I've got a splitting headache. I'm going to bed. Do you mind?"

"Not at all," he pushed himself to his feet on his cane, his bad leg giving him a twinge. "Take a couple of aspirins and turn in. That'll do you all the good in the world. Good night."

"Good night."

Thud, thud, droned the ship's engines. *Thud, thud. Thud, thud.* You could feel them more clearly because of the calmer sea. The clock rang with chimes, and struck ten. Max continued to smoke while the lights were put out, turning over more than one speculation in his mind, until the reproachful hovering of the steward roused him. He finished Valerie's brandy and went through the Long Gallery into the lounge.

Having prepared himself with a couple of novels, he settled down in a corner where he could keep an eye on the main staircase. Hooper drifted through on the way down to bed before eleven, and Lathrop a little later.

"I hear," remarked Lathrop—his voice sounded loud, though it was not—"I hear they got an oil-tanker ten miles behind us today."

"You can hear anything in these ships."

"Ho! You seem pretty cool."

"Just ordinary," said Max. He spoke casually. "Do you happen to know the number of Miss Chatford's cabin?"

Lathrop forbore to make any comment, especially a jocose one; his was never the obvious way.

"By gosh, I believe I do!" he exclaimed, after a pause. "Not that I could tell you 'em offhand, but hers is a chemical formula. C-20: that's it! I remember her laughing about it, and saying it was a chemical formula. Or did she say a chem-

131

ical formula turned the wrong way round? Anyway, it's some kind of gas."

"Thanks."

"Be careful," said Lathrop; and drifted on.

Thud, thud. Thud, thud. Still no sign of H.M. At half-past eleven Max could no longer disregard the lounge-steward's turning out the lights. He slipped down to the purser's office, but knocking got no reply. His original impulse was to go to cabin C-20 and make sure Valerie had turned in; but he thought his motive might be misinterpreted, so at the last minute he changed his mind. Returning to the main hall on A Deck, which they were more or less bound to keep lighted late, he sat down grimly to read.

The clock on the wall clicked with each jump of its hand.

As with most people aboard this sealed-in ship, the heavy air once more did its work.

He dozed off in the chair. Then he awoke with a start, how much later he could not tell. But it came over him suddenly. His skin was crawling with the apprehension of danger—danger intimate, personal, striking to the heart—and he had a distinct sensation of being watched.

He looked round warily. A dim light burned in the roof of the main hall over the staircase; someone must have extinguished the rest. Not a whisper breathed aboard the *Edwardic* except the creak of the bulkheads and the dim churn of the engines. When Max glanced up at the clock over the lifts, the same clock which had marked time for Estelle Zia Bey's passing, he saw with a start that it was ten minutes to three.

He must find H.M.: that was his one wish. He couldn't go to sleep still wondering, puzzling, tossing on the edge of anguish to find out the solution. He must find H.M.

H.M.'s cabin was on the boat-deck, and whether his danger were real or fancied, he must go out there.

His head feeling light from lack of air, he moved over as softly as his limp allowed to the black-out doors. Again he had the sharp sensation of being watched or followed. But he could see nothing. The doors creaked and cracked, an explosion of sound, as he wormed through.

It was not difficult to find the companion-way tonight. He emerged on the boat-deck into a windless, clear, wintry night of stars. Darkness still pressed in from the sea; the light overhead was bluish, with distorting shadows, yet he could

132

faintly distinguish objects at a distance of some feet. It was so quiet that he could hear one of the look-outs whispering and a stir of feet as of rats. Yet the apprehension of danger remained: he almost smelt it.

Something moved and darted ahead of him.

Though the boat-deck was blurred and imprisoned by shadows, the white fur coat gave her away. He knew it was Valerie Chatford before he grasped her wrist. In her hand, just visible, was a faint bluish shine which marked the barrel of the electric torch.

He heard his voice whisper out harshly, an eerie noise which seemed to proceed from his brain rather than his mouth.

"Give me that torch."

No answer. The insistent whisper muttered again.

"Give me that torch," he said. "If you try to press the button I'll have to slosh you. Haven't you done enough already?"

"Are you mad?" she whispered back. "You don't think I was trying to—?"

"Give me that torch?"

The slapping and hissing of waves had become a monotone, in time to the movement of the great gray-black funnel above them, and the swing of the foremast against the stars far ahead. Max's heart felt physically cold. It was the turn of the night, in the hour of suicide and bad dreams. Shortly you would be able to scent the dawn. He kept his hand clamped round her wrist, and wrenched the torch away.

"Listen!" said Valerie.

Both of them whirled round. Feet began to pound on the deck some distance away. The voice they heard was clear, not loud, but it split the quiet of the night like a blow against the brain.

"Submarine off starboard bow. Torpedo co-oming!"

*   *   *   *   *

Twenty seconds later, shatteringly, the alarm-bells began to ring through every corner of the ship.

17

Max thought: well, here it is. Now what happens?

No more than that. No emotion which he could afterward remember. In the space of twenty seconds before the blare of alarm-bells, a hundred speculations went through his head. He wondered what the explosion would look like and sound like. He wondered whether the ship necessarily went up wherever the missile struck, like a spring toy he had had as a child, or whether there might be parts of the hull where it could burst without igniting the cargo.

Then the alarm-bells ran under the deck like fire.

"Run!" he said. "Get down to your cabin, grab a blanket and anything else you may need, and go to the dining-room. Got your life-jacket?"

"You don't think," Valerie screamed at him, "I was trying to signal a—"

"Never mind what I think. You can move faster than I can. Hurry!"

"Don't we go for the boats?"

"Damn your soul," said Max. "You heard what the third officer told us. You obey orders. Go on!"

A torpedo in motion through the water, someone had once told him, made a kind of chuckling and clicking noise. If you sighted it enough distance off, he had also been told, a ship readily responsive to the helm on a zigzag course might manage to dodge it. That would be the first one.

Valerie had gone.

The alarm-bells were still blaring, drowning thought. Max hurried down. He fell twice on the journey, flattening out on the deck, without consciousness of pain. But he did not run. He told himself that he ruddy well wouldn't run.

The lower decks were astir. A sailor walked quickly but quietly past, coiling rope. Max took the example. Fastening on his life-jacket, he went into his cabin, which now seemed to him unendurably hot. Taking his notecase from the dressing-table drawer, and the passport he had that morning redeemed from the purser, he glanced round for anything else that might be of service. Gloves. Extra cigarettes and matches. Finally, gas-mask and blanket.

One part of his mind always listened, as tense and acute as a microphone. He was waiting for the torpedo to strike. Why didn't it? Perhaps it had already struck; but that was impossible.

Leaving the cabin, he was clean out and down the passage before he recalled that he had forgotten one of the most important things of all: his overcoat.

He went back for it.

It vaguely surprised him that he was no longer afraid. Get out of here, he said to himself. What are you delaying for? Don't look round the place again. The thing's coming in half a minute, and then there won't be time.

On the way out for the second time, he met his bedroom steward, who asked him if he had got everything, and was reassured. The steward nodded and moved away. You still had to shout under the din of the alarm-bell. When he reached the dining-room, some of the passengers were already there. The third officer, standing by the door with a watchful eye in counting, nodded and grinned at him as he passed.

The many little mosaic mirrors of the dining-room pillars glittered under lights, and repeated images. Cloths were on the tables. Hooper, bundled up in life-jacket and blanket, wearing a green Tyrolese hat with a little feather in it, sat placidly at a table and drummed his fingers on it. Lathrop, wearing his gas-mask, sat at another. Dr. Archer came in quietly, and Kenworthy smoking a cigarette. Both, after consideration, took chairs. No one spoke to anyone else. The last to appear was Valerie.

The clatter of the alarm-bells stopped; and stillness was a blow.

Still no one moved or spoke.

Max removed his life-jacket in order to put on his overcoat underneath, after which he replaced the life-jacket. Valerie—across the table from him—was fumbling and twisting at the strings of hers; so he set it right for her.

She was the first to speak out in the hollow, bright, still room. *"I'm afr—"* she began, a sharp sound. Max closed his fingers round her shoulder and gripped as hard as he could. Her shoulder-muscles remained rigid, but she seemed to grow calm.

One of the doors to the kitchen squeaked. The water in

the glass carafes on the tables tilted slowly back and forth with the motion of the ship; Max could feel no difference in speed.

Lathrop lifted his gas-mask to speak loudly. "They must have missed us."

"Ah; looks like it," nodded Hooper. "My son," he added to the third officer, calling across the room, "dashed if I haven't forgotten the present I was bringing for Lou's little one! Can I go back upstairs and get it?"

"No. Please remain where you are."

"But what in hell are they waiting for?" demanded Lathrop.

"Steady, please."

Kenworthy, looking narrowly at each passenger in turn, continued to smoke his cigarette and smile. It was like a gesture of insolence. Dr. Archer thoughtfully checked over the contents of his pockets: torch, cigar-case, flask, lighter, and two bars of chocolate. The doctor's hand shook once; he darted a quick glance round to see if anyone had noticed. Hooper sighed as though bored. They made 'em tough in Somerset, Max thought. Hooper calling, "My son, can . . ."

Max sat up straight.

Where was Sir Henry Merrivale?

The whole ship seemed alive with moving and dragging noises; it was all the intimation they had of what might be going on outside. Lathrop smote his gloved hands together. Dr. Archer poured out a little water into a glass and drank it.

"Mr. Cruikshank!" Max called sharply, and everybody jumped. "We're one short. We—"

"Quiet, please!"

Footfalls clacked loudly on the staircase outside. There were two sets of glass double-doors opening into the dining-room. At the doors on the starboard side, the third officer stiffened to attention. Max saw the last person he expected to see: old Frank. Commander Matthews strode into the room, stopped short, surveyed them all in turn, and spoke quietly.

"Ladies and gentlemen, don't be alarmed. There's no danger."

His stocky shoulders went back.

"In fact, there's no submarine. You can go back to your cabins. We've been the victims of a false alarm."

It took about thirty seconds for the meaning of this to settle itself in minds adjusted and eyes focused to look back at death. There was dead silence, except for the quiet trampling of feet overhead: the crew filing back to their quarters. The red lacquer of the dining-room, the mirrors endlessly repeating a picture of old Frank with his hand half raised: Max afterward remembered nothing on the voyage with quite such vividness as this.

Dr. Archer got up with stiff legs from his chair, and sat down. He smiled. Kenworthy yawned.

But that was not all.

"Just one moment!" said Commander Matthews. "Mr. Cruikshank, close the doors."

The third officer went round, closed the double-doors, and bolted them all. He next walked across to glance into the kitchens and make sure they were empty. Commander Matthews, hands in side-pockets and thumbs hooked over the edges, took a few steps closer to the passengers.

"I said you could go back to your cabins," he went on. "That was only in a manner of speaking. To keep you quiet. I'd rather you stayed here a while. The fact is, that false alarm was not an accident."

His tone remained conversational. He approached a table and leaned against it.

"I don't know whether you know it: Every one of you has been under surveillance since Sunday night. There wasn't a move any of you made that I didn't know about. There's a murderer with us. I don't have to tell you that. I was seeing to it that he didn't get away with anything else.

"Unfortunately, there was something I didn't foresee." The captain's lips drew back from his teeth. "He thought of a new dodge. He imitated a look-out and set up a submarine alarm. We couldn't take any chances. We fell for it—nearly ten minutes, we fell for it. Everybody aboard was concerned with his own particular duties in case of attack. Nobody noticed what was happening anywhere else. Sort of cover, do you see? I think you do. Under that cover, there was time enough for this fellow to do what he wanted to do. An attempt was made to rob the purser's office."

Commander Matthews paused.

He was now so close that Max could hear him breathe, noisily.

"In the attempt," he went on, "Sir Henry Merrivale was

137

injured; seriously injured, we're afraid. The robber hit him down from behind.

"The purser's assistant, Mr. Tyler—" Commander Matthews hesitated, and moistened his lips—"is dead." He paused again. "Mr. Tyler died in the line of duty. His skull was fractured with repeated blows from some heavy kind of weapon. We think the poker from the fireirons in the smoking-room. Anyway, he's dead. I thought you all ought to know."

Silence.

His hearers were in a kind of paralysis. What the threat of a submarine could not do, a combination of the sick relief of being told it was a phantom danger, and now this news on top of it, nearly accomplished for most of them.

"I'd be grateful," the captain concluded, "if you would just remain where you are for a little while. Except my brother. Come with me, Max. If any of you wants anything to eat or drink, just call for it. Mr. Cruikshank will see you get it."

He turned round.

Halfway to the door, his fists now on his hips, he stopped short and turned round. He appeared to struggle with speech.

"To most of you," he added, awkwardly, "it's too bad. You don't deserve this treatment. You behaved like veterans in what you thought was real danger. Thanks! Come on, Max."

And he strode out, unbolting the doors and flinging them open ahead of him.

Max left behind all paraphernalia. As he left the room, he had a swift vision of Valerie Chatford's head fallen forward across the table, buried in her arms. Commander Matthews was waiting for him in the far corner of the open space on C Deck, by the purser's closed office.

"Well?" said Max. "What happened?"

"Neatest trick I ever heard of," snapped Commander Matthews, almost with admiration. "False alarm, and—murder as quick as a wink."

"They didn't manage to kill poor old H.M.?"

"No. We can't tell how badly he's hurt. The doctor's with him now." Frank Matthews regarded his brother narrowly. "You look a bit green, my lad. I don't blame you." He laughed a little, unamused. "Never mind. We'll get through. Would you like a drink?"

"Not now. What *happened*, exactly?"

"God only knows. It was only by a miracle Griswold himself didn't get knocked off. We're all sleeping in our clothes. Griswold's cabin adjoins his office. When the alarm went, he got up, opened the safe, unlocked the cash-drawer, and 'phoned for his assistant to round up the money and papers while he—Griswold—went to give Cruikshank a hand with the passengers.

"Cruikshank said he didn't need any help, and Griswold came back. He'd only been gone five minutes. But the damage was done. You can speak to Griswold yourself."

Max tried to adjust his thoughts.

Out of confusion emerged a clear and crooked track, which was the murderer's track. Max could see it wind now like the path of a snail.

H.M. had spotted the game, whatever the game was. In some way its purpose, or its proof, was concerned with those little finger-print cards which the purser had locked away in the safe. H.M. wanted to get at those cards. So did the murderer. But Griswold would not even have shown them, much less have given them, to any unauthorized passenger; and burgling a ship's safe is not a very practical course for an amateur.

The false alarm had served a double purpose. It had made the purser open his safe, which he would naturally do in the event of a submarine attack; and it had afforded a screen for the thief, so that in the blind preoccupation of every other person in the *Edwardic* he could take what he wanted. For a spur-of-the-moment plan, it had realistic genius. Max wondered savagely why he hadn't anticipated some such thing.

Commander Matthews opened the door of the purser's office.

"Come in," the purser said dully. "Take a look at the holocaust. Poor old Tyler!"

The office was in confusion. The improvised cardboard files, in which the purser's assistant had stored the finger-print cards of officers and men, were scattered all over the floor. It seemed carpeted with black finger-prints on white cards, and spidery signatures. The drawers of the desk were pulled open. So was the cash-drawer. A light steel box containing money and papers, its lid up, stood on the desk. The safe was open.

Griswold sat on a newly mended swivel-chair in the corner, his head in his hands.

"Five minutes!" he growled. "Five minutes!" And he got to his feet as the captain entered.

Max looked sideways out of the corner of his eye. Beyond a half open door he could see into the purser's cabin. A human body, covered by a counterpane, had been laid down on the bunk with its knees bent. The counterpane covered its head as well.

Young Tyler had not bled much. There were very few stains in the office, except on the finger-print cards.

But Max shut his eyes for a few seconds before he turned to the purser.

"So," he said, "our murderer stole a march. He got into the safe and stole the finger-print cards."

"No, he didn't," retorted the purser. "He never even touched the safe."

"What?"

"That's just it," insisted the purser, extending a pair of fervent hands as though he held something in them. "The old boy . . . Sir Henry . . . how is he, sir?"

"I don't know," said Commander Matthews. "You might hop down and see. Dr. Black is with him now."

"The old boy," resumed Griswold, wiping the back of his hand across his forehead, "warned me somebody might try to crack that safe. I laughed at him. Nobody could crack the safe, if you see what I mean. I told him so when I talked to him tonight.

"Cripes, I can see what happened as plain as day! The old boy suspected something fishy about that submarine-warning. He came chasing down here to make sure nothing was wrong. The murderer caught both him and Tyler; must have sneaked up on 'em, for they were both hit from behind. Then the murderer got what he wanted. But I'll take my oath he didn't touch the safe. Look."

He pulled the door of the safe further open. It had a number of compartments and pigeon-holes, some of the compartments equipped with tiny doors and locks. From his pocket the purser took out a bunch of keys at the end of a chain; his hairy hands shook so that he had difficulty in selecting a small key, with which he opened one of the compartments.

"There you are," he explained. "Untouched. All the cards inside. Wrapped up in a handkerchief, just as I left 'em. The bloke seems to have gone through all the other cards, and not to have bothered with these."

Max hesitated. "Maybe he couldn't get at 'em. You had the compartment locked."

"Ah! But I didn't have it locked then. I only locked it up—later. After Tyler was killed. Locking the stable door: something like that. It wasn't locked at the time of the—the funny business. Oh, and another thing. He's pinched all the passports that hadn't been reclaimed by their owners. But if he was after them, why? Just what in blazes do you make of that?"

Max whistled.

"That's going to make it difficult for people when they land at the other side, isn't it?"

"Damned difficult," conceded the purser. "That is, if any of us ever do get to the other side."

"Mr. Griswold!" said Commander Matthews sharply.

"Sorry, sir. I meant—"

"Whose passports were taken?"

"Mr. Lathrop's, Miss Chatford's, Captain Benoit's, and Mrs. Zia Bey's. It won't bother the last two, but it may be serious for the others. And to cap matters, the only person who had any idea about what's behind this—Sir Henry—is half dead on us. He had an idea. He told me so, though he wouldn't say what it was. And if he doesn't recover . . ."

The purser's telephone buzzed.

Max's wits felt drugged. As Griswold took up the phone, Max saw that the time was twenty-five minutes past four. Then both he and Commander Matthews leaped forward when they saw the expression on the purser's face. It was so quiet in the office that they could hear the voice of Dr. Black, the ship's surgeon, over the phone.

"Dead?" squeaked the voice. "Of course he's not dead."

"He'll recover?"

"Certainly. There's no concussion. He'll have to lie up for a couple of days, and he'll have a headache that'll make him harder than ever to handle; but that's all."

"When can we talk to him?"

"Tomorrow or next day. Not earlier. Isn't that good enough for you?"

Griswold replaced the receiver. The breath of relief, and of hope taking on life again, was as palpable in the office as though a hag-ridden spell had left their minds.

"Got him now!" snapped Commander Matthews, rubbing his hands together. "Look here, I've got to cut along. Mr.

141

Griswold. Max. I leave you in charge. Question those people in there, if you like: I must go. It now seems only a matter of time. But carry on as before."

Never had it seemed to take so long, after that, for the heavy night to grow into morning. More than once, while Griswold took one passenger after another into his office—all without result—for questioning, Max thought the clock had stopped. The thin hours wore away, water dropping on nerves. Yet Max's feeling of buoyancy and hope persisted. At twenty minutes past seven he and Griswold were startled by a wild yell from the direction of the dining-room.

It was not until they arrived in the dining-room, plunging into the midst of an excited group still imprisoned there, that they realized it had been a cry of jubilation. One of the portholes had been raised; the gray light of dawn streamed through it, touching faces grown pallid by artificial light. The other passengers were gathered round it. Grinning, the third officer beckoned Max to the porthole.

The morning wind blew cold and drowsy on his eyelids as he peered out. Smoking with mist, the blue-black sea plunged and ran as the *Edwardic* dived in a long swell; spray stung Max's face. The horizon was being unveiled in gray. He saw the shapes along it. Small and purple at first, with smudges above them on the sky, they grew from dots into outlines. Max saw the single funnels coiling with black smoke, and the long low hull slipping beneath the line of the forward gun-turret. Stripped and lean, fast as terriers, the destroyers kept guard.

Hooper took off his life-jacket, and dropped it on a chair. He clapped his hand on Max's shoulder.

"We're through, lad," he said simply. "The navy's here."

18

"This here wallop over the onion," observed Sir Henry Merrivale, not without modest pride, "is a beauty. It'll probably spoil the contour of my Shakesperian skull for good. But I never had anything like it since I played rugger for Cambridge in '91."

He pulled the bed-clothes up round his chest, and settled back among pillows. He did not move his head unduly. Yet his expression—for H.M.—was almost affable.

His companion stared at him.

"Look here," Max said, uncomprehending. "Is anything wrong with you?"

"Wrong? Sure there's something wrong! I'm an invalid, that's what I am. But I never was one to complain, was I?"

"You're sure," inquired Max, "it hasn't affected you permanently? I expected to find you raving and cursing the place down. What's the matter?"

H.M. looked surprised.

"Nothing's the matter. It's a scar of honor, son. The first I've had in the way of business for twenty-five years. Also, I got everybody aboard this ship jumpin' like a scorched cat at the least word I say. Ho! Chicken broth. Gobble gobble. Wines not served to passengers. Anything I want. Y'know, I bet you—" his expression grew thoughtful—"I bet you if I asked to have my picture taken, in brass buttons and a cap with gold braid, standin' on the bridge and giving orders to everybody, I bet you the skipper would let me do it. No, I'm all right. There's only one thing I can't stand. There it goes now."

Who-o-o! went the blast of the ship's whistle, doing duty as a fog-horn. H.M. winced and put his hands to his head, glaring malignantly at the roof.

Up here in his cabin on the boat-deck, the fog-horn had a deafening loudness. The *Edwardic* was creeping so slowly that you could hear the water wash as though in a gentle lake.

Max attacked.

"Listen, H.M. The others are coming up here to burst in on you in a minute. I thought I'd get in ahead of them. Do you know what day this is?"

"Thursday, maybe?"

"It's Friday afternoon. You've been out of action since the early hours of Thursday morning; the doctor wouldn't let us see you until today. People are now in a stew wondering when we're going to land, and where. Some say we're going to land tomorrow, though Sunday seems more likely to me."

"I hear we got a convoy."

"We're being escorted, anyhow. That's the point. The dan-

143

ger isn't over, but at least it's so much lessened that people are beginning to get pretty wild about something else. I mean this triple murderer who's making hay of the whole ship."

"So?"

"When we sighted those destroyers on Thursday morning, we were all pretty pally. Then we remembered, and we're half afraid to meet each other alone in a passage. You've got to do something about it. Do you remember what happened to you when we had the false alarm of a submarine attack?"

H.M. settled back among the pillows and adjusted his spectacles. He twiddled his thumbs over his stomach. "Oh, yes, son. I remember."

"Did you see who hit you? Or killed the purser's assistant?"

"No."

Max's spirits sank.

"But if it's any consolation to you," added H.M. quietly, "I didn't need to see. I can tell you who committed the murders, and why, and how. I can tell you where the ghost's finger-print came from, and why it was put there, and what the game was." His expression grew still more somber. "You trust the old man, son. Let me play possum. I know what I'm doin'."

Who-o-o! went the fog-horn overhead, and H.M. winced again.

"One person's responsible for all this?"

"One person, and one only."

"Anyway, what happened on the night, or morning, the purser's office was robbed? Will you tell me that?"

H.M. sniffed. "I daresay you can guess for yourself. I warned Griswold (burn me, how I warned him!) someone might try to do it. I wanted him to get the finger-print cards for me in the evening. But, oh, no. He was busy. Tomorrow would do just as well. There nearly wasn't any tomorrow. When I heard that alarm-signal go, I thought it might be a have. I went scrabbling down to the purser's office. There was the young lad—decent feller, too—at the safe. We had our backs to the door. The next thing I knew, the ceiling fell on me. The last thing I remember, all in a kind of fire-cloud, is the look on young Tyler's face when he turned round and saw who was standing behind me.'"

H.M.'s big jaw tightened. Settling back still further, he pulled the bed-clothes round him.

"I hadn't seen the murderer's face," he explained, "but

144

young Tyler had. So he had to be disposed of. It was a messy job. The murderer hadn't much time."

"But hang it all, what did the murderer want there? He wasn't after any of the passengers' finger-print cards!"

"Wasn't he?"

"No. He didn't even touch 'em."

Again the whistle roared, shaking the air with physical pressure against the ear-drums. The blacked-out porthole of H.M.'s cabin stood partly open. Wisps of white mist, as clammy as damp wool, drifted through the crack and faded away like the smoke of breath on cold air.

A dim light burned at the head of H.M.'s berth, shaded by a heavy berth-curtain. He motioned Max to close the port-hole, and exposed the light fully.

"Y'see," he went on apologetically, "I haven't been quite frank with you. You're not the first visitor I've seen. The captain's been here. And the purser. From the captain I got this." Reaching across to the bedside table, H.M. opened the drawer and took out a .45 caliber service revolver, which he laid in his lap. "From the purser, I finally snaffled these." This time he held up the passengers' finger-print cards, which he spread out fan-wise. "I have an idea I'm goin' to need both before I'm many hours older."

Max studied the revolver. Uneasiness crawled into the cabin as clearly to be felt as the touch of mist.

"What are you going to do, exactly?"

"As soon as the captain can get time off," answered H.M., consulting his watch, "he'll be coming round here. I'm going to explain to him what the game was, and how it was worked. Then there are two courses for him. He can either nail the murderer straight away, as he'll probably do. Or else—but that's an idea of mine. In either case, I warn you we've got the swine taped. There's hangin' evidence, son. He must be pretty blind and desperate by this time."

Who-o-o! went the fog-horn, its noise first blasting the mist and then strangled by it as the echoes trembled away.

"Now hop it," said H.M. mildly. "And lemme stuff cotton-wool in my ears and keep the top of my head from comin' off."

"But—"

"I said hop it. Your brother'll tip you off when he's coming."

Max shrugged his shoulders and gave in. The last thing he

145

saw, as he went out into the narrow passage running broadside across the boat-deck, was H.M. settling down with ferocious sternness to read a comic-paper. He closed the cabin door. Then he pushed open the outer door down the passage, and breathed fog.

It moved and curled like smoke. It first tickled and then stung the nostrils; you drew it into your lungs, and coughed; you brushed it from your face, and left a sooty dampness there. Though objects were invisible at fifteen or twenty feet, an outline of them would drift out or retreat into obscurity as the mist moved. Max groped aft from the forward part of the deck (which passengers were forbidden to visit), passed a little iron gate, and emerged into free territory.

Despite the fog, there had been a different feel about the air all day. They were coming home. You could almost smell land. Their whereabouts nobody knew except the officers, who did not tell. For the past two days Max had been talking with Valerie Chatford, and playing table-tennis with Valerie Chatford, and swimming in the ship's pool with Valerie Chatford, and racking his brains about Valerie Chatford . . .

Bump.

He stopped short.

He heard the noise, muffled by fog, from somewhere ahead. Quivering, the blast of the whistle drowned it out, but when that explosion died away, he heard it again. *Bump.* A sound like leather against wood, with savagery behind it.

Some distance ahead of him, forward of the open space for deck-tennis, a door led you into a small gymnasium. Nobody had used it so far. On the open deck outside the door —mist blotted out everything now—was a small cage for practicing golf-strokes, and a punching-bag hanging from its wooden roof. Somebody seemed to be standing in semi-darkness and, at intervals, letting drive a fist at the punching-bag. And Max sensed, in someone's heart, a fury of terror and despair wordlessly expressing itself.

Bump.

"Hello!" he called. There was a final thud of the bag against the wooden roof. You could almost feel the anger of it. A door closed. When Max reached the entrance to the gymnasium, the punching-bag was still swinging, but the other person had gone.

That was the atmosphere now engendered in the *Edwardic.* When he went downstairs, he found Valerie crying in a

146

corner of the Long Gallery. She would not speak to him, and went off to her cabin. Something like a row took place between Lathrop and Hooper. Challenged to a game of darts, Lathrop refused; darts, he said, could turn into murderous weapons if used properly. Max tried to read, bracing himself for each roar of the fog-horn as evening drew on. At half-past six, sooner than he expected, the purser accosted him in the lounge.

"Going up to the old boy's cabin?" Griswold bent close to mutter. "They've just sent for me to come up."

"Now?"

"Now. Any idea what they asked me to bring? I'll tell you. My ink-roller, and that rubber-stamp pad of Benoit's. They're outside." Griswold himself braced his muscles for the fog-horn. "I think something's going to blow up. And soon."

When they knocked at the door of H.M.'s cabin, it was Commander Matthews' voice which told them to come in. The cabin, which had a private bathroom, was now brilliantly lighted. Commander Matthews, very much ill at ease, smoked a cigar. H.M. was propped up to a sitting position in bed; the collar of his old-fashioned wool night-shirt was buttoned round his neck, and, headache or no, he smoked his black pipe. He had a drawing-board across his knees, with sheets of paper and a pencil. On the bedside-table Max noticed with some surprise a small portable radio set, a folder-plan of the *Edwardic,* and a clean handkerchief.

"Come in," growled H.M., taking the pipe out of his mouth. "Got the doings? The ink-roller and the ink-pad?"

"Right here," said the purser.

"Sit down, then," said H.M. with a certain grimness. "We got quite a lot of official business in front of us. Damn that fog-horn!"

"Can't be helped," Commander Matthews pointed out. "Well? Have you got anything?"

For a time H. M. leaned back and eyed the roof-light, drawing slowly on his pipe and letting lazy clouds of smoke drift up. Round his mouth there was the edge of a sour smile. But his eyes remained grave even when he began to rock back and forth with ghoulish mirth.

"I was just sittin' and thinkin'," he said. "It's the funniest thing I've come across in a long time."

"What is?"

"This," replied H.M. broadly. "The way the murderer's been deceivin' us."

Commander Matthews changed color.

"You may think it's funny," he said. "But I'd use another word for it. By God, it's not funny to—" He stopped. "Deceiving us how?" he demanded.

"With his faked finger-prints, for one thing. But that's the least of it. The very least of it."

The purser interrupted. "Sir," he said fervently, "I expect to get sat upon. I'm waiting for it. And yet I'll take my dying oath, here and now, that the bloody thumb-prints in Mrs. Zia Bey's cabin were *not*—n-o-t, not—fakes."

"Admitted, son."

"But you just said they were!"

"Not exactly, son. No, no. I said they were faked. I didn't say they were fakes."

Commander Matthews, Griswold, and Max stared at each other.

"Not?" inquired the captain. "What's the difference, then?"

"Well . . . now," muttered H.M. argumentatively, and scratched his forehead. "It's a matter of hair-line definition, maybe. But it can make an awful lot of difference in drivin' people loony over the solving of a problem. The easiest way out of the tangle is not to argue over what constitutes the proper terms. The easiest way is to show you how the trick was worked. Now!" He smoked for a moment in silence, the ghoulish amusement still distorting his face. Then he nodded toward the drawer of the bedside-table.

"The cards with the various passengers' finger-prints," he went on, "are in that drawer. Will you get out the card bearing my own right and left thumb-prints. *My* finger-prints, mind!"

"But, sir—"

"Do as he asks, Mr. Griswold," said Commander Matthews.

Still shaking his head, the purser opened the drawer, riffled through the little heap of cards, and selected the card with H.M.'s sprawling signature across it.

"Good!" said H.M. "Now, son, are you prepared to swear that those are my finger-prints? That they're the prints of my right and left thumb, taken in front of you and the third officer, and signed by me?" As Griswold's look of blackest suspicion deepened, H.M. held up his hand. "Hold on, son!

148

Word of honor, there's no trick about this part of it. I'll tell you: yes, they are my real, honest-Injun prints, taken in front of you. Is that satisfactory?"

"If you say so."

"Uh-huh. All right. Did you bring your magnifyin' glass with you?"

"Got it right here in my pocket."

"Also good. I'm goin' to ask you to take my prints all over again. Have you got any more of those little cards?"

"No, I'm afraid not."

"Well, that won't matter," said H.M. "We can just use this sheet of white paper. No, no: burn me, it's all right. It's an ordinary sheet of paper. It's not prepared in any way. Use one of your own, if you like."

Again Commander Matthews, Griswold, and Max exchanged glances. Putting his pipe down in an ashtray on the table, H.M. arranged the drawing-board across his knees. He pushed a sheet of paper to the center of it.

"Got your ink-roller there, son?"

"Ready for you, sir."

"Then let's get on with the printin'. . . . Cor, this is messy stuff! Gimme that handkerchief. . . . So. Push that sheet of paper farther toward me. . . . So. I'm now goin' to record my prints. Right thumb. Left thumb. There you are. Now take the paper. Get out your magnifyin' glass. Compare the prints on this paper with the prints on that card."

There was a silence.

Griswold, his jowl still full of suspicion, took the drawing-board from H.M.'s knees and sat down at the foot of the berth. He set the card and the paper side by side. The bright roof-light, misted by tobacco-smoke, shone down full on the drawing-board. Taking a large magnifying glass out of his pocket, the purser started to study them.

His glass moved from side to side. His painstaking study seemed to drag on for interminable minutes. Once he stopped, looked at H.M., and started to speak; but thought better of it. He begged a pencil from H.M. Then he began to make annotations, like proofreader's marks, from the arches, loops, whorls, and composites of one set of prints to the arches, loops, whorls, and composites of the other. They saw the perspiration glitter on his forehead as he bent over the board. A drop of it fell on the paper.

Commander Matthews was impatient.

"Well?" the captain prompted. "What about it? They're the same, aren't they?"

"No, sir, they are not."

"They're not—" Commander Matthews stopped. His cigar had gone out, and he dropped it into the ashtray. He got to his feet. "What did you say?"

"I will take my oath," replied Griswold, *"that these two sets of prints do not belong to the same man."*

Again nobody spoke. The purser, seeking something to mop his forehead, picked up the inky handkerchief H.M. had discarded. It left a smudge over the purser's eye, but he paid no attention. All of them were looking at H.M.

"You're positive of that, son?" the latter asked.

"I am."

"Swear to it, would you?"

"Yes."

"And yet," H.M. pointed out, picking up his pipe and whacking it on the edge of the ashtray, "I made both sets of prints with my own thumbs, you know."

19

For the first time in minutes, Max had not been conscious of the fog-horn. Now it hooted out in a kind of vast derision and seemed to shake the cabin.

"I suppose we're not all mad?" inquired Commander Matthews, pushing back his cap.

"No," answered H.M. more soberly. His face pinched up. "It's time to stop foolin' you. But don't rub your head in ashes. Walk proudly. Once upon a time, that very same trick almost fooled the laboratory of technical police at Lyons; so you needn't crumple up with shame if it deceived you. In their case, it was the result of an accident. In ours—oh, no!

"Lemme show you how it works.

"Now, imagine you're going to take my thumb-print. You take it in an inked surface. The surface of any human finger —like this, for instance—consists of a series of tiny ridges in the flesh, comprising arches, loops, whorls, and composites, with hollows in between. You follow that? When you look at a photograph of a finger-print, the black lines represent the inked ridges, and the white lines represent the hollows between. Got it?"

"Well?" demanded Commander Matthews.

H.M. re-lit his pipe.

"Now suppose," he resumed, "your ink-roller, or ink-pad, or whatever you use, is faulty? Suppose it's got too much ink on it? Or suppose a zealous candidate pushes his finger all over an ordinary ink surface, and accumulates too much ink? (Just as I did, a minute ago.) He finds his finger is messy. It's soaked. It may give a blurred print. What does he naturally do, and with all the naturalness in the world?

"Why, he picks up a handkerchief and wipes it off. (As I did.) That's all right. He's simply cleared his thumb of too much ink, that's all. Ink remains. It'll still give a good, clear print. *But what happens then?*"

H.M. paused. He looked round the group.

And Max Matthews, with a mental groan, caught the clue and saw the picture take form.

"Don't you see?" insisted H.M. "On that surface of microscopic lines on his thumb, he's rubbed the ink the wrong way. The ink's still on his thumb. But he's rubbed it off the *ridges* and into the *hollows*. When the print is taken, it's now the hollows which appear as the black lines, and the ridges which appear as the white lines. Just the wrong way round. Like the positive and the negative of a photographic plate.

"Of course, the result is a print very different from one taken with a proper ink-surface, and without hocus-pocus. In particular the 'pockets,' or small core at the center of the whorls, will be so totally different that even an amateur can swear they're not the same. An expert would be still more positive. In France, years ago, the very same thing happened by accident: and very nearly cost one woman a whole lot of money, because they wouldn't believe she was herself.* For years now I've been waitin' for some clever blighter to apply the same dodge to deliberate crime; and, lo and behold, somebody has.

"You follow it now.

"The murderer killed Mrs. Zia, with the deliberate intention of leavin' false finger-prints on the scene of the crime.

---

* *Clues and Crime: the Science of Criminal Investigation,* by H. T. F. Rhodes (John Murray, 1933), pp. 105-107.

He took along a bottle of ink: intending to spill it, as though by accident or in a struggle, and leave fine prints after he'd carefully wiped his thumbs. Instead, he changed his mind and used blood—which is better stuff than ink for the purpose. So the ink was discarded; the Sign of the Shocker appeared; and the bloody thumb-print affronted our be-dazzled eyes. There's the explanation of your ghostly fingers, my fatheads. That's all."

His audience had been listening with varying degrees of emotion. The purser again mopped his forehead with the stained handkerchief. The captain sat like a man thunder-struck: presently, feeling the same heat, he took off his cap and began to fan himself rapidly with it.

"As easy as that, eh?" asked Commander Matthews flatly.

"As easy as that."

"And all very simple," mused Commander Matthews, "when you know the secret."

"O tempora!" howled H.M., shaking the pipe in the air. "O mores! O hell! Sure it's simple—after I've told you. I'm always hearing that. Never mind. Hasn't anybody got any comment to make?"

There was a new note in his voice. Max felt that he was watching them narrowly; that he was asking for something; that he was prodding their imaginations, with gentle persistence, to take a step still further.

Max, whose own eyes were on the portable radio set, found something else troubling him. Though the light burned behind the dial to show that the set had been turned on, no sound issued from it: not even the atmospheric shrieking you usually get at sea. But he did not concern himself with this. He hardly even heard the fog-horn now. He said:

"H.M., it's all wrong."

"So?" queried H.M. softly. "What is?"

"This finger-print business. You say the murderer delib-erately left the fake, or faked, prints when he killed Mrs. Zia Bey?"

"I do."

"But is he crazy?"

"No. Far from it. Why?"

If his finger-nails had been longer, Max would have gnawed at them. "Well, it's difficult to explain. Something like this. If the murder had been committed on shore—or nearly anywhere else except aboard ship—I admit it would have been a stroke of genius. Kill your victim. Plant your false prints. Then watch the police go haring off after somebody who doesn't exist, with millions of possibilities everywhere. They're more or less bound to give up, with such a number of people it *might* be. But aboard ship . . ." He hesitated, and turned to Griswold. "Tell me. Does every ship's purser have to have a working knowledge of fingerprints?"

"They should." Griswold frowned. "And most of them do. Why?"

Max frowned in reply. "All right. The murderer knew, of course, that the finger-prints of everybody aboard would be taken; and compared. He himself will simply have his real finger-prints taken in the proper way, and they won't match with the blood-stained ones. Is that the general idea?"

"It is," agreed H.M.

"Then that's the point. His real prints won't match. But neither will anybody else's! All he's done is commit a ghost murder. He's upset his own apple-cart. He's deliberately called attention to the fact that there's something very fishy somewhere. Where's the advantage? Why leave any prints at all? For, mind you, if anyone once tumbles to the trick, he's done for. Unless he just wants to be spectacular, isn't that risking too much for too little?"

Commander Francis Matthews, R.N.R., raised his arms in the air and uttered a snort of weary impatience.

"Stow it," he said.

"But, Frank—"

"I said stow it," repeated Commander Matthews. He turned to H.M. "I was telling Max the other night, he's the one in our family who gets the funny ideas. All imagination. No stability." The blood rushed into Commander Matthew's face. "What I want to get straight is—"

He stopped short, for H.M. had begun to rub his hands together with every evidence of evil satisfaction.

"Ah! Aha!" chortled H.M., looking at Max. "Now you're beginning to use your brain. Mind, I still say the murderer did just that: deliberately left hocused prints on the scene of the crime. But *why* did he do it? That's what's caused me all the difficult sittin' and thinkin.' Find the reason why, and you'll tear the wrapping-paper off one of the slickest and shrewdest crimes I ever had the pleasure to grapple with. Think, now!"

"Stop," said Max, so sharply that even his brother jumped. "Well?"

"Benoit," Max began, with vivid but confusing images in his mind. "How does Benoit fit into this? After Mrs. Zia Bey was killed, Griswold and Cruikshank went round to get Benoit's finger-prints. There Benoit was sitting, with an ink-pad—a messy ink-pad—carefully prepared, on which he wanted to take his own prints. Only they wouldn't let him. It sounds as though Benoit wanted to give them a set of faked prints then! What in God's name was he doing?"

Silence.

"But Benoit's dead!" the purser protested.

"Oh, sure. Benoit's dead," agreed H.M. "And yet, lads, Benoit's character, Benoit's ways, everything about Benoit, is the key to this whole problem. Don't you see it?"

"No," returned three voices.

"Then lemme sort of trace it out for you," mumbled H.M., with one drowsy eye on the ceiling, and taking slow puffs at the pipe in one corner of his mouth.

"On Sunday night, just before Benoit was murdered," he went on, "Max Matthews gave me a full and detailed account of everything that had been happenin'. There was where I got the first real suggestion of rumminess. H'mf. Young Matthews was tellin' me about a mysterious character wearing a gas-mask, who wandered about the passages looking into people's cabins. It was one of those pig-snouted civilian gas-masks they served out to all of us. I asked whether the character in the mask could have been this person, or that person, until I mentioned the Frenchman. Then I realized that wouldn't do. I said, 'But a French officer wouldn't be wearing . . .'

"And, oh, my eye, did I get a mental wallop when I thought about that! For I *had* seen, seen for myself, the Frenchman wearin' a mask just like that. I was watchin' from a distance, out of the picture, but it stuck in my mind. Don't you remember that boat-drill on Saturday morning? Don't you remember how Benoit appeared there, wearin' just such a mask?"

Max did remember it.

"So the question was," said H.M., with emphasis, "where was Benoit's service respirator?"

"His what?" demanded Max, merely bewildered. But Commander Matthews translated.

"His Army gas-mask," said the captain.

"Exactly," said H.M. "I couldn't believe my eyes. Every member of the fighting forces is equipped with a service respirator, much larger and more elaborate and comprehensive than the civilian ones, and carried in a canvas case slung round the neck. Every soldier in uniform *must* carry his respirator at all times. Yet here was Benoit walking about in an ordinary civilian gas-mask.

"Oh, gents! That was so rummy that I yearned for a look at his cabin. And, when I did look at it, the service gas-mask wasn't there. It wasn't anywhere. On the contrary, there was the little civilian mask carefully put down on a chair with life-jacket and blanket.

"Which wasn't all. I opened the wardrobe (you remember?), and got the shock of my life. There was the feller's spare uniform hanging up, bold as brass. And the insignia on that uniform was all wrong."

Max, still partly dazed, entered a protest.

"Wait!" he requested. "What was wrong with it? It's three stripes for a captain in the French army—I'm positive of that. And Benoit had 'em."

"Ho ho," said H.M. "Yes, he had 'em. But he had 'em in the wrong place. He had his stripes on the shoulder-epaulettes. Listen, son. A French officer wears his stripes in just two places: round his cap, and round his sleeve. Never on the shoulder. Look it up in a military dictionary. I hadn't got a close look at Benoit's clothes before, so I didn't notice until then. But there it was. I even, if you recall, picked up the sleeve of the coat and had a good look at it; because I couldn't believe my eyes.

"But, combined with the gas-mask question, it was conclusive. Benoit was a fake of some kind. He wasn't a French officer; he knew nothing about the French army, and probably blinkin' little about any army at all. Even then—with six good-sized clues starin' me straight in the face—I still didn't tumble to it. But Cruikshank suggested that he might be a member of the French Intelligence service. . . ."

H.M. paused.

Max, listening with the back of his mind for the roar of the fog-horn, heard instead something which made him jump up out of his chair. The portable radio was speaking to them.

"*Captain! Sir Henry!*" it whispered softly, amid a sudden buzzing and at the end of a sharp click. Max thought he recognized the voice of the third officer. *"Get ready. I think your man's on his way up."*

H.M. calmly pulled open the drawer of the table, took out the revolver, and weighed it in his palm.

Commander Matthews got to his feet, stock and menacing. He had to clear his throat.

"Just what in hell," he wanted to know, "is this?"

H.M. was apologetic. "It's the murderer, son," he explained, pointing to the little pile of finger-print cards. "He's got to snaffle one of those cards, or he'll hang as sure as the Lord made little apples. He's in a corner and he's desperate. I sort of thought he might take a crack at it while everybody else was supposed to be at dinner or on the bridge, and I was supposed to be still crocked-up. If you want to see some action, duck into that bathroom, all three of you. Turn out the light and hook the door open an inch or so, to make sure it won't swing. Don't come out unless something happens."

They obeyed.

Max was in such a state of maniacal curiosity and perplexity that he feared even to breathe might make his shoes scrape on the tile floor of the bathroom. Cramped into that confined space, he and Frank and the purser steadied themselves close to the door. They turned out the light. With the door hooked open, they could see a segment of the cabin—in a narrow vertical opening—which included a part of H.M.'s berth.

Who-o-o! went the fog-horn.

Except for a bumpy jerkiness, and the very soft thump of the engines at dead slow, the ship hardly seemed to be moving at all. H.M., sliding the revolver under the bedclothes, lay back nearly at full-length on his pillows, folded his hands across his stomach, and closed his eyes.

Silence.

It lasted for fully three minutes, unbroken except for a soft slap-slap of water outside, the fog-horn, and a hundred imagined noises in Max's brain. Smoke misted the bright light of the cabin. H.M.'s stomach rose and fell slowly, as though in sleep.

There was a soft tap at the door.

H.M. did not move.

The knock was repeated, more loudly. After still another pause, Max heard the squeak of hinges, and then a longer, slower squeaking, as the door to the passage was pushed open.

It was closed with equal softness and stealth. Max could see H.M.'s nostrils distend and contract as though breathing in sleep. This lasted for thirty seconds more.

"That'll do," said H.M., opening his eyes. His hand, which had slid under the bed-clothes, emerged snakily with the captain's revolver held steady. "Better get your hands up. *Damn you, don't be an ass!*"

Whoever the newcomer might be, he was as fast as a rattle-snake. A wooden chair, with a red plush seat, was flung across the room full at H.M.'s face. The watchers saw it flash past their line of vision. They even saw the bullet-hole spring up in the red plush seat as the revolver exploded in H.M.'s hand. Thrown partly wild, the chair missed H.M.'s shoulder, struck the portable radio, and brought both down with a crash. As Commander Matthews, Griswold, and Max tumbled out into the cabin, H.M. fired again.

The door to the passage slammed shut behind a retreating figure.

Commander Matthews yanked it open in time for them all to see the trap close in.

A man was standing in the longish, narrow, white-painted passage which ran broadside across the ship, and had a door leading to the outer deck at each end. The man was half doubled up, and had his hand pressed to one shoulder. He glanced first left, and then right: first to port, then to starboard. At each end of the passage, the black-out curtains stirred over the door: in each appeared a stocky A.B. with fingers crisped and shoulders set ready. They did not move or speak.

The man cried out. He took a step, turned, cried out again, and stopped.

"Got him," said H.M. softly. H.M., looking dizzy and rather white, crawled out of bed in his old-fashioned night-shirt, tumbled into slippers, and lumbered out.

"I ought to have shot to kill," he added. "But, burn me . . . at the last minute I couldn't face it."

Max paid no attention. He wanted to rub his eyes at the vision of the man who stood, rocking and doubling up still more, right hand pressed to left shoulder. Fingers and sleeve were growing dark red—a much darker red, for instance, than the top of the man's army cap with the gold braid on it. His uniform was khaki, his brown boots were polished. His

157

brown complexion and small dark mustache were turned away from them; the edge of the jaw shone.

"H.M.," said Max, "that's Captain Benoit!"

"Oh, no, it isn't," said H.M. quietly.

"I tell you it is! Ask Frank! Ask anybody!—But you said Benoit wasn't alive!"

"He isn't alive, son," said H.M. somberly. "That's the whole story. He never was alive. Your friend Lathrop kept sayin' one thing, as a joke, that was as true as gospel: Benoit was a ghost. He never existed. In other words, one person aboard this ship was playing two men's parts until Benoit 'died' on Sunday, and . . . grab him, boys!"

The sailors closed in, while their captive squealed. Each took one of his arms. H.M. approached the wiry figure. He removed the cap with the red-and-gold top: to show not dark hair, but loose fair hair underneath. He ran his fingers along the chemist's sun-tan of the face. He touched the dark mustache, and had difficulty in detaching much of it from the upper lip, while the captive still squealed. But other features, other turns of lip and eye and jaw, emerged one by one to show a new face.

They were looking into the bitter, retreating, spectacleless eyes of Jerome Kenworthy.

20

There will be, said the notice on the bulletin-board, *a short religious service at eleven a.m. Disembarkation is expected to take place about two p.m. Will all passengers please obtain their landing-cards from the purser's office.*

"H.M.," said Max Matthews, "you're going to tell us all about it before this ship docks. If you don't, all these people"—he indicated an interested audience—"are going to tear you in pieces. Do you understand that?"

"Ho ho," said H.M. modestly.

On that bright, cold Sunday morning, with all the portholes open, H.M. sat by the fireplace in the smoking-room. His tipple was whisky-punch, an old favorite. Round him sat Max, Valerie, Hooper, Lathrop, Dr. Archer, the purser and the third officer.

Griswold shook his head stolidly.

"I still can't get over it," he declared. "Young Kenworthy! And I still don't understand what in blazes his game was. But I feel hard done by."

Valerie opened fierce eyes.

"*You* feel hard done by?" she cried. "I'm the one who should do that. I told you the perfect truth about those letters he wrote to Mrs. Zia Bey! And nobody would believe me. I actually saw him, dressed as Benoit, leaving the scene of the murder with the letters in his hand! And nobody would believe me. In all innocence I went out of my way to provide him with an alibi! And you all thought *I* was the perfect liar."

Hooper pursed his lips doubtfully.

"Ah," he admitted; "but I'm the one the chap put upon, look. I swore there were two persons on that dark deck on Sunday night, when all he did was shoot a dressed-up dummy and pitch it overboard. Eh?"

Lathrop bridled.

"He got me worse than any of you," Lathrop declared. "Because I practically solved the thing without knowing it. I kept on telling you 'Benoit' was a ghost. I said we hardly ever got a single glimpse of him, except at meal-times, and then he sat at a table by himself. Even then we never saw him except by artificial light. I said (didn't I, now?) that it seemed funny for a French officer always to wear his cap indoors."

The third officer, wrinkling his forehead, would not agree to this.

"No, I'm the victim. There were only two occasions, sir," stated Cruikshank, "when *all* the passengers—every one— were supposed to be present: when the gas-masks were distributed, and at the boat-drill on Saturday morning. Those were the only times that flum-diddling might have been spotted. It wasn't terribly important, the first time, when both Miss Chatfield and Kenworthy didn't appear—I saw them later in their cabins and give them their gas-masks. Naturally, I wouldn't notice that 'Benoit' disappeared immediately we were through in the lounge. But, at the boat-drill, as soon as I insisted that Mr. Kenworthy had to be brought on deck seasick or no, the Frenchman shot away and disappeared; and I didn't stop him. He was wearing his gas-mask, too, because that was the only time he had to face daylight instead of artificial lights."

The purser raised his hand imperatively, and turned his George Robey eyebrows with sinister effect on them all.

"Steady! After all," asserted Griswold, "*I* knew the fellow. I admit I only knew him on one crossing, months ago. Still, I thought I knew him. And yet I actually talked to him, as Benoit—or rather Cruikshank did, when we were getting his finger-prints—without spotting who he was. Do you know why I never spotted him?"

"Well, why?" asked Cruikshank challengingly.

"Because he spoke French," returned the purser. "I've just thought of it. That's the one perfect way of disguising your voice. It's a funny thing: when you hear somebody rattling away in another language, all voices sound alike to you. All identifying ideas go out of your head. Try it sometime. And it was a double safeguard for the fellow to pretend he knew no English, because it would give him an excuse for not talking to people. He—"

"*Hoy!*" roared H.M.

There was a dead silence after this blast. H.M., gobbling whisky punch, glowered back at them with an injured and dignified air.

"Do you want to hear about it, or don't you?" he asked in outraged majesty.

"Sorry, sir," apologized the purser hastily. "Yes, we do. Start where you left off when you were talking to the captain and Mr. Matthews and me the other night. You said you got worried when you had a look at 'Benoit's' cabin; when you found he hadn't got a service respirator, and was wearing the wrong kind of uniform. Go on from there. You knew Benoit was a fake. But what made you decide he was a ghost?"

"Mostly," answered H.M., "it was a shaving-brush."

He was silent for a time, sniffling. He eyed the porcelain cat without favor.

"Well," he said, "that came later. "On the Sunday night when he was supposed to be murdered, and I examined 'Benoit's' cabin, I didn't tumble to it. Even aside from the uniform and the gas-mask, I was as bothered as blazes by all those little shifty twisty points you've just been mentioning.

"Now our friend Cruikshank suggested that Benoit might be a member of French Intelligence, powerfully stimulated by a long harangue Benoit delivered about some woman being a 'traitor.' But that, obviously, was pure eyewash. All members of Intelligence on a service like that are drawn from men who have served, or are serving, as officers in the regular army. Anybody who'd been a French officer at any time wouldn't be wearin' such a weird uniform. But that prompted another startling thought: Would *any* real Frenchman be wearing such a uniform?

"Remember, every Frenchman alive has got to do his military service as a young man. Lord love a duck, would it be possible for any feller to serve nine months in the ranks and later forget the number of pips he had to salute? If he ordered a captain's uniform from some tailor, would he have the tailor shove the stripes on the shoulder instead of round the sleeve? That was where I began to get a strange, burnin' sensation at the back of the skull.

"It looked as though he mightn't be French at all. Cruikshank thinks he speaks English—though the feller won't let on. Why? Why won't he let on? Why is he so shy of bein' seen in public, or speaking to people? Why does he keep his hat on all the time?

"Mind you, he was up to dirty work of some kind. He clearly staged that business with the inky, inky ink-pad in front of Cruikshank and Griswold. He looked 'guilty' when they went in; and gaped like a fish, as though his plans had gone wrong, when they went out. And later, while I'm sittin' and thinkin' and pitchin' quoits on the boat-deck, Valerie Chatford up and says she saw Benoit come out of Mrs. Zia Bey's cabin just after the murder. . . .

"I'd already decided that somebody was tryin' the dodge of reversed, or positive-and-negative, faked finger-prints on the scene of the crime. Who was it? Benoit? If so, why did he later try to take his own finger-prints on an obviously messy ink-pad—in front of the purser and the third officer, as though he wanted to produce *another* set of faked thumb-prints? I ask you, why? He first fakes his own prints in Mrs. Zia Bey's cabin. Then he gets all ready to fake 'em again, when they stop him and take the prints properly instead.

"Why?

"And then I remember the shaving-tackle.

"It's awful sad, and I was awful dense. I handled both the razor and the shaving-brush in Benoit's cabin on Sunday night, but the old man was too full of other ideas to notice: though I did think it was a bit rummy that the feller should

161

have a straight razor without either a razor-strop or a whet-stone to sharpen it with.

"Musin' dreamily, I went to the barber's late Wednesday afternoon. I'd met this fiend before. In fact, I'd been in his shop, for an interrupted shave, only a very short time before Benoit was 'murdered' on Sunday night. Whereupon the barber, with accents injured, informed me that when he started to shave me on Sunday night, I was the first customer he'd had. He added something about lather on the brush, and . . .

"Cor! That was when I remembered, with burnin' clearness, that the shaving-brush in Benoit's cabin had been bone-dry."

H.M. paused.

Max remembered very vividly H.M., in an absent-minded manner, fingering the dry brush in Benoit's cabin. And again he saw the plan take form.

"You fellers," rumbled H.M., pointing sternly round the group. "You fellers who have only one shaving-brush, as most of us do. Is the brush *ever* quite dry? Don't it remain in all its glory, from day to day, just about half damp? Benoit's brush, obviously, hadn't been used for a week. Neither had his razor. He hadn't gone to the barber. Yet this spick-and-span feller, always smoothly shaven except for his mustache, had gone from Friday afternoon until Sunday night without a single sign of stubble sproutin' on his face.

"There was where I woke up. All the bits of funny business began to assemble at the end of a shaving-brush.

" 'Captain Benoit' was somebody else.

"That's why he spoke only French: to disguise his voice. That's why he always wore his cap: because no wig ever invented will stand scrutiny at close range. That's why he kept out of everybody's way, and only appeared in the softest of artificial light. But could he keep up that deception long? No! *Only long enough so that he could murder Mrs. Bey, leave evidence to incriminate a phantom Captain Benoit, get himself confronted with that evidence in the rôle of Benoit, and break down and confess. Then Benoit, having confessed, shoots himself and drops overboard. A character has been created, and is now destroyed. The case is closed. And next day the real murderer appears languidly in his proper character, safe forever.*

"You see how a ghost was to get the blame?

162

"The rôle of Benoit was made up lock, stock, and barrel: with fake clothes, fake family photographs, fake passport, fake handwriting carefully practiced, even fake trunk-labels. It was done with care, and, burn me, some artistry! It was too bad the whole scheme went wrong.

"But, once you've decided that was the game, it's a very simple matter to decide who the impersonator must have been. There were certain qualifications the feller had to have. Thus:

"*One.* He had to be a passenger. No officer or member of the crew, with official duties to attend to, could possibly qualify.

"*Two.* He had to be a man who had been confined to his cabin, and was never seen on deck until after Benoit's 'death.'

"*Three.* He had to be a man who spoke very good French.

"*Four.* He had to be a man who had never been seen in Benoit's company, or at a time when Benoit was also in view.

"And that, my fatheads!—that tore it! There was only one possible person."

H.M. broke off to gobble the rest of his whisky-punch. With deep and evil satisfaction, he took a cigar out of his pocket, sniffed at it, drilled its end with a match, lighted it, and settled back. But he also produced the folder-plan of the *Edwardic,* which Max had noticed in his cabin on Friday night.

He went on:

"I'll take those points in reverse order, if you got no objection. A little side-questionin' elicited wonders on this subject. You can supply the corroboratin' information yourselves.

"Very well. Now, you've seen (in the dining-room, for instance) Mr. Lathrop in the presence of Captain Benoit. You've seen Mr. Hooper in the presence of Captain Benoit. You've seen Dr. Archer in the presence of Captain Benoit. You've seen Max Matthews in the presence of Captain Benoit. But did any of you—at anytime, or anywhere—ever see Jerome Kenworthy in the presence of Captain Benoit? You can bet you didn't.

"Speak good French? Did you know Kenworthy took high honors for the Diplomatic, and was in the Diplomatic until they kicked him out of it. (Ah, I see the gal nodded there!) Well, the one supreme crowning qualification for the

163

Diplomatic Service, the *sine qua non* of everything, is an excellent knowledge of French. That fits in too.

"And as for being always in his cabin for the first couple of days?

"I hardly have to tell you that. It was notorious. Hey? But that's not all. He's carefully trained his cabin steward (didn't he tell you this himself?) never under any circumstances to try to barge in unless summoned. Is that correct?"

Both Griswold and Max nodded. The purser groaned.

"His cabin steward," continued H.M., "seems to have been worried as blazes because Kenworthy—apparently—hadn't eaten a mouthful of food in several days. But he had! Remember, 'Captain Benoit' appeared only at meal-times, and not always then. He ate his food. He then returned, and as a rule made himself sick (genuinely, violently sick) by deliberately swallowin' nux vomica or somethin' else that'd do the work. His illness wasn't a sham. It was rather a brilliant alibi. You don't expect a man half-dead from seasickness to worry about cuttin' people's throats. But he was never actually *sea*sick at any time. Don't you realize that these thin rangy blokes, who slosh down booze all day, seldom are?"

"But, sir . . ." began the purser.

"Hold on. Durin' his brief appearances in public as Benoit, he locked the door of his own (Kenworthy's) cabin, and kept the key. Again a part of his alibi. Nobody likes to pester a seasick man. If anybody knocked while he was away, he could just say later that he'd refused to answer. And there was another thing."

H.M. pointed his finger malevolently at Max.

"You!" he said. "The number of Kenworthy's cabin?"

"B-70."

"Uh-huh. And the number of Benoit's cabin?"

"B-71."

"Just a second, there!" interposed Lathrop, frowning. "How is it that they weren't side by side, then? If I remember, Benoit's cabin was on the starboard side, and Kenworthy's on the port."

H.M. unfolded the plan of the *Edwardic*.

"Sure, son. That's the whole point. This ship is built on the plan of nearly every other liner afloat. That's to say: the cabins with even numbers are on the port side, and the cabins with odd numbers are on the starboard. Cabins with following numbers aren't side by side: they're directly opposite each other, with the width of the ship between 'em.

"And what constituted the width of the ship at that point? What runs straight through there, with one entrance near the door of Kenworthy's cabin and the other entrance near the door of Benoit's cabin just opposite? Think!"

"The lavatories," answered Max.

"That's right. Bulls-eye. The lavatories. So if Kenworthy wanted to nip across quickly to Benoit's cabin, or Benoit wanted to get home safely to Kenworthy's, the feller had a short-cut straight through there without showin' himself anywhere else in the ship. Also, it was a place where either of 'em could appear without suspicion. Oh, Kenworthy is mustard! Every move was planned as craftily and innocently as a campaign by our friend in Berlin.

"He had only two really ticklish or difficult moments, as I'll show you when we recapitulate. Long ago, I got rather a strong idea, long ago in New York Kenworthy made up his mind to kill Estelle Zia Bey—"

Dr. Archer spoke quietly. "Why, Sir Henry? I have a particular reason for wanting to know that."

H.M.'s weary expression indicated that he faced once more that quality which he likes to call the blinkin' awful cussedness of things in general.

"From the evidence we've picked up," he said, "you ought to have a pretty good guess. This gal here ought to be able to tell us, anyway."

Valerie was annoyed and nearly tearful.

"Oh, b-b-bother all of you!" she burst out. "I've *been* telling you all the way across the Atlantic. And not one of you would believe me! You thought Jerome was the chivalrous gentleman and I was the worm! I *knew* my facts were right. This Zia Bey woman confided to two or three of the girls at Trimalchio's that she had a whole pile of letters from Jerome . . . letters admitting something or other . . . I don't know what . . ."

"Would it be askin' too much," suggested H.M., looking at her over his spectacles, "to inquire who you really are? And what in blue blazes your game was all along?"

Valerie braced herself.

"Yes," she said, "I'll tell you. I'll tell all of you! And why? Because that beast stole my p-passport, and now I shan't even be able to land in England. And I don't care, because

165

I don't think I want much to do with the Kenworthy family—now."

She braced herself still more.

"My name's not Valerie Chatford, though I've lived all my life in Mr. Chatford's house, first when he was single and then when he married Ellen Kenworthy. I—I went to school with Valerie. She died a year ago. But I'm not related. My real name—" here she braced herself for the third time—"is Gerte Vogel."

"Vogel!" said H.M. His eyes narrowed, and he whistled. "So! Are you by any chance a relation to the Mrs. Vogel that was housekeeper for Chatford? The housekeeper who caused all the scandal when Chatford married Ellen Kenworthy? (You heard of it, the rest of you.) Old Lord Abbsdale, Jerome Kenworthy's old man, was shocked to the bottom of his Puritan soul, and disowned his sister for good. Any relation to that Mrs. Vogel?"

"Yes, I am. I'm her daughter," retorted Valerie. "She's dead now, so don't you say anything against her."

H.M. again whistled softly.

"And Valerie's dead, too," the girl went on. "And Mr. Chatford, my courtesy Uncle Arthur, has been drinking himself blind and green. He's an *awful* spectacle. And my Aunt Ellen has turned into a shrew. Both of them have been at me to do something for them, after all they've done for me. They said Aunt Ellen's brother, Lord Abbsdale, was as rich as Croesus, whereas we had nothing. Aunt Ellen said her brother had disowned her, and he was a narrow-minded old so-and-so who'd never take her back. And she wept. And—oh, lots of things."

She drew a deep breath.

"Then they conceived the great idea. They said why didn't I pass myself off as Valerie Chatford? After all, he might take a liking to Ellen's daughter, because he'd liked the daughter as a child. Better still, if I could do the old boy some great service, or some service to his son . . ."

Color came into her face, and she twisted her fingers together.

"You know how rottenly I played my part. I wasn't really trying to help Jerome Kenworthy. I was only trying to make him, and everybody else, *think* I was trying to help him so he'd be grateful. That was why—" she whirled round to Max —"on the night Mrs. Zia Bey was killed, I told you about the

166

letters and most horribly naïvely asked you to get an envelope from the purser's office. I knew you wouldn't. I knew you'd pass it straight on to the captain. That would bring me into the middle of it. And then presently I could break down and confess that I'd been trying to help Jerome. I didn't see any harm in it! I knew *he* hadn't done the murder . . . or at least (don't you see?) that's what I thought, because I had seen the Frenchman . . . and I should be getting his gratitude.

"But all the time," she concluded wearily, "it *was* Jerome after all. What a world."

H.M. chuckled, and corrected himself with a cough.

"Vogel," he mused. "Vogel. That's a good German name."

"Yes, it is," said Valerie. "That's another thing. My f-father was born in Germany, though he became a naturalized Englishman and as good a citizen as anybody. But I can't help having some sympathy for my father's stock, can I? Then—" again her eyes fixed on Max—"when they began sneaking up on me, and saying, 'Heil Hitler,' I didn't know what dreadful things they mightn't be thinking. They even hinted I was signaling a submarine on the night of the false alarm. Me! When I'm so terrified of submarines that I was only up on that boat-deck because I couldn't sleep for fear of them. I'd never have traveled aboard this ship in a million years if Aunt Ellen and Uncle Arthur hadn't said I'd got to follow Jerome, and get in with him."

"Now, now!" said H.M.

"I'm an awful flop, though. You didn't even believe me about the letters, when I was telling you the truth?"

H.M. opened his eyes. "Didn't I, my wench? Y'know, I think you underestimate the old man."

"But did you?" demanded Max. "I thought—"

"Looky here," said H.M. wearily. "Aren't you forgettin' independent testimony? Aren't you forgettin' what your own brother told us? Aren't you forgettin' that Mrs. Zia Bey's cabin stewardess confirmed the fact about there bein' a packet of letters in the handbag?"

"By George, she did!" muttered the purser.

Again Dr. Archer intervened. A frown ruffled his classic brow, and he waved a hand in vague dissent. "Yes," he persisted. "But I am still curious about Mr. Kenworthy's motive for wanting to kill the lady. Compromising letters. Er—isn't that (if you will excuse the term) rather a Victorian sort of menace in these days?"

"Sure," agreed H.M. "But Lord Abbsdale, Kenworthy's father and sole source of revenue, is rather a Victorian sort of bloke. As you'll admit if you've listened to what we've heard about his character."

The doctor ignored this.

"But there," he smiled, "I can probably assist you. Everybody has contributed something to this discussion so far except myself. Now I enter. As I told you up on the boat-deck on Wednesday, I conducted a post-mortem. I told you I found results which were surprising." He paused. "I did not say I had discovered the lady was poisoned or drowned. I did discover, however, that she was going to have a child."

H.M. snapped his fingers.

" 'Letters,' " he quoted from Valerie, " 'admitting to something or other.' Jerome Kenworthy's child, for a fiver. And Estelle Zia Bey was goin' straight to old Abbsdale. Oh, my eye." He blinked at Max. "Of course. Didn't she tell you, when she was tight, that she was goin' to see someone *'in the Adm—'*, which is Admiralty for a fiver? Didn't she say she had her proofs? And there, for our third fiver, is motive.

"Which, ladies and gents, about seals up the case now.

"We can pretty well reconstruct. When Mrs. Zia Bey decided to cross the ocean and pour out her woes on Abbsdale's shoulder, Kenworthy calmly made up his mind to kill her. If I had to guess here, I'd guess that he was very charmin' about it. I'd guess he persuaded her to take this ship, and said he'd go along. I'd guess he only begged her to keep quiet about bein' a great friend of his until he made up his mind what to do."

Lathrop interrupted.

"Whoa there!" Lathrop said. "Suppose she told somebody aboard that she was a friend of his?"

"Well," said H.M., "suppose she did? What of it? I think you'll have noticed that Estelle Zia Bey, for all her merry garrulousness, was an exceedingly close-mouthed woman about mentionin' personal details—even when she was reelin' drunk. And observe that she didn't trust Kenworthy an inch: she pretended to seal up those letters in an envelope for the purser, and probably told Kenworthy she'd done it, whereas actually she kept 'em in her handbag. Unfortunately, he saw through that.

"But even suppose she had said Kenworthy was a pal of hers? Remember, this crime was to be the work of Captain Pierre Benoit, of the French Tirailleurs. There was never to be any doubt about that. Captain Benoit was to be caught, literally red-handed, with bloody finger-prints. He was to confess. He was to leave a suicide-note, and kill himself. End of case. How could that concern the innocent son of Lord Abbsdale?

"Kenworthy planned with exceedin' great care. His uniforms and the other frippery, as Benoit, he undoubtedly had made in New York. He booked two cabins, carefully chosen, in two names. Benoit's trunk was sent aboard; but the personality of Benoit never walked aboard: it appeared later. Kenworthy simply dropped Benoit's steamship ticket and passport on the berth in cabin B-71, where the steward could pick 'em up. (It's the steward, you remember, who collects your ticket after departure; you don't have to give it up at the barrier.)

"Now I don't have to load your minds with details of his double life aboard, which you can imagine for yourselves from what I've already said. He couldn't have kept it up for long; but then he didn't have to. What he had to establish was a blurred impression, on the minds of worried, unobservant other people on a gloomy first night, that one of their fellow-passengers was a dark-complexioned man in a French uniform. The first night he also spread a little disquiet with some spectacular knife-throwin': which was *intended* to catch attention, and implant in our minds the idea of some half-loony feller with a fanatical grudge against a woman. And he nearly, but not quite, got caught at the boat-drill.

"On the second night, he was ready. I doubt if he meant to kill Mrs. Zia Bey quite so early at night. Thinkin', d'ye see, that she was safely away getting sozzled with Max, he slipped round in Benoit's character to have a search of her cabin. She surprised him when she went down to get her coat. But she didn't yell out, because at first glance she didn't recognize him as Kenworthy; and the spectacle of a strange man in her cabin, for purposes to be guessed at, wouldn't either upset or even displease her. When she tumbled to it, it was too late. He stunned her and then killed her, probably with that razor.

"He'd taken along that bottle of ink, not quite decided whether to use it or blood. But he substituted the ink for the

169

bulge of letters in her handbag, wiped his thumbs, and left careful faked prints for the sleuths to find. Then he left.

"Mind you, he didn't even care if he got some blood on him! Or if he was seen approachin' or leaving the scene of the crime. That would be all to the good later, when 'Benoit's' guilt was established.

"But now would come the really ticklish part of the scheme. The question was, when would they find the body? When would the hounds start bayin'? When would they begin to chase finger-prints? He didn't think it would be so soon as that night: certainly not within an hour: and it was a reasonable assumption. He got back to Kenworthy's cabin, shed his disguise, swallowed another dose of the rank stuff that had been keepin' him genuinely sick for two days, and crawled groanin' in to bed. And no sooner had he settled down than . . ."

The purser finished it. "*I* walked in," Griswold said gloomily.

H.M. nodded.

"Yes; on your first visit, as you said, to his cabin. But what else? Just to sweeten the imaginary situation, Kenworthy told that ghost-story about a feller in a gas-mask wanderin' about. No sooner has he told that, than in walks Max Matthews. By what Max tells the purser, it's thunderingly obvious to Kenworthy what has happened. They've found the body! The captain's already roaring for action! Kenworthy must have felt a cold sweat in his brain as well as his stomach. Remember—" H.M. looked at the purser and Max—"in what a blistering hurry he chased you out of there? Remember how he nearly had a fit when the purser suggested sending for a doctor? Remember how he swore he wouldn't be disturbed again that night no matter what happened?

"Now for the real, true, acid-test.

"He turned himself into Benoit again, locked the door, and slid through the lavatory-way to B-71. Here he sat down to play with his rubber stamps, havin' the ink-pad all prepared.

"Here was how he intended it to work. Somebody, maybe the captain himself, would come round askin' for finger-prints. Good! Benoit, with the ink-pad in front of him, would agree and press his thumbs to his own messy ink-pad. Then he would show annoyance, wipe his thumbs on a handkerchief, and make in the presence of witnesses *the same faked thumb-prints he'd left in B-37*. All this time, as though

170

they'd trapped him, he would manage to look and talk as guilty as hell."

This time it was the third officer who interposed.

"Excuse me," said Cruikshank. "But all that jabbering of his . . . about 'that woman' and 'her' being a traitor . . . ?"

H.M. grunted.

"Bogus motive, son. He wanted to instil into your mind just the idea he seems to have done: that Estelle Zia Bey was a Nazi spy, and that he'd killed her. Y'see, I'm dead certain it was Kenworthy who wrote the skipper that anonymous note warnin' him there would be a woman espionage-agent aboard.

"Well! With the thumb-prints taken in Benoit's cabin, he thought his plan would be complete. It wasn't likely that they would compare finger-prints in his cabin, on the spot. They'd just collect 'em first, and take them away for comparison. When they'd taken the prints away—that very same night—'Benoit' would write his suicide-note, stage his fake suicide with a dummy dressed up, and disappear. Nobody would see him again after the purser and the third officer had left the cabin. 'Benoit's' prints would tally with the bloody ones. His confession would be there. Finally, no other finger-prints taken aboard that ship would be anything like Benoit's, because Kenworthy's own prints would be taken in a proper manner. The beauty of that twist, y'know, is brilliant. And the whole imposture would be finished in forty-eight hours."

H.M. paused, and sniffed into his empty glass. His cigar had gone out, but he did not re-light it.

"Only," he said sourly, "it went wrong."

"Because," said the purser, "Cruikshank and I got excited over all his jabbering, and refused to let him use his own ink-pad. So we took his prints in the proper way. And he was dished."

"Dished?" roared H.M. "No wonder he had that funny look on his face when you left: the look you couldn't quite describe. His whole plan was royally, crisply burnt to a cinder. Don't you see how?

"We'll pass over the events of the next night, when 'Captain Benoit' was becoming a graver danger each minute, and had to be disposed of before he got caught out. Kenworthy dressed up a dummy (he says he made it of a blanket and some rolled-up newspapers), fired a shot, and tipped the 'body' overboard, knowin' quite well the lookouts would see it fall. The 'body' would come undone in the water, of course, but no one would ever know that. He was still tryin' to salvage his plan, y'know. Captain Benoit really did leave a suicide-note, confessin' to the murder: but it got thrown out. And Mr. Hooper swore to two people on B Deck.

"We'll also pass over the appallin' shock Kenworthy must have got when, staggerin' up after having disposed of the dummy, staggerin' up to get his first drink and let his stomach settle again, staggerin' up for the first time in his proper clothes, he ran into a girl who said she was Valerie Chatford, his cousin—and had come to save him from the menace of the letters!

"Oh, my eye.

"But don't you see the huge, the hangin' evidence that had now got him round the neck with regard to the thumb-prints?"

Valerie looked puzzled. "No, I don't," she returned. "After all, nobody's prints were the same as the bloody ones on the scene of the murder."

H.M. stretched out his hands as though pleading.

"Listen, my wench. For the love of Esau, think! In the purser's safe were eight little white cards, each bearing the left and right thumb-print of a different passenger. But 'Captain Benoit's' prints had been taken properly. Kenworthy's had been taken properly. Consequently, *there were two cards on which the thumb-prints were exactly the same.*"

"Dished," repeated the purser. "And for good."

"Yes. Nobody, so far, had thought to compare the various sets of prints with each other. If you had, you'd have found that Benoit and Kenworthy were one and the same person. But, once this ship got to port and the official police took over, a howler like that would be spotted first crack. Kenworthy had to pinch the card bearin' Benoit's prints. He had to, or he was done for! So he set up the submarine alarm, attacked the purser's office, and—"

"—And didn't touch the cards in the purser's safe," supplied Lathrop, pouncing. "Why? If he wanted one of those cards why didn't he bother the safe?"

"If we ever wanted," grinned H.M., "the last, the ultimate clue which indicated that the guilty feller was Jerome Kenworthy there it is.

"He didn't look for 'em in the safe because he didn't know

they were there. And he was the only passenger who didn't know that. Looky here: think back to Wednesday morning. All of you, except Kenworthy, were up on the boat-deck when the purser told us what he'd done with the passengers' cards. Kenworthy only appeared later. He thought they were in those cardboard files which had been left out in the open, all very invitin'. So he ransacked the files, and let the safe alone. He pinched a handful of passports at random in order to cover the theft of Benoit's *forged* passport. But he didn't get the card he wanted.

"Thinks I to myself: you'll have another go, my lad. So I let it get noised about that I'd taken a much worse conk on the onion than I had. I let it be known I had the cards in my possession. You know what he did. As for makin' up again and puttin' on Benoit's uniform, the feller was desperate. He was watched: that was why he had to set up the submarine alarm when he raided the purser's office. He'd now tried every dodge. He was up a tree. But it was a foggy night. If he put on Benoit's spare uniform, and anybody caught a glimpse of him, everybody would believe the witness had a bad case of nerves and was seein' ghosts after the best sea-farin' tradition. He had a shot at it. And," said H.M., his face growing tired and bitter and rather white, "I had a shot at *him*. That's all."

There was a pause.

It was bright winter sunlight outside. Reflections of it on the water played through the open ports and trembled across the ceiling. They were moving up the Channel. Since yesterday, when they sighted the Seven Sisters along the English coast, it had been known that the port was London. Headed for Tilbury Docks, the *Edwardic* moved through quiet waters toward home.

"There's just one thing," muttered the purser, shaking his head, "that I still don't understand. Kenworthy's seasickness —when he traveled with us before—"

Again H.M. peered at him over the tops of the spectacles.

"You're a stickler for detail, ain't you?" he inquired. "If I got to make what's merely another guess, I'd like to bet that his seasickness for the first few days on the other trip was caused chiefly by the tail-end of a roaring, swinging hangover. They feel exactly ali—*hurrum*, that is, so I've been told. I can certainly tell you, though, that he used that reputation of his with good effect. Everything he knew about this ship:

his own reputation, the position of the cabins, your acquaintance with fingerprints: had all been carefully worked into his plan. He's rather a clever feller, y'know. That's what they thought about him in the Diplomatic."

"Clever?" echoed the purser. "He's a perishing genius!"

"And yet," said Valerie, "he seemed so *nice.*"

"Sure," agreed H.M. "Many murderers are. That's not a paradox or a piece of cussedness, though it always seems to startle people. It's cause and effect. Women think they're nice, so they get into trouble with women. And then they have to get out of it. You've heard such a story before. You'll hear it many times again."

The soft-footed and confidential smoking-room steward moved across to their group.

"Destroyer going past outside," he confided. "If any of you would like to see it?"

There was a concerted rush for the doors, leaving behind only Valerie, Max, and a glaring H.M.

"That's gratitude," said H.M. "Phooey!"

"We're all grateful to you," said Valerie, shading her eyes with her hands. "Especially, I am. But—well, a more horrible and hypocritical nine days I don't want to spend in a hurry. And I've got to go back with this ship, too. They won't allow me to land in England without a passport."

H.M. glowered at her.

"Who says you won't be able to land?" he demanded. "I'm the old man, ain't I? It may take me a day or two to wangle it, that's all. Curse it all, if Lathrop can come askin' me to do the same thing when Kenworthy pinched and destroyed *his* passport . . . throwin' everything overboard, just as he threw his weapons . . . then I can do a little something for you, can't I?" He looked at Max. "Do you want her to land?"

"If she doesn't," he said, and meant it, "I'm going back with the ship too."

"I thought you were beastly," said Valerie. "You thought I was beastly. Maybe we still both think so. But if they don't let me go ashore, and *you* go, I'll jump overboard and swim after you." And she held her hands to him.

*   *   *   *   *

They went quietly into the lounge when they heard the ship's orchestra tuning up. A Sunday quiet held the ship.

Commander Matthews, holding the Bible clumsily, stood by the improvised rostrum and watched his passengers assemble. Again he read the Twenty-third Psalm; and read it, Max thought, very well for old Frank. There were no hymns. There was no prayer. But, as the orchestra struck up at a signal from Commander Matthews, they sang *God Save the King*. And never had those words been sung more strongly, never was more sincerity poured from the heart, than when those strains rose to the roof, and the great gray ship moved up the Channel; and, steady as a compass-needle in death and storm and peril and the darkness of great waters, the *Edwardic* came home.

JOHN DICKSON CARR

The man many readers think of as the most British of detective story writers was born in Uniontown, Pennsylvania in 1906. After attending Haverford College, Carr went to Paris where, his parents hoped, he would continue his education at the Sorbonne. Instead he became a writer. His first novel, *It Walks By Night,* was published in 1929. Shortly thereafter, Carr married and settled in his wife's native country, England.

The Thirties were a highly prolific period for Carr, who was turning out three to five novels a year. Some of these were published under what became his most famous *nom de plume,* Carter Dickson. (Because the Dickson novels contain a great deal of a certain type of comedy, many of their earlier readers attributed them to P.G. Wodehouse. Could an American write like this? Never!)

In 1965 Carr left England and moved to Greenville, South Carolina, where he remained until his death in 1977.

In his lifetime, Carr received the Mystery Writers of America's highest honor, the Grand Master Award, and was one of only two Americans (the other was Patricia Highsmith) ever admitted into the prestigious — but almost exclusively British — Detection Club. In his famous essay "The Grandest Game in the World", Carr listed the qualities always present in the detective novel at its best: fair play, sound plot construction, and ingenuity. (He added, "Though this quality of ingenuity is not necessary to the detective story as such, you will never find the great masterpiece without it.") That these qualities are prevalent in Carr's work is obvious to his legions of readers. In the words of the great detective novelist-critic Edmund Crispin, "For subtlety, ingenuity, and atmosphere, he was one of the three or four best detective-story writers since Poe that the English language has known."